TITLES BY STEPHANIE COLE

AL DENTE'S INFERNO
CRIME OF THE ANCIENT MARINARA

"Everything about this mystery was great. I loved the location, the villa, the characters." —Katie's Cottage Books

"Stephanie Cole does a wonderful job of describing the Italian countryside as well as the way of life there. . . . Her Italian cast is especially delightful." —Criminal Element

"Now more than ever readers will appreciate this extravagant tour through beautiful Italy. . . . [Nell's] dynamic relationship with Pete is a tantalizing joy. Their banter and quips are fast and clever, and one can easily see Nell's temptation to stick it out and develop the best tourist culinary school possible. This is a fun, tasty, and very grounded start to what promises to be a unique new series where cultures blend together to produce an exquisite main course." —Kings River Life Magazine

CRIME
OF THE
ANCIENT
MARINARA

STEPHANIE COLE

BERKLEY PRIME CRIME
New York

BERKLEY PRIME CRIME
Published by Berkley
An imprint of Penguin Random House LLC
penguinrandomhouse.com

ISBN: 9780593097816

First Edition: February 2021

Printed in the United States of America
1 3 5 7 9 10 8 6 4 2

Cover art by Brandon Dorman
Cover design by Judith Lagerman
Book design by George Towne

For Chris and her siblings,
Rich, Anne, Maria, Danny, and Laura—
my real Valentis

1

There were six of us assembled for final preparations in the common room of the Villa Orlandini on a hillside just outside of Cortona, Italy. The villa was home to Chef Claudio Orlandini, his Cornell-educated olive-growing son, Pete, and an assortment of helpful women of the Bari family—not the least of which was the redoubtable Annamaria, the sixty-ish sous-chef who had been keeping the Orlandini household humming along for decades.

Not quite a month ago, I, Nell Valenti, had been trans-atlanticly wooed by a lawyer representing the Orlandinis to come to Cortona, Italy, and develop a world-class cooking school at their villa. Five hundred years ago the property was home to the order of St. Veronica of the Veil, but that was back in the day when the joint was a run-down convent and not the fine, run-down villa it was today. And now, I thought, here we were, on the eve, on the brink, very possibly even on the ledge, for all I knew. Chef, Pete, Annamaria, Rosa, Sofia, and I.

Chef dubbed the theme for our first "intensive" *Marinara Misteriosa*. This culinary virtuoso had found himself longing for the days of his explosive rocketing onto the culinary world stage back in his twenties when his own secret marinara recipe was introduced to Italian sauce lovers the world over, who instantly proclaimed it the finest advancement in marinara development in the last two hundred years. Love, fame, and money followed.

But now?

I had my doubts. How many people, I argued, are going to spring for round-trip airfare plus our fees, not to mention clear their own schedules at short notice, for four days at the villa to learn something they could probably figure out at home just by popping the lid on a jar of Newman's Own? The answer came within days of launching the website: five. Five Americans signed up. When I announced to Chef, the Baris, and Pete that Marinara Misteriosa was a go, Chef kissed both my cheeks.

And now here we were, meandering around the common room with our hands in our pockets, taking care of last-minute tasks, eyeballing the beautiful changes to the space, on the afternoon before the five Americans showed up who were paying top dollar to be in the presence of the first real celebrity chef—well, from Tuscany, under two hundred pounds, and born less than five years after the death of Mussolini.

To make my life a little easier, I decided to go with Cucinavan, owned and operated out of Florence by Manny Manfredi, whose gastrotour services would include handling the money, coordinating airport pickups and drop-offs, transportation to and from the villa—and whatever foodie hot spots and shrines he could offer to our students along the way. At two p.m. the next day, Cucinavan was arriving from Florence with our first class of American gastrotourists. Four days, five students, learning at the sauce-stained knees of renowned chef Claudio Orlandini—how hard could it be?

And if we hit a few snags, as Chef himself would say, *Tutto fa brodo*—Everything makes broth. The first time I heard Chef use the common Italian phrase, I knew we had our brand, and it gave me a little frisson of pleasure. *Everything makes broth.* Three weeks ago, that outside wall had been stripped of its peeling wallpaper, washed, dried, and painted a bright teal in chalkboard paint. I found a sign painter in Siena who did the lettering in gold leaf centered high up on the gorgeous teal wall: TUTTO FA BRODO, with plenty of slants and serifs to make the Orlandini Cooking School brand glisten with all the agelessness of a fresco.

I crossed my arms, amazed at the changes. No more *muschio*, the moss that had been providing the 3-D effect on the moist walls. No more mildew. Luscious rugs in geometric whites and golds offset the wall hanging, stainless steel worktables doubling as desks glinted in the daylight, and Bauhaus metal and sling-back leather chairs outdid anything I ever owned, that was for sure. For a moment, my heart picked up a beat, and I thought the Villa Orlandini Cooking School might really stand a chance.

Today, down at the far end of the wall, near where the American foodies would put up their throbbing feet at the end of a tough day with polenta, Rosa and Sofia, Annamaria's sisters who were members of the order of St.

Veronica of the Veil, were fifteen feet off the ground on rickety ladders, hanging a ten-by-twelve-foot tapestry banner in a famous William Morris Oriental design. Clustered below, shouting directions, and gesturing as broadly as a traffic cop, was Annamaria. *More this way, more that way, higher, lower, are you drunk?*

When we all finally agreed that the banner was as straight as we could get it without either a carpenter's level or an infusion of tea, we flopped into chairs and waited for Annamaria to wheel in her tea cart with extravagant antipasti aboard. Nibbling on a peperoncino, the stalwart Rosa thumbed the remote and navigated her way to a cable TV channel, then upped the volume as though she had a twitch, and we all stared at Rosa's daily fix of a close-captioned American show called *Stealth Chef.* "*Ecco Stealth!*" she stage-whispered as though drawing our attention to a shadowy image of the Blessed Virgin on the side of an Arkansas barn.

Stealth Chef—face obscured by a black bandana, hair obscured by a professional black head wrap, voice distorted by a high-tech voice changer—had hit on a gimmick that was sheer kitsch. But it worked, and it sold, and it topped late afternoon cable culinary shows. I had to admit, Chef Orlandini's merry little Tutto Fa Brodo brand looked a little ho-hum alongside Stealth Chef's brand, splayed across the simple set kitchen: Recipes for All.

This anonymous dicer slicer, filming from an undisclosed location in the United States, was dubbed the Robin Hood of celebrity chefs. While waiting for the pasta pot to boil, the disguised voice lost no opportunity to plug the shtick: "Recipes belong to everyone," the figure mincing garlic intoned sincerely, "nothing hidden, nothing withheld, the democracy of a world kitchen, where rich and poor share and share alike." You would swear Stealth Chef was about to break into doomed and righteous song at the barricades in *Les Mis*. All the PC words got gonged: democracy, rich, poor, world, share.

The result in the year Stealth Chef had been on the air was a ratings top spot as unassailable as my own Chef Claudio Orlandini's five-tier tiramisù. But everyone loved Stealthy's mystique. The bandana, the head wrap, the voice changer—pure theater. The problem with all this televised celebrity was that it started to give Rosa Bari ideas. Would Chef consider a gold hoop earring? A fish tattoo? A paisley ascot? A nose job? Thankfully, she voiced these abominations only to Pete or to me, on some level knowing better than to make any direct suggestions to Annamaria or Chef himself.

The two times Chef wandered through the common room when *Stealth Chef* was on the air, he truly stopped dead in his tracks, transfixed as though he had spotted the East African oryx on the Serengeti Plain. He seemed okay with the disguises—after all, Chef's easy charm was probably in the same league as Stealth Chef's bandana—but his eyes widened in shock when the whole concept of Recipes for All got plugged. You would think he was watching either an autopsy or a student with bad knife skills. Right there in front of him. *"Cosa sta dicendo?"* he declared: What is he saying? Then, hoarsely: *"Ricette per tutti?"* Recipes for all? He was baffled. With arms open wide, Chef Claudio Orlandini turned slowly, addressing the walls in broken English. Where, then, is the art? The pricelessness?

Palming a few cubes of fresh mozzarella from the antipasto tray, plus two slender breadsticks, I motioned to Rosa and Sofia to turn off the TV. Sofia, who was in charge of the remote at that moment in time, clicked it once, and both of them headed like long-suffering galley slaves toward the classroom stainless steel tables. We all sat. Pete dashed in and scraped over a chair he flipped around and straddled. Chef's only son was forty, with short dark hair, hazel eyes, and angular cheekbones. He loved his father without losing sight of the man's short-comings, and he became my friend one night over dinner, at a time when a murder too close to home nearly derailed all of us. Over the past weeks, I had been developing both a start-up cooking school and a fondness for this man who could turn a beautiful black Moraiolo olive between his fingers and gaze at it like it had a story and the value of a diamond.

Annamaria, dressed in an elegant navy blue sheath, dropped straight-backed onto a bench and folded her hands prayerfully. A former nun herself, Annamaria slid in and out of this default position. We smiled and tipped our heads at each other as if we were meeting after a very long time away. At length, she began to pour tea. Sofia passed a plate of rolled and speared anchovies. Pete popped a couple of olives. Rosa appeared to be daydreaming.

I had six sets of photocopied information collated and stapled. These I passed out in a silent rustle, setting Chef's next to me until he returned from the *bocciodromo*, the indoor bocce dome, and joined us. He never fretted, sensing, I'm pretty convinced, that when I showed up last month fretting was penciled into my job description. *"I nostri studenti domani."* In my half-baked Italian, I drew their attention to the top sheet. Manny Manfredi of Cucinavan had sent me a nice printout of the Americans who had signed up—not to mention paid up—for Marinara

Misteriosa. Alongside each alphabetized name was age, permanent address, and occupation. I went down the list.

Jenna Bond, 24, Baltimore, MD, barista, Artifact Coffee
Zoe Campion, 34, Chatham, NJ, outdoor educator, Walden Trails School
Glynis Gramm, 53, Naples, FL, owner, Gulf Coast Apparel
Robert Gramm, 54, Naples, FL, owner, Gramm's Lams dealership
George Johnson, 37, Brooklyn, NY, server, Fraîche Take Bistro

Annamaria perused the list with a scowl, then swatted it lightly with the back of her hand. "Only one, how you say, cook."

I turned to her. "Which one?"

All three Bari sisters answered at once with many shrugs. "Giorgio."

I looked at the entry for George Johnson, not seeing what to them as they sat with folded hands was obvious. "Why do you say that?" At their blank looks, I tried again. *Perché?*

As she fussed at the clip that held back one side of her salt-and-pepper hair, Annamaria blinked at the ceiling. "Bistro." Sofia and Rosa nodded vigorously at their elder sister's sagacity.

I held up a finger, not my first choice. "Actually"—I raised my voice, quickly muttering out of the side of my mouth to Pete, "Jump in, okay?"—"all we know about Giorgio is that he's a waiter—*cameriere, capisce?*— which doesn't mean he cooks." This brilliant deduction was met with appreciative murmurs from my colleagues. I went on. "Judging by the scant information we have on our first group of students, we can't make any inferences about who comes to us with cooking skills and who does not." Three faces turned in unison to Pete, whose melodious Italian translated my point.

I sipped my tea. Then I launched into what I always think of as my Battle Stations speech, developed over my lengthy career of designing cooking schools (four, total, including this Orlandini gig), and which I'd distilled down to three rules. For these, I pushed back my chair and stood at my place. *"Uno,"* I bleated. "Assume no kitchen skills. They are here to learn, so, we will teach them. Whether they're good or they're bad, show no shock. We work with what we've got." I inhaled and delivered the most craven part of the Battle Stations speech. "Insofar as we can"—I scanned their intense faces—"we give them some tips, we give them some recipes, some wine, time in the presence of our celebrity chef, and we send them off happy. We are selling the Orlandini Cooking School experience."

Their faces hadn't changed.

"Due," I went on, regarding the ceiling. "No fraternizing." In Italian, Pete went on a little long on this point, I thought, ruling out lovers, pals, drinking buddies, dance partners, roommates, and piano accompanists. At that one, I eyed him. He studied a stunted olive. Then I grabbed the list of names and waved it around. "These are our customers. Do you understand?"

"Our students," amended Annamaria, trying for the high road. I think she was privately savoring an image of these five Americans as holy seekers. Had she not been listening to Rule #1?

I pressed my lips together. "Our customers," I repeated. "We will be living here in close quarters"—Pete was all over this half sentence like shine on polyester; Rosa made a cat call—"so we behave with the utmost professionalism at all times."

"No hello?"

"Of course hello. Be cordial and helpful at all times." When I saw how wide their eyes were with this, well, loophole, I fretted. All I could throw on top of Rule #2 was something about thinking of these five American gastrotourists as shoppers who have entered our retail establishment. We want to sell them our goods, but we want to respect their space.

Pete apparently thought it advisable at this point to encourage some role-playing, because before my very eyes, Rosa and Sofia moved quickly away from the table. Wringing her hands, Rosa smiled dementedly at Sofia. "I show you a, how you say, sauté pot—"

"Pan." Annamaria scrutinized her fingernails, as though she had been saying "pan" all of her sixty years.

"Yes," murmured Sofia, flushed with competence, "you do."

Keeping the kind of distance from her customer I recalled from the leper colony scene in *Ben-Hur*, Rosa waved her all the way out of the common room, then turned and curtsied. We all clapped, and clapped again when Sofia skipped back in and took a bow. I debated finessing the performance, but decided against it, finally. They got the basics just fine—sell them on the Orlandini experience, but respect their space.

Pete said, "What's next?"

I nodded at him and sang out *"Tre."* Speared anchovies, cubed cheeses, stemmed peperoncini paused in midair. I had their attention. "Refer all suggestions and complaints to—" For a nanosecond of horror, I realized I hadn't worked out this point. Who was the go-to for the program? Not Chef, not unless it had something to do with asking him whether the dough was stretchy enough. Not Annamaria, although I considered her—she was, after all, inner circle, but even after our short acquaintance I knew this woman's realm was the kitchen, at Chef's side, and she was stunningly single-minded. Not Pete, although he handled the villa accounts, so had a finger on the business side of things. Still, he was chin deep in the olive harvest and could only be called on occasionally as an instructor, depending.

I eyed him.

He scratched his nose and gave me a tight little smile.

In a moment of honesty rumbling deep inside myself, I realized I didn't want to designate him the go-to for live suggestions and complaints because I could just imagine the customers manufacturing suggestions and complaints just to sidle up to him. The bath water's too hot, Chef is too remote, I need more practice with the gnocchi board, the polenta whisk, the pasta maker. That would simply not do, no sirree. Pete seemed to read my mind. Was I that obvious? Leaning closer, he said quietly, "I can take care of myself, Nell." When I was about to sputter something by way of reply, he held up a hand. "I'm happy to do it, if you want me to."

After a moment, my shoulders slumped as I let out a long breath. Then I finished Rule #3. "Refer all suggestions and complaints," I intoned, "to me." At the three other sites where I had designed and developed cooking schools, there was enough staff to lay this disagreeable part of the operation off on program managers or assistants to the chief operating officer. Here, there was just me. No organizational chart. Just, basically, a . . . family. "Hey!" cried Rosa appreciatively. "La Bella Nella."

Before turning to page two of the handout, I shivered—someone must have left the door open—as my gaze slid over the names of our first, small group of American gastrotourists. Jenna, Zoe, Glynis, Robert, and George. At the time, I had no way of knowing that one of them would never make it home.

2

When the antipasti ran out, so did my colleagues.

Even Pete begged off. "I can still harvest a few more trees," he explained apologetically, "before I lose the light." Rosa and Sofia had been helping him in the grove over the busiest time of the olive harvest, but I claimed them for good as the advent of Cucinavan and Marinara Misteriosa neared. He relinquished the nimble and game Bari sisters with good grace. These two were on semipermanent loan from their convent. "The villa," declared the Mother Superior I had not yet met, "can be viewed as in need of our pastoral aid." Although I suspected she was being glib and saw a great opportunity to rid the Veronican community of the restless, youngest two Bari sisters, I was grateful to have them. The remaining sister, Giada, couldn't be spared from the convent.

On the eve of what I could tell from her expression Annamaria saw as the outbreak of the plague, we were all informed we were on our own for dinner. Annamaria had a few last-minute adjustments to the kitchen. As she left the common room, pushing the tea cart, straight-backed, she looked as though she wanted a few minutes alone with the stove and *frigorifero* to exhort them to be brave. *"Nella mattina,"* I called after all three of them, *"discutiamo il primo giorno."* In the morning, we discuss the first day.

From the door to the courtyard, Pete smiled at me. "I didn't even need to translate."

I bucked up. "Can you meet me later in the office? I think we'll be okay if at least you and I understand the day's schedule."

"I'll bring some wine."

Also, it occurred to me: "Chef. Bring Chef." I threw up my hands. "He can't wing it. He's not just cooking for the next four days, Pete."

"I know, I know. He's teaching."

"And inspiring. And charming." What else could I add? "He *is* the cooking school at the Villa Orlandini." I waved the class list like I was clearing the air—which, maybe, I was. "What these five first-timers think of their experience here will make or break us. It's that simple. Their 'reviews' will turn up everywhere—Yelp, TripAdvisor, personal blogs, you name it."

Pete started over to me. "I know Pop can be a wild card, but he'll come through," he said softly. "You'll see."

His trust in his father was so complete it was touching. But what I couldn't gauge was whether it was misplaced. I gave him a wan smile and watched him hurry off to the waiting olive trees, heavy with fruit. The light from the late afternoon sun fell through the common room windows in lovely floating squares, white motes hanging in soft suspension. My eyes settled on the gold leaf lettering,

TUTTO FA BRODO, and although I would never admit it to anybody, I had my doubts.

I had done what I could. But for some reason I felt as gloomy as Annamaria. With her remote, disapproving personality, with Chef's mercurial behavior, and with Pete's cheerful naïveté, I wondered why I ever agreed to this job. On the eve of our first public foray into cooking classes with Marinara Misteriosa, I felt more vulnerable than I ever had, even in the presence of my pushy parents as they laid out all the reasons why I should join the Dr. Val Valenti empire of cable TV psycho-shrinkage.

For the first time—and in all new ways—I was utterly alone.

At the end of each of the next four days, whatever happened, it was on me.

My so-called office had been thrown together out of what had originally been the Veronicans' refectory, the small, communal dining hall just a few steps down from the kitchen. Now it sported one whitewashed stone wall, a great, soft area rug in a pattern of a medieval rose mosaic, an executive desk with plenty of scrollwork in an antique platinum finish, and a floor lamp that Rosa let me know was particularly cool but which reminded me of a giant tampon. Little by little, I would sneak in a file cabinet and a bookcase from the Ikea in Florence.

Turning on the tampon lamp, I sat at my fancy desk and awaited Pete and Chef. I had downed—of all things—a meatball sub I had put together for myself in the kitchen empty of any Bari sisters, and settled into my temporary office, with a brief glance out the single, arched window.

It was one of those soft Tuscan nights I had come to love in a very short time, when you just know the stars will emerge if you wait long enough, and then there they'd be, silver speckles that sharpen before your very eyes. I spread out the paperwork I had prepared on Marinara Misteriosa, pulled closer the diffused light of the oven mitt–style table lamp, and looked it over.

I didn't have to spend a long time with the agenda—after all, I had designed it. But I wanted to hit the most important spots, especially for the first day, with Chef and Pete. Over four days, Chef was demonstrating a few essential marinara sauces, made distinctive by subtle differences, and culminating grandly with his demonstration of the incomparable *prima marinara*. In the online description, we added several teasers. Will Chef Claudio Orlandini unveil a new marinara sauce, outdoing even his own famous marinara magic of fifty years ago? Will you be there when he unlocks the legendary Orlandini recipe vault? Will you be there when he divulges at long last the secret ingredient of the *prima marinara* sauce that rocketed him to fame on the culinary world stage?

I banked on the mystery, the closely guarded secret, the unassailable fortress of a recipe being a draw for enrollment. But I was learning. What's the sweet spot number of years gone by when a mystery either gets enshrined in the public imagination or is just plain forgotten? The class we limited to five students filled, sure, but there were only two others on what I liked to call the Waiting List. Two. But not two hundred. Maybe puzzles like secret ingredients just get old after fifty years. It's not like bad behavior in the royal family. Or the whereabouts of Captain Kidd's buried treasure.

Still, I had to believe we'd catch on. So much—regardless

of the field—depended on word of mouth. And over their few days with us, Zoe, Glynis, Robert, George, and Jenna would sample the best of Tuscan wines, go truffle hunting with the dog Stella, tour Pete's Silver Wind olive grove, go mushroom picking with Chef's stately sous-chef, Anna-maria, dine together in the chapel, stroll the streets of hilltop Cortona, and spend so much time in the kitchen with Chef Claudio that they would be awash in marinara and terrific stories of his life in *la cucina*. The Orlandinis' dream had become my dream, too. That quiet little truth came to me as a shock, as I sat there next to the diffused light from my oven-mitt lamp, and I shut my eyes. Outside the night was so still I could hear the churr of the nightjars, the tentative bark of a neighbor's dog.

"Nell?"

I opened my eyes. Backlit in the doorway to my short-term office was Pete. A wonderful addition to the quiet evening of barks and churrs and readiness. "Hey!" I said, pushing back my chair as he stepped into the office, scraping his fingers through his hair.

He winced. "Don't you have any lights in here?"

Outside my immediate desk area, there wasn't much. I gave a gentle whack to the tampon floor lamp, which upped the light a notch, which was when I noticed Pete was alone. My watch surprised me: 9:12 p.m. He was an hour late. An hour late and—I craned my neck—alone. "Where's Chef?" When he slumped down against the wall just inside the door, I got the message this was a bigger question than I had thought. "Pete?" I stood up. "What's wrong?"

One backlit arm lifted a bottle. "At least I brought the wine—"

"Where's Chef, Pete?"

"He's fine. I left him at the hospital."

"The hospital?" I yelled, pulling myself to my feet on muscle-free legs. "What happened?"

"They're setting his arm."

"His arm?"

"He broke his arm playing bocce." I didn't even ask how that was humanly possible. It's like shuffleboard with balls. "I just came home to tell you, and then I'm going back. Preferably with Annamaria."

"That'll fix him," I approved.

Pete nodded slowly. "That'll fix him."

"But good," I added with something as close to glee as I could muster.

Now to get the full report. With shaking fingers I pulled out two wineglasses from an otherwise empty desk drawer, then managed to ambulate over to where he sat. I had to know the worst. "Which arm, Pete?" I whispered. It all seemed terribly important.

He pressed his eyes shut. "His right."

And then the full measure of the disaster hit me. The glasses were forgotten. Sinking down next to Pete, I took a swig from the bottle, then, in a small voice I didn't know I had, I asked: "His whisking arm?"

Pete lowered his head miserably. "His whisking arm."

All right, I told myself, all right, now you know, Nell. Sure, instructional whisking videos starring Chef Claudio Orlandini had been standard educational tools for years at the finest culinary schools. The man's whisking approached the speed of a Major League pitcher's fastball. Urban legend has it that when Chef whisks his *bescia-mella* sauce, it is impossible for mere witnesses to see when he changes direction. And now. And now. Well, I couldn't bear to squint down whatever the long road to recovery might bring. Anything short of Chef's permanent disability would be welcome.

But what about tomorrow?

I felt dazed. "We can do this," I said more to myself than to Pete. As I scrambled to my feet, I thrust the bottle into his hands, and told myself the kinds of things that usually buoy one up. I am a professional. I am a strong woman. I am a good person. I am a Jersey girl. I am a size ten, five feet, eight inches, a natural brunette, and I could pull off Ferragamo's cerulean blue leather paper-bag-waist pants. But—but—at the center of the room, I boiled over.

"I am a sap!" I screamed.

"Nell?"

It felt so good, I screamed again. "Why did I take this godforsaken gig?" Flinging open the window even wider, I think I yelled to the nightjars to shut up. And then to the neighbor's dog to bark off. Stiff-armed against the window, I told myself not to take it out on Tuscany. No, not Tuscany. Not Pete, and not the Bari sisters.

Pete put his arms around me. "How could he?" I sobbed. "How could he?" All the time and hard work that'd been put into this start-up. In the past month, we had survived moss on the walls, a resident porcupine in the decrepit dormitory, Chef decamping to Rome to woo his long-lost love—and let us not forget the murder, the investigation, the killer's attempt on my own life, the liberally flung-around suspicions, the bad press, the beef stew.

We reacted to the pounding on the door to my office. *"Fammi entrare!"* It was Annamaria. More pounding. *"Pierfranco!"*

Pete wrenched open the door. I didn't move from the

window, afraid a scene with Annamaria would just exhaust all of us. I wanted this imperious woman in the well-worn pink chenille bathrobe to save all her best work for when she strangled the miscreant in the hospital's emergency room. In rapid Italian, Pete filled her in. She gasped and did a little two-step backward. Then she got control of herself and hissed back at him in Italian, which involved a certain amount of backlit spit. The Spit of Fury. New list, by Nell Valenti: Orlandinis You Can Count On. At the top, Annamaria Bari.

I realized then that this was working out as well as it possibly could. I wouldn't have to go confront Chef. If he turned his limpid Al Pacino eyes on me, never mind he's in his seventies, I'd be toast and he'd get away with having let down our side. Instead, we had the A Team, A for Annamaria. Who needed the Furies when we had Annamaria? Pete called back to say she was throwing on some clothes and they'd go together to collect his pop. Or whatever was left of him when Annamaria got through with him.

My mind already on damage control, I shooed them away.

Immediate goal: finish off the wine and do whatever it takes to keep Chef out of my way until tomorrow morning. I apologized to the nightjars, who didn't believe I meant it, anyway, although the dog in the night moved the barking on down the road. To his credit, he had compromised on volume and direction. From this window, I had no view of the villa's courtyard, vehicles, or drive down through the vine-covered stone entrance gates. Just as well. I wouldn't see when Pete and Annamaria returned with the rat in chef's clothing. Then I sank into my desk chair, booted up my Mac, tapped the tampon lamp for as high as it would go, and opened my file containing the detailed spreadsheet for events over the next four days of Marinara Misteriosa.

Depending on just what kind of shape Chef was in, we'd have to make some last-minute accommodations to the schedule of Marinara Misteriosa. Maybe he was side-lined when it came to whisking, but we could still have him narrate the technique while Pete or Annamaria quietly got the job done. Or—and I sat back, feeling pleased—maybe Chef could call a student up to the stove to receive Chef's one-on-one whisking tutorial. When I realized I was actually turning Chef's inability to live up to his job description into an honor conferred upon a student, I felt slightly ashamed.

Nell, have you become just a spin-o-matic?

When all was said and done, had I inhaled my father's televised marketing brilliance, like so much secondhand smoke? I bit my lip. Then suddenly there was Rosa, pad-ding softly across my mosaic rose rug with a tray sporting brass peacock handles and holding an insulated French press, a demitasse cup, and two chocolate biscotti I knew she had made just that morning. These she set down with a smile so sincere I nearly cried, then, patting the air with a *"tu, tu, tu, Nella,"* she backed away, whispering, *"sta bene."* It's all right. The aroma of espresso rose around me as she soundlessly drew the door shut behind her.

I languidly drew the little demitasse spoon through the coffee. Taking my time, I sipped. Yes, I was most defi-nitely a sap. I took a job full of drama and misapprehen-sions thousands of miles from my home. Accepting that truth, I dunked the first of Rosa's biscotti just to the point that—like me—it softened but didn't fall apart and sink into the rich, dark depths. About tomorrow's official opening of the Villa Orlandini Cooking School, I would figure it out. Because to offset the sap part of me, I had the professional, tough, Jersey girl part of me. Everything was in play. Sap, Jersey girl. Had I achieved a kind of equilibrium? My teeth sank unnecessarily into the espresso-soaked inch of biscotto.

Truth be told, there in that solitary hidey-hole, I was fond of the sap in me.

It kept me safe from spin. The kind of spin that leaves nothing vulnerable in its wake.

3

O pening Day of the Villa Orlandini Cooking School
was a bad time to exfoliate.

Because apparently I had forgotten what the scrub
does to my face.

What I should have exfoliated was Chef. Yes, that
would have been satisfying. But no one was giving me
that particular delicious opportunity. And he thought his
arm hurt. Ha! Just let Nell Valenti at his pores! Fortunately, I came to my senses as I was scrubbing the gritty
gray paste touted as Dead Sea minerals into the top quad-
rant of my forehead, just along the hairline. Suddenly, I
remembered the skinned look I had achieved last time,
and how it took two weeks to settle down. But it was Wee-
hawken in the wintertime, where everyone looked angry
red with the cold, the sleet, the unrelenting gray. There I
fit right in.

As I stared back into the mirror over the bathroom
sink at my horrified eyes, I splashed warm water onto my

face, gently swiping off the hardening goop. Then I put on an off-the-rack beauty, a mink brown wraparound shirt-waist in a cotton jersey fabric with just the right amount of slink. I especially liked the sash, which had enough material that it fell into a floppy bow over my hip. Before too long, light blue Murano glass earrings dangled, a matching bracelet bangled, and Gucci blue suede slides my mother had passed on to me after wearing them twice rose to the occasion of style and reasonably good sense. Cucinavan was rolling in around two p.m., so I was ready to walk out my bedroom door a full eight hours ahead of schedule. It was Game On.

Holding my slim leather portfolio against my chest, I click-clacked my way up the paved path to the cloister walk and the entrance to the main building. The Ape, (pronounced Ah-pay), our little blue farm truck, stood by, waiting for an outing, but the vintage ocean green T-Bird was gone. With incredible sangfroid, I found myself won-dering if Chef had run away again. Perhaps Rome? Per-haps Calabria, where the shepherds roam? Perhaps back to the *bocciodromo*, to break his other arm? I couldn't possibly care less. We would manage. I pushed open the door into the kitchen, where I caught Annamaria and Chef in a hug, or, half a hug, considering the sling. When they saw me, they sprang apart guiltily.

Clearly, someone had to be the Annamaria in the room. "That's telling him," I said icily.

Annamaria looked as if she had been exfoliating, too. While Chef played for sympathy by turning those Pacino peepers on me, she scrabbled for some Italian equivalent of a high road. First she sniffed, and then if she lifted her chin any higher it could turn on the hood fan over the range. "I apologize to Chef," she explained with an elegant shrug, "for bad things I say." Or, more likely, I smirked, the battery of *malocchi* she had flung like Zeus at him. A man could stand just so many curses.

Chef saw his chance. *"È vero, è vero, Nella."* Then he crossed his heart with the claw-like fingers of his immobilized arm. In my head, which was starting to ache, I expunged the name of Annamaria Bari from the list of dependable Orlandinis. The only name left was Pete's. I was beginning to feel my Zen, null set, black hole equanimity seep back into my cells. And then Chef tucked his head in around his collar in what he thought was a conciliatory manner. In English he tried, "You look very pretty today."

My nose started to twitch. I wanted to hoot and blather in gibberish in his face, but in a reasonable voice, I responded, "That's as may be, Chef, but we have work to do." I turned, blinking, at Annamaria. "Are there scones?" Wordlessly, she opened one arm in a priestly half benediction, drawing my gaze to the platter on the table. Two scones. Hoarded, probably, for those fallen from grace in the kitchen. Instead, I claimed them. Let them eat toast. Daring the two with a mere look to stop me, I took a cloth napkin, gathered up both scones, the coffee carafe, a cup, and my portfolio, and announced I would be breakfasting in my office, and would see them both at nine a.m. for final instructions.

On my way out, just trying to hang on to all the things I was taking with me, I paused. "Chef?"

"Sì?" came his satisfyingly small voice.

Without turning, I spoke. "I recommend changing into the Lagerfeld shirt for the first day."

* * *

*A*t nine, more or less—this was Italy, after all—Baris and Orlandinis assembled in my office. Pete had brought Laura and Lisa, two more of Annamaria's sisters, over from the convent to lend a hand during Marinara Misteriosa. These two were twins with bowl-cut bangs and chin-length hair, sturdy women with the kinds of hands you see in boxing gyms, who fell somewhere in the middle of the Bari birth order. They could make beds, sanitize bathrooms, lug fifty-pound sacks of potatoes, and knock heads together if necessary. Sadly, they seemed to go in fear of Chef himself, which seriously limited their ability to crack their twenty collective knuckles with gusto and keep him in line.

I handed them each a single sheet, the agenda for day one. In English. While they stood shuffling from foot to foot in front of me, I sat with my fingers steepled on my desk. Pete made his way in Italian down the agenda items.

Manny Manfredi—which somehow Pete managed to make sound like a scourge—arrives at two p.m., at which time we make introductions and show our students to their lodgings. At six p.m., we convene in the common room for Chef's official welcome (from the look on his face, which he disguised quickly, I could tell it was the first he had heard of this duty—which, of course, it wasn't); following this inspiring welcome, all students receive their course packets and are given a tour of the villa facilities by Pete and Nell. At eight p.m., dinner in *la cappella*, thanks to Annamaria Bari, who provides an array of the marinara sauces they will be learning during their stay. Visiting sommelier and vintner Theresa Franchi will be on hand to decant a selection of local wines.

Pete made it all sound fairly easy, even in Italian.

Everyone left, including me. On our way out, I noticed they seemed clear on last-minute jobs, and Chef loped off toward his apartment, presumably to write the welcome speech he had left to the very last minute. Considering he was right-handed, I had no idea how he planned to pull off this task, but I decided to let him wrestle with the problem for, oh, a good two or three hours before offering to help.

For the next few hours, I inspected. I even put on my designer reading glasses to peruse, well, whatever I wanted to peruse. Sofia showed me around the physical spaces the five Americans would be using. In addition to the kitchen, the common room, and the chapel—two formal dinners were planned—there were the accommodations. We booked the Gramms into the converted barn studio apartment. At a higher rate. The other three, Zoe Campion, Jenna Bond, and George Johnson, were "roughing" it in brightly painted rooms on the second floor of the old nuns' dormitory, each outfitted with a twin bed, a dresser, a nightstand, an easy chair, and lush area rugs.

They sparkled.

They gleamed.

True, they smelled a little like ammonia, but that would pass.

The door to the first floor of the dormitory—where Chef's living quarters and Annamaria's room were located—was kept locked, yielding to a keycard system we had installed just three days ago. Since then, Chef had misplaced his keycard five times. Life was long. Life was hard.

Finally, I was back in my office, hoping to meditate (English for "nap") behind closed doors until the witching hour of two o'clock befell us and the Cucinavan deposited five Americans on our doorstep. But at the precise moment I had slid out of Mom's slides and stretched out on the rug, a knock came at the door. Do Do Not Disturb signs mean nothing anymore? "Nella?" It was Rosa, but muffled and wheezy. I always open doors to Rosa. She sings a mean Billy Joel and understands things like irony. Together we were working on absurdity. It wouldn't take long. We were naturals.

But when I swung open the door, patting my hair in place, pulling my snipped lock over the exfoliated part of my forehead, I couldn't immediately find her. I felt like I had tumbled down Alice's rabbit hole and it was a forest of floral arrangements as tall as lemon trees. "Rosa?" I called, and she pushed her way out from behind the closest arrangement, fashioned into an arbor of intense, eye-watering lilies. "What's all this?" I cried, and she gave me a look like she might be ready to graduate from our absurdity study sessions. All I could get out of her was, "Flower truck make delivery then go."

Rosa thrust a card at me. Millefiori was the name of the business responsible for this tasteless jungle of flora. In English, A Thousand Flowers, and I could swear there were more than that many outside my office door. I swatted at them, taking in half a dozen varieties of lilies—Oriental lilies, Turk's cap lilies, trumpet lilies, Easter lilies, daylilies, hybrid lilies—as I brought the card close to my face, wheezing. "Get rid of them, Rosa." There were enough death flowers here for a state funeral. And then I saw: *Congrats on your first day, honey, we always knew you could do it! We love you, Mom and Dad.*

Of course, of course. Dr. Val and Ardis Valenti. Who else? They had been plying me with the lilies they never seemed to recall I'm allergic to for the last sixteen years, ever since the Winter Sports Banquet at my high school, when all I got was a Certificate for Participating on the freshman girls' tennis team. Pretty much my job was running after balls, either with or without a racquet in my hands. My parents had actually hired a handsome young man, dressed in a tux, to present me with an armful of lilies. I learned, in that moment, two things. The girl who had served and forehanded and backhanded the team to the regional finals got a trophy for MVP that looked puny by comparison to my lilies. And I knew it was all wrong. I also learned why these overdone flowers were associated with death and funerals. Because if you weren't dead already, you were—like me as I struggled to breathe—well on the way.

I glanced again at the card. *We always knew you could do it!*

No, they didn't.

And their guilt on that score made them overdo it.

The Bari sisters hauled the death arrangements all the way outside and out of their tender hearts deployed a few here and there. The arbor got positioned in front of the entrance to the main building. The floral "blanket" was arranged over one of the rails in the split-rail fence bordering Pete's olive grove. Standing arrangements flanked the garage doors and the dormitory. The rest adorned the compost heap behind the barn.

Then the sisters cranked and pushed open all the windows in and around my office. Me, I fled to my room, then dug around in my travel bag and took some hits on my inhaler. By the time I blew my nose and blotted my watery eyes, I was feeling pretty restored. Just in time to

greet Cucinavan, which tour operator Manny Manfredi
was swinging in a wide arc around the villa's courtyard,
honking merrily, and finally coming to a stop. Never
mind he was half an hour early.

Pete and I exchanged a meaningful look, and he took
off in the direction of the dormitory. Chances were fifty-
fifty that his pop was groomed (dental bridge in place,
pate gleaming, hands washed, scents applied) and dressed.
Pete would alert him to the early arrival. I had nauseating
visions of Chef bowlegging it toward our five American
foodies dressed in his form-fitting spandex bocce pants.
If just one person can be a welcoming committee, I was
it. Fortunately, I had remembered my slim portfolio.

The door on the driver's side of the Cucinavan swung
open without so much as a complaint from a hinge, and
Manny Manfredi alighted. He had thinning hair and a
thickening paunch, and he was dressed in a way that suggested Cucinavan might be making a detour through Bo-
tswana. Safari vest with ten thousand pockets for every
little thing, nylon rip-corded pants that could zip off into
daring Bermuda shorts, and a bushwhacking brimmed
Tilley hat with an adjustable chin strap.

"Manny?"

"Nell?"

We shook hands.

Still smiling, he threw open the sliding side door to the
van, and out climbed the five American gastrotourists. I
think I said more hellos and *benvenuti* than a van full of
strangers had any right to expect.

First out was the youngest, Jenna Bond, the barista.
Strawberry blond, blue eyes, white pullover sweater, jeans,
looking like she was feeling out of place. Brainstorm:
Chef should bring Jenna Bond up for his one-on-one

whisking tutorial. Or . . . was I acting as dim as my tele-floral lily-sending parents? To be determined.

Next out of the van was Zoe Campion, a pretty brunette in a white V-neck T-shirt, pussycat gray capris, and a lightweight charcoal cardigan. No jewelry, no nail polish. On her feet were a pair of dusty white Crocs. We shook hands.

Then out of the van came Robert, "call me Bob," Gramm. Half the Gramms. He had white, well-cut hair, clearly white earlier than most people's, narrow restless eyes, and a thin and short upper lip, the kind I always associate with cruel schoolyard boys. Like Jenna Bond, he was wearing a white pullover sweater, only one with a Polo logo, and jeans that looked like someone had—could it be?—ironed them.

Whoever that was, I could say for sure it wasn't his wife, Glynis, who stepped down from the van with a throaty laugh and a good-sport kind of artlessness I liked right away. She had wavy hair with highlights, and demi-bangs that didn't seem to be covering up anything at all, not even wrinkles. Her clothes were a long-sleeved navy blue shirt, slim beige pants, a nubby sweater tied casually over her shoulders. At least Glynis Gramm looked like she knew she was coming to cook, not hunt big game or sashay around a country club.

Last out was George Johnson, with a second-look kind of face. Put him in a crowd, and you'd never see him. Under six feet tall, average build, black hair combed back and let fall willy-nilly, dark eyes that presented absolutely no competition to either Pacino's or Chef's. In a crowd, he'd be the one you'd peg for forty years as a letter carrier for the USPS—maybe with a passion for some wet, solitary thing like fly-fishing. In a crowd, nothing. But up close was when you'd catch the little changes of expression that made you wonder what could possibly be going on inside. A microscopic eyebrow ripple, a nanosecond of a lip pucker, a millimeter swerve of his gaze. Because his voice was quiet, you'd listen hard for a joke or an observation.

The conversation was pretty general and everybody piped up at once. I kept smiling.

"This place is gorgeous."

"Our renovations are ongoing." That was Pete.

"But we're ready for you!" That was me.

"Old convent, eh?"

"Is there a dungeon?"

How do they think nuns spent their time?

"Any walking trails?"

"Can't wait to get started."

"Glynis made me come."

"Look, look, look."

It could only be Chef. We all turned to look as he stood at the top of the winding stone steps of the dormitory. How he got there was anybody's guess, considering his own living quarters were on the first floor. *"Benvenuti, tutti"*—he spread wide his Lagerfeld-clad left arm in a Pope kind of way—*"alla Villa Orlandini."*

Bob Gramm muttered, "Oh, God, is he going to talk Italian the whole time?"

4

A nd then, never taking his eyes off us, Chef began his descent in a murmur of appreciation from us mere mortals in the courtyard. The man definitely liked to make an entrance, even if it reminded me of Norma Desmond making her way down the grand staircase in *Sunset Boulevard*. Zoe stepped up beside me. "He's coming up on his fiftieth anniversary, isn't he?"

I was impressed she knew it. We had soft-pedaled it a bit in the promo materials, not entirely sure how that little fact would play—virile Chef, doddering Chef, hard to say—but it had got through to this leaf-gathering teacher from Chatham, New Jersey. "He is," I said, tensing suddenly when it looked like the descending Chef nearly missed a step. "Although Chef was already cooking professionally earlier, it was fifty years ago that his secret recipe for *prima marinara* debuted."

"The culinary sensation of the year," Zoe pointed out.

When Chef reached the bottom and bounded over to his waiting fans, the noise level increased. There were shrill questions about his poor arm—"not your whisking arm, I hope," teased Glynis Gramm, which showed me she had some knowledge of Chef Claudio Orlandini, and when he declared with what to me sounded like crackpot bluster, "All my arms whisking arms," a roar went up from the group. Even Zoe Campion, eyeing Chef sideways, nodded in appreciation. I alone, apparently, was left to wonder just how many arms Chef had.

New questions arose. Can we see the place where that guy got murdered? Can we see the famous recipe vault? Can we see the bathrooms? The Bari sisters emerged from the main building, tucking their chins shyly, elbowing each other not so shyly. Only Annamaria was missing, no doubt awaiting their pilgrimage to the kitchen. Like an old-time vestal virgin, keeping the holy fires tended.

I corralled Manny Manfredi as he busied himself toting suitcases to the center of the courtyard. "Where will you be staying?"

"Cousins in town," he rattled off negligibly. "Will you be needing me before pickup on Tuesday?" He seemed half interested in the possibility.

"Probably not," was the best I could give him. "Not unless we add something to the program that requires van transportation."

"Eh," he temporized, "could happen. Call me."

"Seems a good group," I tried, not entirely truthfully. Too soon to form any real impressions. But I was hoping he'd open up and tell me about any red flags he saw fluttering. Tidbits he'd overheard, idiosyncrasies he'd observed. "Anything you can tell me?"

For half a minute, we stood in silence, each of us gazing off into some great distance. "Glynis Gramm," Manny announced. "Nice lady." Which told me exactly nothing.

Then Manny got a bit stern. "You should convince Robert to put his valuables in your safe. He carries too much cash and flashes more jewelry than his wife." I aahed, struck that to my knowledge there wasn't a safe anywhere on the villa grounds, recipe or otherwise. Note: Talk to Pete. "Jenna Bond, now, there's a sweet kid. But sooner or later Robert will catch her eyeing him, and—and—" He gestured kind of impotently.

"She's got a crush?"

"I don't know. Maybe. And it's none of my business, but—"

"Okay, I'll keep an eye," I said, suddenly feeling like the dean of students at a private girls' boarding school. "What else?" I asked. "Zoe Campion?"

"Another nice lady. Carries her own stuff." We stood nodding at nothing.

Finally: "George Johnson?" I prompted him.

"Oh. Johnson. A loner. But friendly. If you told me he's an undercover cop, I'd say sure."

"Well," I said genially, "back home he's a waiter."

Manny lifted his shoulders. "Undercover there, too."

"*I'm* guessing," I said, "he's George Johnson, waiter at a Brooklyn bistro, here to spend some time with marinaras." My imagination, I had to admit, sometimes wore brown lace-up oxfords with orthotics. I sighed. So, the world according to Manfredi just deposited with us two nice ladies, a flashy husband, a sweet kid with a crush, and a friendly loner. All were here almost at the drop of a hat to learn some very focused Italian cooking skills and recipes from the best.

For reasons I may never know—oddly, this was the first time I ever had this thought—marinara means something to these five Americans. Partly, I wondered, looking at our first class, what the world was coming to. I would tell no one that back home there were days I wouldn't go any further toward putting on the old feed bag than to trot down to the corner store to buy a jar of factory-bottled marinara to throw over some pasta. Yet here were Glynis, Jenna, Zoe, George, and Bob who had just dropped a few grand to come to the Orlandini villa to make some tomato sauce from scratch.

It was not a good time for me to doubt what I was doing for a living. I had already made the exfoliation blunder.

Five sets of eyes swiveled over to me.

"Andiamo!" I called to the group, my arms spread wide in a rare Zorba the Greek moment. I worried I was setting a tone I wouldn't be able to keep up. "Let's get you settled in." I broke off with a couple of wheezes. "All right?" So far, everyone was happily chattering away. Chef, with a courtly little bow, shouted, *"Alla cucina!"* —*To the kitchen!*—and everyone watched him go like dutiful little fan girls and boys. At the heavy door into the main building—where he glanced bemusedly at the arbor of lilies—he proved a little graceless with his broken wing, trying to swing the door open just far enough to wedge his body through. Finally, he worked it out, yelling one more lusty *"Alla cucina!"* at us, and hobbled into the building and out of sight. Not certain whether they were expected to trot after him into the kitchen, everyone turned to me.

Pete and I widened our eyes at each other.

"Chef is speaking generally," I extemporized with a broad smile. "We see the kitchen later."

When in doubt, stick with the program. It was Dr. Val Valenti's watchword and it had served him well. When Manny Manfredi honked and waved as he drove the

Cucinavan off the villa property, I felt wistful, remembering the day a month ago that Pete Orlandini picked me up from the train station and brought me there on that September day when the teals and ochres of Tuscany were sharpened by a light rain, and the beauty of this rather ramshackle villa struck me.

Ramshackle back home in New Jersey usually meant a sagging frame house that didn't have much style when it was built back in the 1920s. But here in Italy there was still a sense that ramshackle was something that had outlived bombardments and sieges and abandonments and centuries of the changing purposes of fickle humans. True monuments, with no descriptions. Even ruins had style. But on that day a month ago I had pangs of aloneness. I had signed myself on to a job at this unfamiliar place for . . . who knew how long?

Today, on the other hand, I stole a look at our five newcomers who had only four days ahead of them in this unfamiliar place. For four days, I believed anyone could rise to the occasion. It would be packed with just enough truffle hunting, mushroom picking, and sauce stirring that they wouldn't feel the aloneness. Not at all. I would hope things like the lambent moonlight and ochre hillsides would seep into them almost without their being aware, and that they would leave Tuscany feeling they knew the place. Feeling they fit in. And were right at home. After four days, they wouldn't even know how wrong they were. And that was a good thing.

"Glynis, Bob." I stepped over to the Gramms. "Let me show you to your lodgings."

"Absolutely," gushed the wry Glynis, who gamely took the handle of her roller bag.

Her husband raised a manicured hand. "Glyn," he said

authoritatively, "leave it. It's their job to handle our luggage." At that, he folded his hands in front of his crotch, and looked around as though he were waiting for his porter to materialize.

His wife snorted softly at him. "Get over yourself, honey. We're here to cook."

I wasn't entirely sure how that answered his luggage-toting remarks, but I liked her for it. Punctuating her point, she snapped her handle into place and smiled at me as her husband said with an edge, "You're here to cook. I'm here to let you." He actually snapped his fingers in the direction of Laura. "Oh, Boy. You there."

Titters and elbow jabs went around the tight little circle of Bari sisters.

Laura squared her shoulders and, with a look like she was about to fillet a fish, headed over to us. Her walk was about as menacing as any nun could make it.

Glynis leaned in. "Bob means he's just keeping me company. I've badgered the man for years to come with me to Europe for cooking classes."

"Well," I said diplomatically, "I hope he discovers you were right."

She waved a hand. "To be determined, for sure," she told me. "If he isn't selling Lamborghinis to Floridians, he's bored." As her appreciative eyes took in everything we passed, she added, "Don't know what made the difference this time, but here we are."

I murmured something unintelligible, determined to stay professional. Glynis Gramm and I started toward the barn, her roller bag rumbling behind her. I gave her the side-eye. Glynis had game, no denying, unperturbed that her husband who "let" her come was walking on ahead.

He told the long-suffering Laura that the rumbling roller bag bothered his sensitive ears, so she needed to carry it by the side handle.

For the first couple of hours, all was quiet. The newcomers were invited to rest or wander the villa grounds. I tried sitting in my office, in my desk chair, at my desk, with the door open, just to foster the impression of approachability. No one approached. There was still a faint smell of lilies in the corridor, and as I fanned my office air with the liability waivers Manny Manfredi had given me, I strolled restlessly to the window, where I caught soft blue and vermilion streaks as the day headed toward sunset. Then I noticed some activity out on the grounds. Pete and Jenna Bond were strolling in his olive grove. Glynis, on the highest bit of ground I could see, almost out of range, was by herself, turning slowly with travel binoculars up to her eyes.

No sign of Bob Gramm, who was probably connecting to the villa wi-fi and checking in with Gramm's Lams back in Naples, Florida.

No sign of Chef, but raised voices from the kitchen located him for me.

No sign of George Johnson. The man might well be the only one of the group who had the opportunity to stretch out in the room we styled the "Dante," for a famous Tuscan of yore. Very yore. Jenna's room, the "Puccini," was next door to George's. And Zoe Campion's, across the hall, was the "Galileo." Standing empty, the "Vinci," the fourth renovated room, stood empty awaiting future rich Americans. Lisa Bari, who enjoys metalworking when she isn't singing the lowest harmonies in the sisters' new Billy Joel cover act, had fashioned small brass plaques with the room names engraved by hand.

A knock at my open door startled me.

George Johnson wasn't resting in his room. He was standing in my doorway.

I was startled. "How did you find me?" Not the most gracious of welcomes . . . "No, really," I went on. "I've been here a month and I still have a hard time finding my way around."

He laughed. "I found a trail of nuns. They were very clear on things like mortal sins and where your office was."

I beckoned. "Come on in, George."

He did. For my part, I teetered in Ardis Valenti's cast-off Gucci slides over to my desk, where I quickly put about two hundred pounds of distressed wood between this man and me. I sat, but he stood, his hands in his pockets, taking in every bit of my office. "I keep waiting to find a secret passage."

"Ah." I held my coffee carafe aloft. He nodded. I poured him an espresso. "The villa's five hundred years old. It doesn't yield up its secret passages easily."

"No arrows?"

"Or neon." I watched him decide to take a seat, and went on, "The only subterranean passage I know about is a short hop to the wine cellar." I pointed vaguely in the direction of the kitchen. "Past the kitchen. We'll see it, oh—" I checked my agenda. "Tomorrow."

He sipped appreciatively. "Your doing?"

"The wine cellar or the espresso?"

He held up his demitasse cup.

I nodded. "I like my coffee too much to entrust to others."

"Even Chef Claudio Orlandini?" His gotcha look wasn't at all threatening.

I bit my lip, deciding on whether to sidestep or tell some truth. "Chef's coffee is quite good," I equivocated. Then I actually wrinkled my nose at this Brooklyn waiter. My voice dropped. "Mine's better." There was an economy of motion about George Johnson that I liked. No nervous movements, no distracting gestures. It made for a kind of grace. "Just my opinion."

He made a detour. "And tonight?"

I handed him the single sheet on villa letterhead that detailed their arrival day. At that moment the voices from the kitchen got louder. The daily Chef and Annamaria battle over one or more menu items. I felt myself stiffen, wondering how to block it, when George raised a hand. "I'm in the food service business, Nell," he said with a tolerant smile. "Believe me, I know about kitchen histrionics."

I relaxed. "Thanks."

"You're from Jersey."

I sat back and narrowed my eyes at the man sitting across from me. "You looked me up."

"That I did. You were easier to find than secret passages."

"So true."

"I'm no sleuth, Nell. The Villa Orlandini Cooking School website had your short bio." He nodded at the papers spread out on my desk. "I'll leave you alone." He smiled, glancing back swiftly at the sheet. "And I'll find some cozy nook to read up on what to expect our first evening at the Villa Orlandini."

I decided to get into the spirit. "Oh," I told him, "that's just what we let you think you can expect. Here"—I smiled, feeling like I had all my own secret passages—"there are always surprises." And no sooner had I said it than I knew, with a little frisson, it was no banter, it was a deeper truth about this place. I remembered the night not even a month ago when I stumbled over the body of another guest of the Villa Orlandini. Murdered. And it hadn't shown up on any of our agendas.

O ver free time the first day, the five of them stuck to-gether because it didn't occur to any of them that they didn't have to. So when on the spur of the moment I suggested walking into Cortona, all of them clamored up to me, begged a few minutes to change shoes, and I was stuck. When we headed out of the gates of the Villa Or-landini, I passed out pocket flashlights for the walk home. It was a rumpus on feet. Some tried giving trite Italian songs full throat—"When the moon hits your eye like a bigga pizza pie"—some opened up about travel misadven-tures, and a few tried bellowing about their Dreams and Goals.

Where the road came close to a gentle, sprawling drop-off that lent us a panorama of the Val di Chiana, and even farther away, a streak of a meandering river, it was Jenna of all people who stepped up to the edge and shouted so hard she bent over, "I don't want to be a barista forever." As she turned to us, Glynis commented gently, "It's clean, honest work, Jenna."

Jenna put an end to that with a snort. "It's what you have to do when you don't have a meal ticket."

It seemed like a slam on Glynis, who cocked her head and took a step backward.

I put in, "Maybe it's just what you have to do when you hit adulthood, after Mom and Dad—"

"Assuming you've got them," she muttered, and moved to the outside of the group.

George tried, "Well, what was your major in—"

"There was no money. No money, no college, not in any real way. I don't want to talk about it."

When Zoe stepped up to the edge to shout her dreams and goals to this Tuscan valley, the others went with her. Jenna was left standing close to me, but when she said softly, "My dad died nine years ago," it seemed she was barely aware of me.

Poor kid. "I'm sorry," I said.

Next, George stepped up, then side-armed a stone out over the drop-off, like he was skipping it across a river. For him, for him, he called, just the good luck to keep doing what he's doing.

"Cop-out," sneered Bob Gramm.

Glynis spoke up. "I know what he means. I love what I do. I love my boutique." She gave a happy shrug and didn't even need to blast it out across the Val di Chiana.

Bob shoveled his wife a sour look as he strutted to the drop-off. "Penny-ante stuff, Glyn."

She was merry. "I brought in more than Gramm's Lams did last year." Turning to the rest of us, Glynis went on, "Apparently more tourists would rather buy high-end jewelry made by local artisans than an imported sports car with a base sticker price of two hundred grand."

"I would," agreed Zoe.

"Why not both?" quipped George.

Bob raised a hand and gave rather a shopworn explanation. "Imports hit tough times a few years ago—"

"Ah." That was me and was about the extent of my interest.

But Bob wasn't finished. "Over two years we got rid of all the chaff."

"Rhymes with staff," offered Glynis, meaningfully.

"And hired a strategic consultant—"

Out of the side of her mouth, Glynis translated, "Bankruptcy attorney."

Somebody tittered. Maybe me.

"What about you?" George Johnson put me on the spot. He jerked his inscrutable head in the direction of the drop-off. "Come shout your dreams and goals, Nell," he declared with false heartiness. This was met with some unwanted enthusiasm, like that moment at summer camp when all the other girls in your cabin are flapping around in sixty-four-degree lake water, eyeing you, the last one to take the plunge, shivering alone on the dock in the windy gloom.

I demurred, which may be the first time ever I got to use that word. "No, no, no, this is your drop-off, your Tuscan valley, your"—here I started shoveling it—"wishing well. No coins required." I had learned the art of airy demurrals at my father's Ace-bandaged knee. Occasionally someone in his studio audience would shoot him a tough question, like has he ever smoked weed or cheated on his wife. It was Dad's opportunity to deflect in a way I came to think of as shrink sleight of hand. Zoe, Jenna, Glynis, Bob, and George all nodded, just as happy, it seemed to me, to get moving toward town and the Bar dell'Accademia and a shot at some refreshments that had nothing to do with wine.

I noticed two things as I loped to the front of the group.

I might not have a five-year plan I wanted to share with this group, but I could at least assume a mantle of leadership. When out of the corner of one eye I saw George unobtrusively thumb his phone, I had a strong feeling he was recording us. Out of the corner of my other eye, I saw Jenna Bond shivering alone on the edges of the group.

She might just as well have been in last year's worn-out bathing suit on a day of windy gloom up in Canada, staring into the frigid lake water. In that moment, I felt close to her, but couldn't tell her why. I sidled over and took her hand. "Let's go to the head of the class," I said, feeling only glib and small, my throat tightening up from what I recognized as my life spent saying within the earshot of anyone only as much as I needed to in order to move things along.

I could walk hand in hand with her, I thought, sliding a look at Jenna. But at the end of the day, the plunge was the only way off that stuck place on the dock.

5

My scout pack was so enchanted with Cortona, I have to admit I was worried they'd all ask for cooking school refunds, check in to hotels on the piazza, and spend their four days drinking grappa and bellowing "That's Amore." Forget slaving over sauté pans just to come up with marinara! Such a bother! To tell the truth, I wasn't sure I would try to talk them out of it. In fact, I was thinking I might join them. When it became clear to me that they all wanted to spread out and poke around in the local shops, I told them I'd meet them—here I pointed unequivocally to the signage over my head—in, yes, thirty minutes right here at Bar dell'Accademia. Settling into an outdoor café chair, I watched them scurry off helter-skelter, like I'd turned on a light in the kitchen of a prewar building in the Bronx.

I didn't even take note of where they went, but I swear no two were together. Had they scoped out the closest shopping possibilities that quickly? Apparently so. Motor-bikes buzzed by, dogs and children wended, selfie sticks got wielded like batons—all while I, Nell Valenti, set the timer on my phone, sat back, adjusting myself so a slant of sunlight hit my upturned face, and waited. In twenty minutes, I felt restless, and decided to stroll the perimeter.

I only saw two of my charges: Jenna, standing outside La Dolceria with her nose pressed to the windowpane like the Little Match Girl, and Bob, inside Tesori della Toscana—Treasures of Tuscany—what looked from the glittering window display like a high-end jewelry store, along the lines of what I imagined his wife owned back home. While Bob glanced furtively from side to side, a clerk was wrapping up a gold bangle bracelet, presenting it in a velvet drawstring bag to the rich Americano, who began trying to find just the right spot in a jacket pocket to hide it.

It must be hard to buy jewelry for Glynis, who's probably seen it all, and can get any of it at a discount. But I thought he'd made a good choice. I scampered out of sight just as he turned toward the open door. Taking the long way around the cobblestone piazza, I caught a glimpse of George, smack-dab in the center of Piazza Garibaldi, snapping some phone pictures of practically everything. In that unguarded moment, the guy looked like a tourist.

Maybe he was.

Then, just as I started to turn away, I realized he had suddenly steadied his phone and was taking what had to be multiple pictures of . . . me. I had the distinct impression the man had just been waiting for the perfect opportunity. Then he lowered the phone, made a little bow at me, and slid the phone into his pocket. My skin prickled.

Otherwise, the walk back to the villa was uneventful.

I can't say the same for the next four days.

In contrast to Chef's theatrical entrance down the

stone steps to the courtyard, Annamaria Bari did her queen-in-exile act in the villa's common room. She was in her natural element, standing there with her pale pink-sleeved arms folded, her fine head still and level, her smile serene, if not exactly warm. As we collected for the formal welcome from Chef, I could tell our marinara-seeking Americans were quick to pick up something magnetic about this stranger, Annamaria Bari. She stood immobile against the backdrop of the whitewashed stone wall, and the whole effect was like a fresco. Someone gasped, not, I'm pretty sure, George, and I don't believe Bob Gramm even noticed her.

Pete had a fire going.

Rosa had strategically lit wall sconces.

Someone had taken the trouble to aim two of the overhead track lights toward the warm gleam of the painted brand, TUTTO FA BRODO. This, Bob Gramm acknowledged. "Whoa, dramatic, huh? What the hell's it say?"

At the sound of Chef's voice, we all turned. In the door to the kitchen, but still wearing his Lagerfeld outfit, he intoned in his lame English: "It say . . ." A pause as he moved to the center of the room, without looking at the sign itself. "Broth . . . is . . . everything." At that moment, I wanted to crawl under my pricey desk and pretty much stay there for just about as long as I could and still sustain life. Instead, I had to stand there and take it with a fake smile.

How on earth could Chef not even know the translation for his own brand? The man didn't deserve anything, anything nearly as cool as what we'd given him. Tutto Fa Brodo, Everything Makes Broth, says something about life—here I glared a silent *You idiot!* at my employer. His translation makes it all about soup! I couldn't bear to look at Pete. I was about to make him a fatherless child. Just one of those villa surprises I promised George Johnson.

Channeling my inner Laura, I moved like a menace through the group toward Chef. Pete stepped between us. "Yes, Chef," he pointed out, doing several things at once—clamping an arm around my shoulders, pulling me close in what could pass for esprit de corps, and shooting Chef and the whole wide world a brilliant smile. "Broth is everything, and everything makes broth. Both are true, and we welcome you all to Marinara Misteriosa. Please, Glynis, Jenna, find seats." Then, shifting his gaze, "Bob, George, Zoe, please." He completely defused the situation. Day one, gaffe one. I opened my slim portfolio and made a brief note. *Explain brand to Chef. Congratulate him on narrow escape.*

Right now all I had to ponder was why our American foodies were chattering happily. But I am not one to dwell on what appears to be working. Glynis commented on the beauty and comfort of the common room—"We're in good hands!" George registered everything, at least twice—"Clever updating of the old multipurpose room concept!" Bob commented on the evening's use of the stainless steel tables: "Christ, I could use a drink!" Jenna liked the fire. I came to some early conclusions about our guests. Bob Gramm was happy being unhappy. George Johnson kept his happiness to himself. Glynis Gramm's happiness had some foxed edges, like old books. Jenna Bond never assumed any happiness, and Zoe Campion apparently invented it.

As Pete took his place at Chef's side, and back one step, as translator, Chef launched into the official welcome—in robust and rapid Italian—to our guests, touching on what sounded like his "beautiful staff," casting his free left hand in the direction of Annamaria and all the rest of us, and hitting on the word *marinara* about two dozen times more than they would ever have time to learn and prepare. He managed to make the word *marinara* sound faintly obscene. Each time he uttered it, greedy murmurs rose from the group.

Now Annamaria's eyes were moving and a furrow appeared on her brow. It was as if every misgiving she had about American tourists was being paraded in front of her. Chef appeared to be promising marinara *"con acciughe"*—he slapped his palm for emphasis ("anchovies," translated Pete)—*"con capperi"*—another slap ("capers," said Pete)—*"e con olive"*—another slap ("olives," Pete said with a shrug, sure they could figure that one out for themselves). Chef's voice rocketed up an octave as he spoke even faster. To that first list he added, kissing his fingertips, the original marinara from hundreds of years ago, the Australian marinara with fish stock, and finally something called *sugo finto*, known as the poor man's marinara.

As Chef started to go into more particulars about why *sugo finto* is fake marinara, George Johnson raised a hand. "Chef?" He was polite, but he seemed to appoint himself the spokesperson for the group. "When will we be learning your world-famous *prima marinara* sauce?"

I think my heart stopped for just a moment, suddenly convinced Chef Claudio Orlandini, who apparently didn't even know his own brand, might now divulge he had no intention of disclosing the never-before-revealed recipe for the marinara that nearly fifty years ago launched his own stellar career. Or he could fall down in a fit. A hush fell across the room. Bob Gramm muttered something about having forked over thousands of buckaroos—"U.S.

currency, not these so-called euros"—to learn the poor man's marinara. "Oh, shush," retorted Glynis. But the man had showed some grasp of irony.

And then two lifesaving things happened. First, Chef exploded with glee, "On the final day!" Then he laughed uproariously at the fun fact he had hidden up inside his one good sleeve—he hadn't forgotten the whole point of a pricey Marinara Misteriosa workshop, after all, and he had practiced the Big Reveal in English. What a scamp. Then the second lifesaving thing occurred, the bright "pop" of Rosa's uncorking a fine prosecco Chef had chosen from the wine cellar. Clapping and whistling broke the rest of the hush. Everyone gathered around the drinks table as Rosa poured and Chef welcomed all to the villa, inviting them to enjoy the buildings and the grounds during their stay.

And before I knew it, suddenly over the sound system came the slow, ceremonial opening chords of Billy Joel's "Scenes from an Italian Restaurant." Recognizing it, Glynis flung her head back with a whoop, Bob indiscreetly shared something with Pete along the lines of that song was playing the first time he and Glynis . . . and the rest was drowned out by the sister act unable to resist joining in with Billy when he came in, singing, "A bottle of white, a bottle of red, perhaps a bottle of rosé instead."

Jenna held her glass with two hands right in front of her chest, like she was warming a little bird. All Pete and I could do was exchange hit-upside-our-heads looks at this unplanned musical addition. Who was the happy culprit? It had to be a Bari, and I suspected Rosa herself. As I stood shaking my head, I turned slightly—and caught George Johnson backlit by the firelight, controlling a smile, but his eyes were on me, and they were twinkling.

I suddenly knew who he was. Unless I missed my guess, our "George Johnson" was just another private eye my dad had hired to watch over me. Better already than the last one, Hal, from three weeks ago, oh yes, better. That guy just tailed me. This one, this one—as George watched me, I pointed my finger at him fiercely, mouthing *I know who you are*—this one went deep undercover, inventing a Brooklyn waiter persona, signing on for the very first set of classes at the Tuscan cooking school I was designing. With his head tilted, and his lips pursed, George Johnson gave me a quizzical look.

Fuming, I wanted to stalk out. A bad way to start our opening weekend.

Do the job, Nell, I told myself. Just do the job.

And George Johnson—or whatever his name really is—can do his.

I mmediately following Chef's welcome speech in the common room, I solicited information we needed to know from each of the guests, "to serve you better," touching on matters like allergies and any other "challenges" we could address to make their Villa Orlandini experience more enjoyable. With my pen poised, I got more than I bargained for, but these were early days for the beauty pageant smile, and I endured. Bob Gramm was gluten-free, he announced in a no-nonsense voice, and elaborated by adding, "And I do mean gluten-free."

Dropping my voice, I asked, "Celiac disease?" The sort of thing that should be on the application to enroll in the cooking school. Yet another form to revise . . .

"No," he had to admit with a whine, "not officially." I caught an eye roll from Glynis. At that, he prissily straightened his sleeves and asked if we were prepared to offer gluten-free pasta. We were. "My health has been delicate since getting over hepatitis last spring."

After allowing for a couple of sympathetic murmurs from the others, Glynis told us she slept better with a memory foam pillow, and Pete told her we'd get right on it. Jenna professed a sensitivity to preservatives and chlorinated toilet paper. I made a note, somebody tittered, and glowers were tossed around. Finally, George Johnson mentioned a latex allergy. At which Bob Gramm elbowed him, looked bug-eyed at the man's crotch, and blared, "Got some blisters, didja?" He alone was hoarse with laughter.

"I'd rather not say," answered George, still good-naturedly.

I sneezed three times and found myself wondering whether I had a Bob Gramm allergy.

Last up was Zoe, who looked sheepish. "No allergies," she told us.

As I shut my portfolio, I concluded we had a fine bunch of neurotics for our first group. I reminded them to check the communications table just inside my office door for daily updates to Marinara Misteriosa. Then, Pete and I announced a hasty tour of the villa grounds, dealt the five of the them our easy reference maps, and got them out the door at a cheerful trot. The day was cooling, and in the dusk, Jenna's sweater, Bob's hair, and Glynis's diamond earrings caught the last of the light. After charging around all the key buildings, we came to a huffing halt in the courtyard. Valiantly trying to keep to the schedule, Pete ended up pointing vaguely toward his olive grove, the truffle woods, and the rest of Italy. Orientation, over.

I gave it my heartiest. "And now," I said as though I

were revealing the big prize on a TV game show, "let's go find Chef in his kitchen." Glynis was so downright eager she nearly toppled me, and off we set, with Bob, Jenna, Zoe, and George right behind. No protests, since it was clearly the source of the heady aromas swirling into the corridor.

"Dinner tonight is very informal," explained Pete as he made his way to the front of the group. Holding my breath as I passed through the gauntlet of lilies—Zoe expressed the opinion that they were lovely—we stumped back into the main building where lamps cured the chill. As they made their way toward the kitchen, I caught a glance of George trying the doorknob to the door marked Wine Cellar. "Tomorrow," I called. He gave me a pleasant look, and when I thought he was about to start over to me, I held up my hands in a crow-eating manner. He stopped. "So sorry, George, about before. If I seemed angry." If? I hitched my shoulders in an *aw, shucks* way meant to quell any conversation. He nodded, folded his arms, and waited to see what else I would say. Whenever that happens, I have a hard time just leaving well enough alone. I'm never quite sure I actually believe in the concept of well enough. Does that make me a perfectionist? "I just mistook you for someone else." With a disarming wince, I finished up, "Sorry."

Had Rosa been around, she would have recognized that reason for the absurdity it was. It made no sense whatsoever, but George Johnson seemed inclined to take a generous view of things, and waved it all off with one hand. We exchanged smiles. His: *If you say so, you adorable flake.* Mine: *Best I can do and not kick you and your blistery privates clear out of Cortona.*

"Shall we?" he said softly, gesturing toward the

kitchen, where the door stood open and out wafted the heady scents of garlic, a happy clash of opinions in English, and Pete himself, standing half in the open doorway. Against the outside wall was our beautiful commercial range with six burners that suddenly seemed inadequate. Two pasta pots bubbled and steamed. Four saucepans kept their secrets simmering.

Suddenly, Bob Gramm raised his hand, waving our handout of the evening program. Nobody called on him, but he asked anyway. "According to the evening's agenda, there will be wine?"

Pete moved farther into the room. "Yes." He glanced at his watch. "Theresa Franchi, our local vintner, should be arriving any minute."

Bob Gramm scowled. "Pairings?"

After a beat, Pete said reasonably: "An introduction to our regional grapes. And then, a couple of uncorked suggestions for good choices to drink with your different sauces."

Bob got oddly belligerent. "I'm interested in wine."

"Since when?" said Glynis, barely audible.

He turned to her with a stony look. "Since I have to eat tomato sauce for four days."

6

My heart sank a little when I realized how crowded the kitchen looked, what with—I counted silently—twelve people: Annamaria, Rosa, Pete, five American foodies, Chef (given how his energy can suck the oxygen out of any room, I counted him as three people), and me. Aside from the dervish in a black toque, all the others stood relatively still as Annamaria described the menu of four marinaras as though she was reciting it for posterity.

Rosa beamed. But at that moment in the crowded kitchen, I wondered what was going to happen in the morning, when the predictable kitchen chaos set in as the bustle of culinary students erupted. To navigate a working kitchen required more than five senses. You needed to anticipate atomic bombardment in ways invisible to the naked eye, including the sudden movements of knives and sizzling hot pans. Some chefs in training came by it naturally. Others through mishap and heightened anxieties—all of which affected their cooking.

"Only four sauces? Aren't we learning seven?" That was George Johnson.

Chef smiled tolerantly. "Tonight is . . . sample."

Biting her lip, Zoe asked, "What have you left out?"

In the breathless hush that suddenly followed, dread got slathered like tapenade on toast.

What were they worried about?

Annamaria took a step forward. "No *sugo finto*," she announced. Then her eyes darted around the others. I could tell she couldn't quite figure the mood. To her, Chef's *prima marinara*, probably the single most persuasive motive for their attendance here for these four days, was just another sauce. "No *sugo finto*," she repeated, flinging up one finger. Then, with a grim look, "No fish sauce," flinging up a second finger. From her expression, I couldn't tell whether she was disdaining fish, sauce, or the English language.

Chef caught on. "Sample include *la prima marinara*."

Widespread relief ensued.

As Chef rattled off the buffet plan of attack, motioning cryptically about how to move with your dinner plate through the room, I stepped back from the fray. Crockery scraped, Americans chattered, forming a line. Rosa and Annamaria drained and served the pasta. Bob Gramm's they drained from the smaller pasta pot and delivered at arm's length to his plate. They acted like they needed hazmat suits. "Glootone free," intoned Annamaria, and drilled him with a look like she was serving him his pet dog.

Pete set out the sauce samples in decorative bowls made by local Tuscan artisans. Descriptive cards—in English—accompanied each. He shot me a wink as they broke formation and crowded around the last bowl in the buffet: All it said was *la prima*. At last! Reverent mutterings took over. George Johnson inhaled *prima* speculatively—this, this was the true *marinara misteriosa*!—and stirred the secret sauce with his left hand, his pinkie raised like it was high tea. "What are you picking up?" Glynis nudged him. "Tomato," he said humorously. Jenna Bond's lip curled at Bob Gramm, who stepped in front of her. A strong reaction, I thought, but maybe the shy Jenna came to the villa with a history of being bullied by line cutters.

A tap on my shoulder.

I turned, and faced Theresa Franchi. "*Buona sera*, Nell." Theresa, who married our vintner, Leo Franchi, three years ago, was an American in her midforties who had been knocking around Italy for a few years, working restaurant jobs, until she happened onto a grape harvest in Sicily and fell in love with viticulture. She'd tell whoever asked that she was just one more expat in a long history of American expats, one more leaf in the wind whose single greatest bit of luck was running into a Tuscan vintner named Leo Franchi. Admittedly, Leo was pretty great, a tenderhearted old bachelor "*troppo occupato per amore*"—too busy for love. A third-generation vintner whose vines were his offspring. And then he met Theresa. In Cortona, the Franchis were a couple with mystique.

Still getting to know each other, Theresa and I lightly kissed cheeks. Hers, I noticed, were stiff with the kind of worry I had seen on her from the first Theresa sighting. The Villa Orlandini had been a small customer of Leo's age-old indescribable wines, but now we were poised to give them a lot more business, if the cooking school took off. I hoped it would help. Over the month I had known her, I watched her brush off the rainy spring, the hot summer, the ailing soil, the increasing competition—and the beloved but aging Leo.

Since their marriage, Theresa had taken over the books, but bookkeeping software wasn't making much of a difference. To me, she had a hunted look, like what she was always thinking, just below the surface of pleasantries, was *It's just a matter of time, just a matter of time.* I had seen that same look on the faces of hollow-eyed restaurateurs just waiting for their concepts to catch on. Only, someone on the outside of their difficulties, like me, could never say what would happen when that time came. Better times? Doom? More of the same, just hanging on?

Theresa had let herself into the chapel, the site of the Orlandinis' dining room, and set up five bottles of wine and ten glasses on the elegant antique sideboard. "How's the first class?" she asked me as she uncorked the first bottle, 2016 Chianti Colli Senesi. Her eyelids fluttered with the effort of just being sociable.

"Good, I think."

Together, we looked over our shoulders at the sounds of approaching voices. The aroma of Chef's "samples" announced their arrival.

"Come in!" I gushed.

Every single one of them looked reasonably happy, even Jenna, even Bob. They flowed into the chapel, spreading out a little, and held onto their fragrant, steaming plates with two hands. Pete stayed in the doorway, tacitly turning over the next program item—dinner!—to me. "Before you find your seats"—I gestured to the beautiful long table, set with soft linen placemats and napkins in the Tuscan sunset vermilion they had all just witnessed—"I'd like to introduce you to our local vintner, Theresa Franchi, who is providing the wine for the evening's meal."

I heard Glynis say, "Lovely."

Zoe threw in, "Nice to meet you."

Setting down the uncorked bottle, Theresa turned with a bright smile that would convince any onlooker there was nothing better in this world than to be a Tuscan grape-grower and winemaker. As she surveyed the hungry group of Americans, what started out as a bubbly *benvenuti* caught in her throat, and I watched Theresa's face lose all its color. She took a step back, her hip meeting the sideboard, and didn't speak.

"Theresa?" I said in a low voice. "Everything okay?"

Then her voice dropped, and her troubled eyes turned to me. "Nell," she said, "I forgot my notes." She bit her lower lip. "I can't do this without my notes." Suddenly remembering her job, she sang out, "Hello, everybody!" She brandished a bottle with the green and gold Franchi vineyard label. "Welcome to a short tour of Franchi Estate Winery, without ever leaving your seats." If it sounded a bit hysterical, I don't think the others noticed.

"Oh, she's American," Zoe said softly to no one in particular.

"I'd say from the South," put in Bob Gramm, smiling, and pulling out a chair.

"Very cool," commented George, but I for one was unclear what he was referring to.

"Pretty bottle." That was Jenna.

As they found seats for their first meal of Marinara Misteriosa, I motioned Pete over to us.

Pete drew alongside me. "What's up?"

Theresa straightened up. "I forgot my notes, Pete. I need my notes. My memory's crap these days."

"Are they out in the car?"

But I already knew where it was going. Your face

doesn't lose all color if the solution is a matter of steps away. She lowered her eyes. "They're at home."

Behind us, our guests were digging into the separate hills of Annamaria's handmade pasta—and Chef's four-sauce sampler—and passing the water jugs, the salad bowl, the sliced ciabatta. I had an idea. "Theresa, you will pour, Pete, you will narrate—"

He said confidently, "I know these wines."

To Theresa, I whispered, "Jump in wherever you can add something of interest, okay?"

Bob Gramm was pointing to his plate with his fork as if it was exhibit A. "Excuse me." He overrode every other voice in the room. "Excuse me!" I shot Pete a look that said, *I'll take it.* "This is not gluten-free pasta. Did I not make myself clear?"

I stepped closer to the source of the aggravation. "Yes, Bob." The *you jackass* went unspoken. "You did."

"I am gluten-free," he orated, slapping the table with every syllable. "Is that so hard to accommodate?" He looked around with a load of righteous indignation. "These, these"—he eyed his plate with his nose turned up—"are sections of garden hose."

Pete intervened easily. "It's gluten-free, Bob. It's just not handmade. We found out about your allergy less than two hours ago . . ." Smoothly putting the responsibility right back on Bob Gramm himself. "It was my pleasure to open the gluten-free pasta box for you."

"Well, then," he mumbled, "just find somebody out there"—he made the kitchen sound like the Siberian tundra—"who can properly cook the stuff."

I noticed Glynis scrutinizing him with no illusions.

Slowly, her husband returned—oddly placated—to his sections of garden hose.

Theresa, Pete, and I made a little scrum against the sideboard, our faces turned from the diners. Setting one hand on her chest, she said, "I pour."

"I narrate," said Pete.

Sliding my eyes in the direction of Bob Gramm, I whispered, "I drink."

With that, we turned back in unison.

The noteless, nervous Theresa came through.

The dependable Pete came through.

And every single student in our Marinara Misteriosa class was captivated. Theresa uncorked and poured half glasses, nimbly making her way around the diners, while Pete supplied the stories about the regional grapes, and which wine paired best—strictly his opinion, he told us— with which of the plated marinara sauces, and why. While our hungry Americans sampled, rolled their eyes, and purred, Theresa added color commentary, mainly funny little stories about the Franchi family history in viticulture. She started to loosen up, and the color came back to her face.

As our Americans tasted the weekend's great teaser, Chef Claudio Orlandini's *prima marinara*, I witnessed dish devotion to the *prima marinara* by Zoe, George, Glynis, Bob (okay, maybe not so much), and even Jenna, which was something to behold.

"Marjoram," voiced Zoe, chewing reflectively; "Chervil," countered Glynis, moving a forkful around inside her mouth.

Chef entered to applause. I found myself wondering what it really meant to this man, to know he was finally opening what outsiders had clamored for: his recipe vault. I felt a little frisson on Chef's behalf—in three days he'd be handing out a recipe he had kept secret for a lifetime, and to me as I tasted that glorious marinara sauce for myself, it felt like an admission of mortality. It felt like he was making out a will.

We ate, we drank, we spoke in half sentences, and we finished. As Rosa and Sofia cleared, the Orlandini chapel became a kind of dream sequence, as we all moved off languorously. As I pushed in my chair, I noticed the candlelight brightening a lamb in one of the stained-glass windows. From speakers overhead came the opening bars of Miles Davis's "Kind of Blue," which always felt inquisitive . . . *Now let's see, where did I leave those keys?* I saw George Johnson press his lips together appreciatively, his eyes darting around, trying to find the chooser of the non-Italian exit music. My money was on Rosa, whose tastes occasionally opened up enough to include someone other than Billy Joel. Left to the classical Annamaria, we'd all be listening to the death scene duet from any of a number of operas.

Zoe paired herself up with Chef, following him into the kitchen. He was pleased.

Theresa came over to me. "We had a disaster today," she confided, stepping me out of earshot.

"What happened?"

"The workmen knocked down the last twelve bottles of our 1985 Rocciosa." Leo and Theresa were expanding the tasting room at the winery, in hopes of attracting more "wine and cheese" events, but it meant carving space out of a very old area of their wine cellar. The Rocciosa was Leo's grandfather's experiment—not the only one in the area—back in the late forties to combine nonindigenous grapes with their native Sangiovese stock, the definition of what became called a Super Tuscan. Strictly for private use . . . until the more robust Rocciosa wine broke out of the family kitchen. A bottle of the rare 1985 vintage brings up to $3,500. Theresa stood blinking. "Leo's heartbroken," she said simply. "Gone is gone for good."

"I'm sorry," I said, giving her arm a squeeze. "No wonder you forgot your notes."

Giving me a grateful smile, she headed for the door.

Glynis, Pete, and Jenna headed toward the common room on Pete's promise of a fire and a nightcap. Bob followed Theresa Franchi out to her car, not helping her carry the unopened bottles.

From my spot leaning on the doorjamb of the courtyard door, I could see nearly everyone, I truly love what I call my "found moments," those unexpected interludes when I find myself completely alone while life goes on around me. No demands, no expectations—no talk. Turning my head slightly, I saw Theresa Franchi standing in the dim light, her arms folded, listening to Bob Gramm bend her ear. Poor Theresa. First, no notes. Then, Bob Gramm. Not her night. Out dashed the slight Sofia, presenting Theresa with her stiff straw tote she had left behind.

Shifting my gaze, I saw the last of Pete and his firelovers disappear into the common room. The lights went on. I sighed happily and, for just a moment, stepped out of Ardis Valenti's cast-off Guccis, letting my eyes shut. Everyone was accounted for, except for George Johnson? Not outside jawing with Theresa and Bob. Not off in the common room sharing fire-making tips with Pete. And then I had it. Off phoning my father, no doubt.

With just an hour left to Opening Day, I was content.

My takeaway had nothing to do with marjoram or chervil. This much I knew: Time and stirring a winebased sauce tend toward the same end. All gets reduced.

I just didn't know an unseen clock was ticking down our remaining time together.

O n that clear, moonlit night, after our American marinara lovers toddled off to their beds, Pete, Chef, Annamaria, and I met for a quick powwow on the next day's agenda. Booked for the first full day was the wine cellar tour with Theresa Franchi, marinara sauces with anchovies, olives, and Chef, and mushroom picking with Annamaria. Then the usual naysaying ensued, at 11:20 p.m. when I could hardly see straight, but naysaying topics turned out to be scanty. Rosa questioned the quality of the anchovies, Chef declared them the finest north of Sicily. Annamaria questioned crowding the wine cellar with all the *studenti* at once, but when Chef agreed with her that perhaps private, one-on-one tours might be better, I could see they were both thinking about Zoe, and Annamaria changed her mind. Finally, the rest of us said our good nights and Pete stayed on to coach Chef on the first cooking class.

Coach? Was it at all possible that in his whole fifty-year career, Chef Claudio Orlandini had never run a cooking classroom? He had run top-of-the-line restaurants, he had run TV cooking shows, he had judged international competitions, he had hosted exclusive dinner parties, he had demonstrated Olympian cooking skills to select friends in the business . . . but, mentally thumbing through what I knew of Chef's career, I couldn't for the sorry life of me picture the guy heading up an actual kitchen classroom. Something this disturbing could only be likened to finding out that your flight instructor was a stupendous pilot who had never actually taught anyone to fly.

In Chef's case, shouldn't somebody here have mentioned it by now?

If anyone ever asks, there is an internal state that goes beyond dread. At that moment, as I stood wheezing under the ridiculous arbor of killer lilies framing the entrance to the main building, I felt a fatalism I had never before experienced. Tomorrow afternoon, Chef Claudio Orlandini would be entering a kitchen classroom for what might very well be the first time in his crazy life. It might take these five foodies no more than twenty minutes into a lesson on marinara with anchovies to realize in horror that the chef they had ponied up several grand to learn from doesn't know how to delegate food prep tasks.

Maybe I should hop to my room and Google legal definitions of fraud.

I collared Rosa, who was heading off to bed, to help me drag the lily arbor to the compost pile at the back of the barn. Between us, we manhandled the thing wordlessly, managing to keep it just off the cobblestones, which would shred the cursed thing as we went. No way I was going to play cleanup. And no way I was going to let the cheerful Rosa play cleanup. We were tired. So we toted the arbor awkwardly aloft, like skulking off with a corpse, and slowed as we neared the renovated barn room and heard the raised voices through the half-open window.

The Gramms were duking it out verbally.

Rosa's eyes widened. I put a finger to my lips, caught between wanting to tune in and not wanting to be outed by my wheezing. Although I wasn't sure they'd even hear it. They weren't shouting, which is oddly what made it sound more vicious. And not at all new. It was Glynis, and she sounded angry. ". . . told me it was over."

"It is."

"What's this, then, a lovely parting gift?"

"Why is it always about—"

"Because with you," she said with feeling, "it is."

"Well," he said, managing to sound high-handed, "maybe you should take a look at why."

"What's that supposed to mean?"

". . . cold-hearted bitch."

A sudden intake of breath. Then came the sound of a slap. ". . . made me one."

"Just one of your many talents." His voice was snide.

"Mine don't hurt."

"Says you." Very high-level, Bob. Wordlessly, Rosa and I inched closer to hear them better.

"What's that supposed to mean?"

"Maybe if you spent more time with me—"

"Twenty-five years is plenty of time. More than plenty."

His voice overrode hers. "—I wouldn't need a Joanne."

"Joanne? Who's Joanne? I thought her name was Sheila. You told me it was over with Sheila." Total silence. No answer. Glynis's voice, when it came was cold. "I see. It is over with Sheila."

"For Christ's sake, Glynis," said Bob Gramm, trying to bluff his way out of it, "none of it means—"

"You're a cliché. You're a mean, middle-aged car-selling flop, and I'm done bailing you out." He let out a cry, and something small clattered onto the floor. "Go home. I don't want you here. Pick up the gaudy piece of overpriced crap and take it home to Joanne. I get your bills, she gets your gold bracelets."

"Look, you, we paid for this stupid trip, and I for one—"

"Oh, yes, you for one. You for one." She let out a harsh laugh. "It's always you for one." And then: "You know, Bob, I think it's finally my turn."

"What's that supposed to mean?"

"I don't know yet. But as soon as I do, I'll let you in on it."

When we heard her approach the door, Rosa and I loped around the side of the barn, nearly dropping the stinking lily arbor, and I pressed my eyes shut, hoping Glynis wouldn't head in our direction while she cleared her head. She didn't, although I couldn't say where she went. I wondered how much of the Gramms' argument Rosa, whose English wasn't very advanced, understood.

So the bracelet from the jewelry shop in Cortona was bought not for Glynis but for a woman named Joanne. The latest in what sounded like a long line. I wished we hadn't listened. Their argument was raw and ugly and full of pain. But in the cool Tuscan moonlight, Rosa and I made our way without a sound toward the compost pile. For the first time, in the distance it looked to me like a freshly dug grave.

7

The day the knife went missing, certain other things occurred that crowded out any awareness that one very long, very sharp blade was unaccountably absent. For me, the day began when the Orlandini family secret—otherwise known as Pete's farmer cousin Oswaldo, who sold us produce—turned up at 7:18 a.m., demanding to see the Americana. Rosa, who happened to be awake and shuffling around the villa kitchen, trying to remember where Annamaria happened to store the coffee, asked the wild-haired Oswaldo exactly which Americana he meant. At present there were four.

When he pranced around with his nose in the air, she told him I was still sleeping, and could he please just leave the order plus the invoice in the corner? He met this suggestion with a look as though he had just understood quantum physics, flung an invisible cloak around his bony shoulders, and stalked out to retrieve the goodies. Which was where I ran into him, as I was heading toward the door to the main building in order to get inside to skulk to my office.

"Buongiorno, Oswaldo," I managed. Even though the lily arbor of death was gone, I swear I could still smell them. Like my parents themselves, they lingered unseen but made their presence forever felt.

He was overjoyed, clamped a fist to his concave chest in some show of fealty, and gestured at the boxes of veggies in the back of his truck. *"Ecco,"* intoned Oswaldo, stepping backward to clear a path for me to retrieve the stuff. It was literally a standoff. We eyed each other expectantly. Did he honestly expect me to haul produce? With a flourish Oswaldo produced the invoice, babbling in high-speed Italian, pointing to a phrase in small print. *"Consegnamo."* Oswaldo enunciated each syllable. Not a word I knew. Related to "consignment"? I glanced at the greens, the peppers, the eggplants. What could that concept have to do with vegetables? I studied Oswaldo, who had pulled himself upright, his tongue keeping all his teeth in line behind his upper lip.

"Non capisco." I don't understand. I used my handiest Italian phrase on him. Did he want a check right this very moment? Very well, I gave him a grim look. First, he can schlep. This I mimed by pointing to him, then to the boxes of produce, then with a grunt I pretended to lift. He approved mightily. With a tepid smile, I turned on my heel to lead the produce parade into the kitchen. No harm done. I could write him a check and get on with my day.

"No, no, no, no!" yelled Oswaldo with such ferocity you would think he was warning me off a minefield.

I faced him. "What?" Italian failed me.

The man drilled me with such an injured look, standing there in a backbend of indignation, that his nostrils were nearly sucked straight up his nose. *"Consegnamo,"* he whispered, slapping his hand. I watched his mind struggle with how to make himself understood. "Dehliffer."

Things were looking up. "Yes, yes, you deliver. Very good. Now come on."

The man stamped his foot. When he kept thrusting his arms at me, I understood that he believed he had met his contractual obligations—eggplants had made it to the villa courtyard. I fumed. Fortunately, considering the early hour, Chef sauntered up to us, dressed in a clinging black T-shirt and classic black-and-white houndstooth pants, his white double-breasted jacket carried over his left shoulder.

In that moment he looked surprisingly youthful, dreaming perhaps of private wine cellar tours with Zoe Campion, and I recalled how beautiful Chef Claudio Orlandini had seemed to me when he made the front cover of three of the top industry trade magazines ten years ago. In the lambent Tuscan morning light, I could tell he had oiled his close-cropped head of hair, and had followed up with something expensive that made his face glisten. Personally, I thought he could have waited until everyone crowded into the villa kitchen for several hours of food prep. Sweat is free.

When he heard from his nephew Oswaldo that the difficult Americana (gesture to me) was insisting on extra (I believe he used the word) cartage, Chef nodded sagely, and then launched into a couple of fake wrestling moves on Oswaldo that led to the nephew's shrieks of delight. When they shuffled around the courtyard in a crazy headlock from yesteryear, the two of them were asserting their familial connection. Winded, finally, the two of them slowed like drunkards, Chef chattering the whole time in robust Italian. Oswaldo's hair got affectionately rumpled, his cheeks kissed repeatedly, and then came the uncle's grand finale—he feinted as though he was going to pants the weirdo. At the end of this display, Oswaldo gleamed, adjusted his pants, and hauled the eggplants into the villa.

Lobbing a one-fingered kiss to Chef, I followed Oswaldo into the kitchen, where I found Rosa, who rolled her eyes at us, dug into the box of produce, and launched into a conversation with Oswaldo that sounded a lot like they were combing through the unsavory personal effects of someone who had died. When I reached my office, I found my two sensible coworkers, Pete and Annamaria, arms folded, heads nearly touching, working something out. Seeing me, they shot me a look. Pete jumped in. "Got a call half an hour ago from Theresa Franchi." He added, "Right after a call from Manny Manfredi."

"Oh?" Raising the blind, I swung open my window. "Tell me about Manny first."

"There's a pop concert in the piazza tonight. He can drive our five if they're interested."

"What did you tell him?"

Pete tilted his head at me. "That we'd let him know. We have to do some shifting around. And it's pretty last minute."

To get the group out of my hair for a couple of hours, I'd pay for the band myself. "We tell them we're moving— not axing, moving—free time to after dinner so they can go. Transportation provided. To accommodate this change—"

"No, no," Pete put in, "not this change, this opportunity."

I nodded. "To accommodate this opportunity, dinner will be early this evening." We beamed at each other. "And Theresa?"

"It's about the wine cellar tour."

"Tell me it's got something to do with notes."

He smiled, his chin lifting in the direction of the scented air floating into the room. Annamaria, dressed in a gorgeous white chef jacket with cloth-covered buttons and black piping, was one of the most intrepid women I had ever met. I think there was nothing she couldn't look right in the eye and vanquish. "It's not notes, Nell, it's just a switch in the day's agenda."

"Namely?" I sat down behind my desk. Unlike George Johnson the day before, Pete and Annamaria stayed standing.

"She wants to switch her wine cellar spot to late afternoon. Something about a schedule conflict this morning. Leo needs her around."

My eyes moved from Pete to our kitchen queen. "That means she's switching with Annamaria, then. Will that work?"

Pushing out her lips, the elegant sous-chef kept it simple. *"Sì."*

Pete went on, "Switching them makes sense, actually, Nell. Now Annamaria will be teaching her mushroom identification class first thing, which means she's then in the kitchen prepping for the first marinara uninterrupted for the rest of the day."

Annamaria closed her eyes. *"Sta bene,"* was all she said.

"And"—I got into the swing of it—"Theresa will be around for the cellar tour at a time of day that makes better sense for wine. Maybe she'll naturally move into commentary about pairings."

"Crazy time in the kitchen, but—"

"I think it'll work. You know . . ." I spread my hands on my desk. "We may want to keep it this way for future classes." As soon as I said it, I realized that Pete and Annamaria were for some reason relieved—even, I'd say, uplifted. Maybe La Bella Nella was staying on? Maybe the cooking school would weather the worst of the events of a month ago? Maybe it would take more than a murder to keep a good cooking school down? I felt a strange kind of power, then, that I hadn't known I had. People were looking to me, Nell Valenti, to set the tone. I got it. If I couldn't stand behind my vision and hard work for the Villa Orlandini Cooking School, why should they? It was all unspoken, but our smiles bucked me up.

It wouldn't last long.

They all seemed game to begin their day with Good Mushrooms/Bad Mushrooms 101. When we explained the schedule change for the day, nobody kicked. In fact, they leaped at the idea of live music in a place as romantic as a piazza in Tuscany, rides provided. So, all settled. Then, with the exception of Jenna, we all pretty much headed to the woods with mugs of coffee. She seemed to take an uptight, academic view of the program, what with a pink spiral notebook and one pen and a spare jammed into the spiral binding. Annamaria looked about as woodsy as she could stand by shedding her chef jacket and donning a cranberry-colored light down vest. She carried a wicker basket that held seven utility knives. Too late it occurred to me it would have been a stellar idea to have brought someone along who could translate Italian with some ease.

Someone, in other words, other than me.

We trooped along like the line heading for the bathrooms in elementary school. I moved up just behind Annamaria, our line leader, who was gesturing airily toward tree trunks, tree leaves, and tree roots, expounding (I was guessing) on the kind of woods we had here on our hands. When she stopped to admire a scurrying quail, insisting how good *la quaglia* is when roasted with olive oil, lemon, and bay leaves, I checked the group.

Bob Gramm, looking some cross between bored and hangdog, scuffing along through fallen leaves, was toward the back of the line, followed closely by Jenna, who was scowling at him so intently that she tripped over an exposed root. Close behind me, apparently all we had in the way of a spur-of-the-moment translator were George, Glynis, and Zoe. Glynis, who seemed no worse for wear after the awful marital clawing of the night before, seemed to think Annamaria was describing the lesser-known, finer attributes of the species quail. George and Zoe exchanged looks with me I couldn't quite interpret. Something along the lines of either *Let's get to the mushrooms already* or *Any fool knows quail is better pan-fried*.

Among the thickest clump of beech trees, Annamaria pulled up short.

We gathered around, watching her find a two-foot-long dried stick, which she brandished like a switch, while favoring Zoe with a side-eye. Maybe it was time to add "Muscle" to my job description. Using the stick to push aside some fallen leaves, Annamaria tapped two leather brown caps of what she declared to be *i porcini*, tasty and edible porcini mushrooms. A soft chorus of "aahs" charged the air. Delighted, Glynis proclaimed them bigger than what she found back home at Whole Foods. Proud as could be, taking silent credit, apparently, for fungi everywhere, Annamaria handed out the knives and shooed the Americans to find sticks to spread fallen leaves and discover their own porcini to harvest and drop into her "wee-care *cestino*"—"wicker basket," I translated.

It was, of course, Bob Gramm who found a twig the size of a hockey stick, with broken prongs at the end of it, which he proceeded to use as a rake. Wielding this thing seemed to take his mind off his troubles, and he dug it along the forest floor as though he were a mountain lion sharpening his claws on his downed prey.

In a moment, Annamaria flew at him, grabbing the offensive makeshift tool and flinging it safely away. Mid-screech, she was explaining to *l'idiota*, from what I could tell, that it was a *peccato molto grande*—a very big sin— to disturb the forest floor. Everyone took a step back. Realizing she might have overreacted, Annamaria shrugged and murmured that using such a big stick was *contro le legge*. "Against the law," I put in.

Bob Gramm was bemused. "These Eye-tals have laws about mushrooms?"

I felt like telling him his ethnic slurs needed some updating.

Annamaria shoved her own dainty, lawful stick at *il idiota*, and everybody got busy exposing the brown leather caps of porcini mushrooms, and then using their utility knives to harvest them. Over the next hour, Annamaria made a tour of the pine and beech woods well behind the villa property, stopping coyly where she knew the mushroom pickers could have some luck. We found some ruffled, funnel-shaped chanterelles, but came up empty when Annamaria described the rare *ovulo buono*—nicknamed Caesar's mushroom—with its reddish cap, delicious grilled with any number of Italians' favorite foods. No luck.

As we were all poking gently at the forest floor with our sticks, slicing off our prizes with our knives, the six of us went very quiet when we noticed Annamaria standing statue-like fifty feet away from us in a copse of beech trees, her head high, eyes closed, arms directing us to the ground. She awaited us with the patience of marble. The woman had an instinct for drama. One by one we made our way over to her, gathering into a semicircle. *"Che cos'è, Annamaria?"* I whispered, figuring maybe she had found a dead porcupine.

"Ecco la morte," she said in her sepulchral voice.

Interested, we drew closer, our little group clustering around . . . a mushroom.

"Surely you exaggerate," said somebody, I think Dob.

"Destroying angel?" breathed another.

Annamaria opened her eyes and looked around the little group. *"Come si chiama . . ."* She paused for effect, then dropped her voice. "Death cap." Several things happened at once. Glynis managed to cut herself on her knife, George crouched as close to the death cap as he could get and took its picture with his iPhone's camera, and Zoe reached down, slowly extending her hand as though to touch it. When Annamaria swatted her hand away, Zoe worked in a laughing, "Just kidding, Annamaria, no worries!"

The horrified Annamaria held up both her hands and

twiddled her shaking fingers at us, shouting brokenly, *"mai, mai, mai senza guanti,"* which I hurriedly put together in English for the rest of us: "never without gloves." Then, tensing her hands in the vicinity of Zoe's pretty head, Annamaria added, *"Sei pazza?"* I knew this meant "Are you crazy?" but when five sets of eyes turned to me, I just shrugged and smiled, lost in an Italian-English wilderness.

Only, naturally, George Johnson seemed to be on to me. And I hated it that he just chewed his lower lip and turned away. I would have preferred it if he'd outed me right then and there. Called in the language police. Done his worst. I didn't want him on my side. In anything. For some reason I didn't want to think about too deeply. He was no more than a spy in the House of Orlandini.

We made it back to the villa's kitchen with no time to spare before Chef began his classroom instruction on the preparation of *marinara con acciughe.* There, in a confused cluster of bodies, we set our knives in the sink while Annamaria tumbled the mushroom bounty out of her "wee-care" basket and set to cleaning them, her fingers flying. After a hasty flurry of thanks to her for her lesson, the five Americans—and I—dashed to the common room. The first thing that caught my eye was a bowl of what looked like dozens of the silvery, staring little fish, sitting out on a stainless steel table.

Ducking my head toward the bowl, I sucked in a breath and detected only the very faintest smell of the Mediterranean. They would do. George, Glynis, Jenna, Zoe, and Bob were busy getting ready in a flutter of laughter and bib aprons, but I noted that it was Zoe who tied Bob's, and George who tied Glynis's. The only husband and wife team in our first class was not much of one. At this rate, it was going to be a long four days before Manny Manfredi pulled in to take them off my hands.

Rosa was cueing up a YouTube video of *Stealth Chef* on the wall-mounted TV, Pete was setting out cutting boards, and Sofia was setting handouts at the places of the five Americans. I knew—after he'd made a speech where he'd no doubt liken haute cuisine to bocce ball—Chef would begin with proper handling of fresh garlic. Nowhere to be seen. "I'll get the garlic," I called to Pete and Chef, "and the knives." Pete smiled and invited the students to take their seats. I swept into the kitchen, where I found Annamaria had set out two bowls of garlic bulbs. But I could tell her mind was elsewhere. For one, she was still wearing her cranberry-colored light down vest. This would be akin to my father, Dr. Val Valenti, turning up on the set in his bathrobe.

With a dish towel clumped in one fist, she was staring at a row of washed, dried, neatly lined up utility knives. A hank of her lustrous salt-and-pepper hair had escaped its slip and was dangling over her cheek. She looked up at me. *"Sette persone, no?"*

"In the woods?" When she nodded once, I stepped closer, counting us on my fingers. "You, me, Bob, Glynis, Zoe, Jenna, and George."

What she muttered was something along the lines of *I thought so.*

Gesturing to the cutlery like she was pitching crap rings on HSN, she pointed out, *"Sei coltelli."*

Six knives.

Seven people.

Even though I could handle that much math, Annamaria

stated the obvious. *"Manca un coltello."* *A knife is missing.* An eyebrow rippled at me. If eyebrows could speak, hers were telling me *No good can come of this.*

With a little smile meant to convey there's a simple explanation, I held up my hand. *"Un momento, Annamaria."* She grunted skeptically. I scooped up the garlic bowls and headed back to the "classroom." As I predicted, Chef was in full throat, with Pete patiently translating as though these were some of the pearls the students with the quizzical expressions on their faces had paid for, and I plunked down the garlic.

Discovering I was pretty fluent in expressions about stalling, I held up a hand and begged, *"Un momento, per favore."* Chef shut up, giving me a look I had seen when he suspected the wine in his glass was on the brink of turning. "Folks," I said, moving around to the end of the worktable, "just a little housekeeping before we continue." Eyebrows lifted. Lips parted. Zoe licked hers, almost unobtrusively. Chef was riveted. I went on, "Did you all turn in your knives from mushroom picking?" By way of answers I got "sure," "of course," "first thing," and "what are you implying?"

"Are you sure you didn't leave yours out in the woods? Not a problem, believe me. Jenna?" I discovered I had decided to ask them individually, like polling a jury. "Sorry." She shook her strawberry blond head. "George?" His eyes narrowed, wondering what was up, and he shook his head imperceptibly. "Glynis?" Half a shrug, then, "Not me." "Bob?" At which he huffed nonsensically, "I don't drop things." I sighed. "Zoe?" She gave me a soft look. "Mine was the first in the sink." As I told them thanks, maybe it was Annamaria (big laugh) or me (the laughter died, which indicated they thought that was where the smart money was).

As Annamaria entered with a tray holding six black-handled chef's knives, I walked it back in my head. *Okay, just one of you.* I kept my face neutral. *One of you*—I smiled at each of them—*is a liar.* While the others watched Chef Orlandini piously unwrap his own set of professional knives that had followed him across the decades, I held my breath as the truth hit me.

One of these five has stolen a knife.

And I couldn't even begin to ask myself why.

8

[ornament]

Despite the busted wing, Chef managed to demonstrate—
while Pete narrated in English—crushing garlic
cloves with a flattened knife blade. George sat thumbing
the tip of his nose, and Jenna scribbled instructions in her
pink spiral notebook. "This technique," translated Pete,
"skins the clove, and crushes it just enough to prepare it
for chopping." Glynis managed to look like she was taking pleasure in this brutality toward poor unsuspecting
garlic, and Zoe actually winked at Chef, who reddened.

Then we moved on to the chopping, and Chef pulled
closer to the skinned garlic target because of the sling.
Setting his hands near the tip and the handle of the blade,
he vigorously rocked the knife back and forth over the
cloves, uttering happy little grunts as he went. Zoe moved
in, George tugged reflectively at his ear, Bob was checking his phone, which he held under the table, and poor
Glynis's nostrils flared. Staring at nothing at all, I made a
mental note to see if Jenna could put in a good word for
me at her coffee shop in Baltimore . . .

As it turned out, skinning and crushing garlic turned out to be a fond memory from this day of Marinara Misteriosa. When the class adjourned to the kitchen, a couple of things happened. First, while Pete inspected the freshly defunct anchovies by the sink, Annamaria had started what she usually did as Chef's sous-chef—namely, sautéing onions and garlic in a drizzle of extra virgin olive oil from Pete's grove while humming something tragic from *Aida*. Before our very eyes, Chef muscled her aside, wrested her long wooden spoon from her hand, and offered it to Zoe Campion. Zoe, who had a twinge, I guess, hit all the right notes: "I'm honored, Chef, but are you sure Annamaria doesn't mind?"

This should have alerted him to his little faux pas, but no. With boundless good humor, he spoke for Annamaria, saying, "She no mind *niente*." Pete appeared to be operating in a state of distraction—wondering how he was going to finish up the olive harvest if he was stuck translating for Chef over the next four days—but I noticed Annamaria's response to what I could call a slight, only that word would never, ever cover it.

This was a woman whose every emotion was worn large on her expressive face. At that moment in the kitchen, though, I saw her fine features shrink, as if happiness could disappear so completely for all time. Slowly, she stepped back from the stove, and turned away, hardly knowing what to do with herself. As a last resort, she stood with her back to the class, her fingers tearing a baguette into tiny pieces. Nobody questioned.

But when Chef anointed Zoe as Sous-Chef for a Day, that left four Americans to pair off as partners for cooking the marinara with anchovies. Glynis and George hastily teamed up, which left Jenna with Bob Gramm, who wasn't about to take this result with anything like good grace. "Oh, so I'm stuck with the special needs kid." At that, Jenna had a hard time controlling her face, not to mention her spit. He wasn't about to give up, and tried, "Whaddya say it's boys against girls, huh? Battle of the sexes!"

Glynis gave him a cold look. "This isn't dodgeball, Bob. You're not back in fifth grade."

George weighed in reasonably. "And it's not a competition. We're all here to learn."

For a snoop, he showed some nice instincts.

"Oh, bite me," said Bob maturely.

It was too much to hope for the aroma of the simmering tomatoes to disinfect the sour air in the villa's kitchen, and I decided to go solve some solvable problems in my office sanctuary. To Pete, who smiled when I sidled up close to him so as not to be overheard, I whispered, "I'm going to get you some help."

"Translating? Or harvesting?"

I winced. "Harvesting, Pete. I'm sorry. I still need you here as Chef wrangler."

"Right now," he murmured in my ear, "Pop seems like the least of our problems."

"I'm not so sure." When he looked at me questioningly, I squeezed his arm. "Fill you in later." Suddenly, into the relationship stink of the kitchen air came Dean Martin singing *"Volare, o-oh oh oh."* Since I admit I have no reliable Cheese Meter, I only cringed at this musical choice, eyeing Chef as the culprit. But Dino seemed to defuse the situation, and before I could hurry out of the Room of Simmering Rages, every last one of them was lamely joining Dean Martin. Except for Jenna, who left Bob to his own sauté pan to stand, shaking, next to George and Glynis. Waving all the goodness of the marinara sauce toward the pretty nose of Zoe Campion, which seemed oddly seductive, Chef wasn't about to make a pitch for sticking with a partner.

Out in the corridor finally free of lilies, I ran into Rosa emerging from the steps leading down to the wine cellar. In her capable hands were rags and a spray cleaner. While everyone else was prepping for marinara with anchovies, Rosa was sensibly prepping the wine cellar for the tour that would follow. Mental note: If I stuck around long enough to do performance reviews, Rosa Bari would get high marks as a self-starter. *"Andiamo."* I cocked my head at her in the direction of my office. Together we trundled. Together we shut the door behind us, at which point she stood at attention. *"Rosa, Pete ha bisogno di aiuto."* This was my one solid go-to Italian phrase, mastered quickly for obvious reasons. I need help, you need help, he/she/it needs help. And so on.

By way of response, Rosa uttered something along the lines of "I lust to help."

I enumerated sisters. *"Abbiamo bisogno di Laura and Lisa, okay?"*

She nodded sagely. *"Per le olive."* She got it in one. For the olives. "Also Pete."

I was filled with renewed hope, pathetic and wan, but hope nonetheless. *"Sì, sì, sì."*

She grinned conspiratorially. *"A che ora?"* Then she tapped her wrist.

"As soon as possible." What my English couldn't convey, my desperation did.

Rosa marched off.

And I was left with more pressing matters in terms of the Villa Orlandini Cooking School than the hurt feelings in the tight space of the kitchen. Find the utility knife that one of our volatile American students had swiped. Bad enough someone stole it, worse still the thief didn't own up to it, and lied to my face. I had no idea where to begin. Make a room-by-room search? And explain that how, to our rich suspects' satisfaction? How could I find the missing knife without alienating all the others who were innocent? In my mind, Yelp reviews were getting worse and worse . . . but then, so were what I was beginning to sense were the secrets and dire purposes of these five American foodies Manny Manfredi had deposited at our villa door.

The hours passed—for me, at least, pleasantly. I applied to myself for a mental health afternoon, which I granted with a smile coated with largesse. I deputized Rosa and Sofia as villa go-tos, explaining as best I could they needed to make a note of any complaints, suggestions, or compliments, not to mention breaking up any fistfights. They worked their jaws in quiet anticipation. Me, I sat with my feet up in an Italian villa sipping from endless cups of French-pressed French roast. I had my own lines in the sand.

As I was earning my keep by doing some design desk work—remove the wall between the kitchen and the storeroom, open things up altogether, or break through with a stone arch? decisions, decisions—Pete stuck his head in. "I'm heading for the bank." He looked tired, and he hadn't harvested so much as a single olive today. "Anything you need from town?"

Without missing a beat, I answered him. "Manny Manfredi." Pete gave a little laugh that made hardly a sound. "Is it Tuesday yet?"

Stepping inside, he ran a finger around his collar as he shook his head sadly. "You know," he said finally, "I think Stealth Chef's got the right idea."

"How so?"

"Anonymity up the wazoo, works with just a sous-chef, no studio audience."

I saw his point. "No drama."

"No drama. The food's the PR."

"Recipes for All."

"Not just now, so Rosa tells me. She tuned in to *Stealth Chef* and it was reruns."

"Poor kid." I made a sympathetic face. Calling the nun on the far side of fifty a poor kid was a bit of a stretch, but there was an odd freshness about Rosa that seemed young to me.

"Yeah," said a weary Pete, leaning against the wall, "Stealthy's got the right idea." His hands went up helplessly. "And look at us. A battery of loose cannons. It'll be week after week of group therapy with tomatoes and garlic."

"It's unfair to expect so much from vegetables."

"Or Oswaldo."

"Agreed." I loosened up my shoulders. At last: some dysfunction I could get behind. With my boots.

"By the way," said Pete, glancing at his watch and straightening up, "he called."

"Oswaldo?"

"He forgot to pick up his pay."

"When will he be here? I can have it ready." And possibly enlist Rosa to hand it to him.

"Oh," said Pete airily, turning in a slow circle, looking around as though wainscoting was infinitely more interesting than anything going on in the kitchen, "just about the time Theresa's halfway through the tour of the wine cellar. Which, by the way, is turning out to be later than we wanted. Leo's got bottling problems."

"Okay, so, when"—I widened my eyes, which ramped up the headache behind them—"can we expect her?"

"Well, let's put it this way, Nell. What she pours the five of them down in the wine cellar, they can carry right upstairs to their places at the dinner table."

Picturing a chaotic scene that was scheduled for three hours from now, I pushed back my chair. Then I gave Pete Orlandini a long look. "You're regretting the whole thing, aren't you?" I felt strangely detached. Maybe I had just lived with the regret longer than he had.

"Not meeting you." The smile lasted.

"But," I added, "I brought a lot of trouble."

He shrugged and found some energy reserves. "You didn't mean to."

I laughed. "Who's doing the cheering up here, Pierfranco?"

He slid out of his chef jacket, stuffed the toque in a slash pocket, and hung it on a chrome hook. "I guess we both are." Then: "I'd better get to the bank."

Going over to him, I landed a quick little kiss-between-good-friends on his cheek. "We can keep assessing this whole project."

His eyebrows lifted. "Oh," he said humorously, "you mean the cooking school."

I gave him a playful shove. Good cover, Valenti, good cover. *"Arrivederci,"* I told him sternly. With a grin, he left my office, and when he was out of sight, I straightened out his hanging chef jacket, then gave it an affectionate little pat. Somewhere along the way, that afternoon, I made a decision not to tell Pete about the vicious argument last night between Bob and Glynis Gramm.

I wouldn't add to Pete's burden unless it turned out—somehow—to be absolutely unavoidable. How far do I go to protect what could reasonably be called our customers' privacy? And just where does that choice damage our own business—or worse yet, peace of mind? From what I could tell, nothing in Manny Manfredi's waiver, or our own, covered the problem. Right then, the problem was unclear, just a vaporous sort of uneasiness.

Tight schedule. If that day was a garment, it would be a straitjacket. Which, with that group, would have come in mighty handy. To be fair, though, whenever I stuck my head in just to be the responsible administrator and to make sure Chef hadn't set fire to anything he wasn't supposed to, everything seemed to be going well. The anchovies, first up, met with some reluctance, Jenna blurting that she had stayed home sick from tenth grade bio the day they pithed the frogs. It ended up being Glynis who did the fish cleaning, expressionlessly. She even did Bob's. Eviscerating and decapitating? No problem. Her eyes were on him the whole time.

I happened to be peeking in when the class was ready for the second marinara of the day, which was supposed to be with olives. The blue bowl with a beautiful quart of Pete's olives was standing by. But then Chef, waxing eloquent on his impressive culinary career, seemed to pull up from the mists of memory a different idea. Very casually he mentioned that the olives could wait; they would be tackling his *prima marinara* instead. Some collective breath holding happened next—including mine—followed by some variation of swooning. Pete widened his eyes at me. They hadn't prepped for *prima*. They had prepped for olives.

The Americans straightened up on their stools, wondering if they'd heard right, while I slapped my hard bright smile in place and took Chef aside. Zoe found some reason to follow, slowly tugging on paper towels from the paper towel dispenser while Pete and I whispered to Chef that we had prepped for olives. "It will take time to make this sudden change in terms of the"—I eyed the lingering Zoe, who was a little too close for my taste, so I kept things general—"ingredients," I said meaningfully to Chef.

He waved me away. "No in the mood for *le olive*."

I pulled him farther yet from the group. "But, Chef, we were saving *prima* for the big finale."

"*L'ultimo giorno,* Pop," tried Pete.

If we served the prize to these five right off the bat, I was worried they'd be checking out the very next day. Even with this group, I couldn't bear it. It felt like an error of, well, syllabus. His eyes were narrow and uncomprehending. For such a fine self-promoter, Chef Claudio Orlandini had some impenetrable zones in his brain. But to him it was clear. His nostrils collapsed from the mighty breath he inhaled, and he thrust out his chest. "*Ma non sono in mood for olives.*" This hodgepodge of English and Italian gave the Americans an opportunity to clamber behind his reasoning.

"Oh," said Bob Gramm, at the end of his short rope, "let the old guy do what he wants."

George piped up. "I can help. Just give me a list—" A little shrug.

Zoe put a comradely arm around Chef, her wad of paper towels fanning out. "I can prep it for you, Chef." From the tone of her voice, I honestly wasn't sure she was referring to the *prima marinara* sauce. At that, I glanced at the silent and inscrutable Annamaria, who was starting to move the blue bowl. She took a misstep, then fumbled the olives, and the bowl fell to the black-and-white-tiled floor, where it shattered.

Pete grabbed a broom, Zoe pulled a dustpan from a utility closet, and they set to work as Annamaria slowly stooped down to pick up the bigger shards, her beautiful face a mask. Sofia appeared in the kitchen and took Pete's place with the broom. While Bob Gramm was swearing and calling someone a moron, I happened to catch sight of Chef, who was standing still and regarding Annamaria with the kind of impassive look I hope never to see aimed at me. By anybody. I felt a pang. There was more than olives Chef Claudio Orlandini wasn't in the mood for, and the only sliver of good fortune I could find in that moment was that I was pretty sure Annamaria hadn't seen his look.

I made a quick executive decision, mainly to avoid any more public back-and-forth about what was planned and what was being substituted. Why did it all feel like such a big deal? What I knew for sure was that we needed to flex. I clapped my hands twice and announced, as though it was a crazy fun switch, that class would be learning Chef's very secret *prima marinara* sauce in half an hour. A joyful shout went up, and Zoe executed a little rumba step. Behind my hard bright smile was a delicious sting, and I added, "Chef himself will prep for the *prima*." He shot me a startled look. "It will be his great pleasure."

Oh, let the old guy do what he wants. Bob Gramm got it right.

For the first time since I arrived at the Villa Orlandini, I really didn't like Chef.

Cradling the bigger shards of blue, as though they were the years of her life, Annamaria Bari looked around the kitchen at the invaders. Her eyes were dry.

* * *

Much later I would be hard-pressed—mostly by Giovanni Battista Onetto, police detective—to recollect the chaos of that late afternoon. In the nearly unworkable crowd of American foodies, plus Pete, Chef, Annamaria, and more Baris than I could shake a stick at, it was a blend of what I came to think of as hush and rush. I saw no reason to insert myself into that happily agitated mix, not when I could get a leg up on office work, but I did have to enter the fray a couple of times. Once I needed to remind Pete to ply the promo blurb for the Marinara Misteriosa workshop by working in the phrases about Chef opening his recipe vault and divulging this closely guarded secret of fifty years.

The quiet part of the afternoon occurred when Chef zoomed off into culinary reminiscences over his long, Olympian career—and it got its quietest both when he breathed the creative process for the *prima* recipe (here I had the strange feeling he was making it up as he went along) and again when he named one of the heretofore secret ingredients. Notepads were scribbled on, pens were tapped. Fresh Roma tomatoes, fresh marjoram ("Ah!"— Zoe's voice—"Pay up, Glynis"), garlic, shallots, red pepper. No surprises there, apparently.

But the exact—if you could call them exact— measurements were colorful and key. A thimble of port. A jigger of Parmigiano-Reggiano. And then—then came the uttering of the secret ingredient that had baffled imitators for half a century. "What's the citrus, Chef?" came Glynis's voice. "I know there's citrus. Is it tangerine?" Over the rumbling laughter of the other four, who knew this was the moment on the brink, that tissue-thin membrane between ignorance and knowledge.

Over the deepest hush came the voice of Claudio Orlandini, with Pete translating. He closed his eyes meditatively. "Juice and zest of one small citron." Cries rose of "how small?" Size of a bocce ball? a tennis ball? a handball? Pete told me later that when Chef named the elusive secret ingredient, he timed it with lifting the lid off a covered ramekin: one small citron. *"Così piccolo,"* Chef equivocated. *This small.* Someone called it the size of a handball. More scribbles. George Johnson sat quietly on his stool, his hands lightly resting on the table.

The revelation of the vaunted *prima marinara* sauce was the highlight of the entire day. While they simmered the treasure, the kitchen got more crowded. Rosa kept up with dishes, the oddly popular Oswaldo turned up to sniff into sauté pans and hobnob with the others and collect a check from me, Annamaria tended two pasta pots, and Theresa Franchi came in to announce the tour of the wine cellar was about to begin. This time she had her notes. "We'll keep it short," she said, raising her voice to be heard, and I mouthed a *grazie* at her.

It was a scene of jostling, elbowing, avoiding hot plates and pots, and shreds of discussion about the unforgettable surprises of this day at the beyond wonderful Villa Orlandini Cooking School. A whole lot of *Bravissimo!* got shouted. Suddenly every one of those Americans believed they were fluent in Italian. Parmesan got grated, citron got zested, palates got tested. Over it all wafted the heady and mysterious aroma of Chef Claudio Orlandini's signature sauce, the *prima marinara*. It made me happy to realize that we can know all the ingredients of something and still not really know it.

They filed out of the kitchen, stripping off toques and chef aprons, following Theresa to the wine cellar. Last came George Johnson, looking quietly amused. As he passed me, he drew both of his hands across the front of my face. "My job was zesting the citron."

"Teacher's pet."

Smiling enigmatically, George Johnson gave me a long look. Without a word, he rejoined the group, heading down the five-hundred-year-old steps to the villa's wine cellar. Just ahead of him was Oswaldo, of all people, who appeared genuinely interested in everything, including the Americans. Turning away to go to my office, I saw Pete, stripping off his chef gloves, watching George, then eyeing me. "Long day," I said, feeling a little odd, a little distant. It was a day, too, I came to see, of wordless moments. Pete said nothing in response, just shot me a tight-lipped little nod and disappeared into the kitchen.

Theresa kept her word. Twenty minutes later, everyone trooped back up the steps, and emerged with stemless glasses of a Montepulciano of recent vintage from the Franchi winery. It was a dealer's choice that day, and we left it to Theresa to choose what to decant to pair with Chef's glorious student-prepared *prima marinara* sauce. The Americans—and the invited Oswaldo—fairly dashed to the chapel dining room to set their glasses at their places, and they returned to the kitchen to plate the day's culinary accomplishments. Chef was insisting on separate dinner plates for each sauce, rattling off some improvised notion about not letting sauces mingle, in the interest of flavor purity.

Theresa entered to hand wine to Annamaria and Rosa, "our kitchen Graces," as she called them. The chaos continued in the dizzying smells of good Italian cooking.

Even Annamaria's handmade linguine smelled, as it drained, like the very first pasta. Everyone worked together to see that plates had the right helpings, that Bob Gramm got his "glue-tone-free" linguine, and that the poor sidelined marinara with anchovies got some love. Annamaria was looking swamped in the day's wreckage of cookware used, stacked, set aside for *dopo*—later. Rosa told her sister to leave it, leave it—*"Hai fatto abbastanza"*—You've done enough. Rosa would stay late or come early in the morning to wash up.

In the happy clash of voices, I happened to pass behind George and Zoe, who didn't notice me. "It isn't right," she practically whispered to him, and I understood she meant the *prima marinara*. I held my breath. "No," he whispered back, "it isn't, is it?" He had the look of a man who's trying to see through the veil of wool over his eyes. "What's missing?" she pressed. But all George Johnson could do was slip her a wry look and shake his head slowly. Silently, then, they found their places at the table and set about cooing over the *prima* sauce along with all the others.

9

When the time came to hop into the Cucinavan for the concert in the piazza, Bob Gramm wasn't hopping. Instead, he was popping some Tums from Manny Manfredi and complaining about how he was paying thousands of bucks a day for meals topped with battery acid. Finally, Bob climbed into the van, And then there was Zoe, dashing up to me to let me know that Jenna wasn't coming. "Oh," I said, figuring it had been a busy day and she was looking for some downtime. "Is she reading in her room?"

"Don't know. Actually, I don't know where she is. She's just not answering her door. Oh! There's Chef. See you." And off she sprang to swing up the van's step just ahead of Chef, who had changed into pleated wool pants and a kind of Cossacks-at-play red silk shirt with billowing sleeves, the right one pinned back to accommodate the sling. From shadows seated inside the van came waves in my direction. I waved back, trying to get some kind of head count minus Jenna.

"Ciao ciao, Nell," shouted Manny Manfredi from the driver's seat. He patted his chest. "At your disposal this evening. Cucinavan," he declared, raising his voice, "meets all needs." In the background came Bob Gramm's querulous comments—"I'm telling you that sauce was off!"—topped by Glynis's smooth overriding that sounded a lot like, "Oh, shut up, won't you!"

"Let me out, let me out," squeaked Bob, lurching his way out of the van. I swear when the man saw me, he adopted a hobble. Representing the Villa Orlandini Cooking School, I stepped up. "Sorry you don't feel—"

Somehow Bob "the Glam" Gramm, who in the lamplight I could tell was sweating, managed to raise his arm in a threatening way at me. "Didn't I tell you gluten-free? Didn't I?" His left arm was hugged tight against his stomach. I know the light was dodgy, but he looked a little green. Joanne should only see him now. She'd need more than a gold bangle bracelet. I stood ready to learn more, to commiserate, and so on, but to my surprise the philandering Lamborghini dealer walked stiffly by me. "That crap dinner wasn't gluten-free. Now I'm in for it," he choked out, his other arm swiping across his quivering mouth, "and I told that hot-shot Chef of yours he's going to pay. I'm Yelp Elite." As he disappeared into the shadows at the barn apartment's doorway, first he muttered, "I warned him yesterday this place is a fraud." Then he called back viciously, "I'll destroy you."

Undaunted, Manny rhapsodized, "I promise transport for all my beloved guests to and from the action in the piazza as needed." He made it sound like he was manning an ambulance at the front lines.

I hollered back, "Much appreciated. Get along, then. Bye-bye."

For a moment, as the van's taillights disappeared to the right at the end of the driveway, I tried to picture Bob Gramm's dinner plate during the convivial chaos earlier. I couldn't imagine the kitchen had made that kind of mistake. All I could hope was that there would be music and dancing and drinks and whatever else I could reasonably expect a piazza to provide to keep that vanload of trouble out of my sight for the next three days. I heaved a sigh. The van would return. Count on it. Like locusts and appointments with the gynecologist. If five students could cause so much trouble, how could we possibly handle ten—or more?

*H*uddled against a cool breeze, I crossed the courtyard just as a small light went on in the Gramms' room in the barn. I made my way upstairs to the second floor of the dormitory. "Jenna?" In the low light, I rapped at the door to the Puccini room. Louder: "Jenna? It's Nell." My ear pressed to the door, I heard nothing. This time I pounded, and waited. Still nothing. I stood unsatisfied in front of Jenna Bond's closed door. Clearly, the kid was suffering from something. Maybe the death of her dad? Maybe a job that doesn't seem to be going anywhere? When it struck me finally that an overdose of sleeping pills could account for the silence inside the room, I heaved a huge sigh that could slow an asteroid in its tracks, and pulled out my master key. "Coming in," I announced.

I opened the door and stepped into the pitch-black room. Fumbling for the light switch, I scanned the room through my wince. No Jenna, alive or dead. Which meant, on the upside, where she was and what she was doing wasn't going to add tragedy to the short, star-crossed history of the Villa Orlandini Cooking School. Or, if it was, at least it wasn't in this room. When it comes to upsides, I, Nell Valenti, will take anything. On the downside, Jenna's absence meant some entirely different kind of bad news that would, before the night was over, entail more searchers and a much bigger net.

But before I succumbed to that next step, I'd snoop. If desperation set in, I'd expose George Johnson—here, I have to admit to a little frisson of double meaning—and enlist his professional help. (Thank you, Jenna. Next cooking class will be free of charge.) When we Valentis hire private dicks, we expect some bang for the buck. (Again, thank you, Jenna. Next two cooking classes will be free of charge.)

So I looked around at her neat little living space for the duration of Marinara Misteriosa. Sofia, who I thought of as informal head of housekeeping here at the villa, had done a spiffy job of making up the bed that morning. I'd recognize those hospital corners anywhere, and that little turn-down topped with a foil-wrapped Baci Perugina chocolate had Sofia written all over it. But Jenna hadn't snapped up the chocolate or slept in the bed. The problem was, I didn't know what to make of anything. Because her purple roller bag was standing open on the floor in the corner, tops, pants, and underwear half tumbling out, that's what drew my eye first.

Crouching, I sifted through everything, my fingers grazing through zippered compartments, coming up empty. Then I spied her pink spiral notebook on the nightstand. Inside all it held were quick sketches of porcini, chanterelle, and death cap mushrooms, with arrows and captions alongside. Quickly jotted fragments of whatever she could understand of Annamaria's lesson that morning were everywhere on the pages. Jenna had really soaked up the info, but there was nothing either useful or incriminating here. She had wanted to learn. One of the pure of heart. No hidden agendas, like George Johnson. No obvious lack of interest, like Bob Gramm. Somehow, this young barista from Baltimore who didn't want to be a barista forever—at this point, I was squeamishly hoping she'd get to be something, anything, forever—had put together the dough to come for these four days of sauce making in Tuscany.

In the jumble of items in Jenna's nightstand drawer was a framed three-by-five-inch color photograph of a younger Jenna arm in arm with—based on the resemblance—what had to be her father, with palm trees and fancy cars behind them. Under the frame were loose newspaper clippings, her passport, a blue plastic report folder with elastic ties, a Mass card for Anthony J. Bondi, and, wrapped up loosely in one of the cloth napkins from the Orlandini dining room   the missing knife. What on earth did she have in mind? Somehow I found it hard to believe that Jenna Bond would steal a five-inch utility knife to slice herself some personal mushrooms. And then lie about it.

Sitting heavily on the bed, I spread out the contents of Jenna's drawer. The only thing that was missing was a Cortona Attractions brochure. Maybe she had taken it with her, jammed it into a pocket and taken it with her . . . to see what, exactly, after nightfall in a strange place, without her wallet, her phone, her eyeglasses, and her Italian-English phrase book? Since virtually everything had been left behind here in her room, I had to assume one of two things. Either Jenna Bond was off stargazing somewhere on the villa property, guided by the lights, and absolutely planned on returning for some sack time and the rest of Marinara Misteriosa . . . or she was in such a bad state that she'd left everything behind because she would no longer be needing it, and would not be returning to the villa or, for that matter, to Baltimore.

I studied the Mass card for Anthony Joseph Bondi, who, according to the dates, was fifty-four when he "entered into rest" nine years ago. On the front, a picture of the Holy Mother, who appeared to be pointing helpfully at the information that the Funeral Mass was to be held at St. Anne's Church in Bonita Springs, Florida, with the time and address. On the back of the card was a thumbnail picture of the innocent face of the fading blond Anthony. Beloved son, beloved father, beloved friend, in business honest, in friendship true. Survived by daughter Jennifer. Survived by. And then instead of "Footprints" or "God's Garden," there were some Andrew Lloyd Webber lyrics I recognized from *The Phantom of the Opera*. "Think of me, think of me fondly / When we've said goodbye / Remember me, once in a while / Please promise me you'll try—"

It felt so sad to me, that poor suffering Jenna was carrying around all this painful memorabilia. The glossy cardboard Mass card had gotten soft with nine years of handling. Pulling out my phone, I GPS'ed Bonita Springs. Fifteen miles from Naples, Florida. Very interesting. Next I peered at the framed photo of what might have been a twelve-year-old Jenna, dressed in a pink skirt and white T-shirt, grinning into the camera with her dad, coconut palms framing the shot.

She was a little overweight, but she was happy, and her hair was pulled back in a spiky ponytail. Her bangs looked like she had trimmed them herself. But back in that day, her hair was brown. Studying the framed twelve-year-old Jenna, I'd say she had played volleyball and didn't drink so much as a cup of coffee, let alone serve up hundreds of cups a day. Had our Baltimore barista grown up in Naples? And then I noticed the swank cars in the background, lined up in what I had dismissed as a parking lot.

But it wasn't.

It was a dealership.

One by one, I read the loose newspaper clippings. *Local Dealership Sells Glamour. Downturn Hits Local Businesses Hard. Bob "the Glam" Gramm Consolidates Ownership.* And on the Police Blotter page from August 9, nine years ago, *Police Respond to Suspicious Gunshot Call.* It went on to report Anthony's death by apparent self-inflicted gunshot wound. What exactly was the cause and effect here? How could I find out? And finally there was a tiny square Death Notice clipping: Anthony J. Bondi, 54, former car salesman, suddenly at his home. What a strange disconnect, I thought. From a suicide in one report to a "suddenly at his home" in another, as if the poor man's heart had just plain stopped, and down he went on the living room carpet.

Who had made the 911 call?

And where had she slipped off to?

I could have spent some time wondering how she had found out Bob "the Glam" Gramm had signed up with his wife for Marinara Misteriosa. Maybe it was just a terrible coincidence. When they all climbed aboard the Cucinavan, had the Gramms not recognized her? I pondered for a moment, and realized for sure that my mother, Ardis Wentworth Valenti, wouldn't recognize the preteen kid of one of Dr. Val's former employees all those years later.

So, with Glynis it wouldn't have been an issue. But what about Bob himself?

I cast my mind back over the interactions between Bob and Jenna the short time they'd been under my nose. No. He didn't show any signs of recognition—no "Hey, gang, wait'll you guys hear this about old Jenna and me!"—but Jenna knew all too well who he was. What else explained her loaded loathing for the guy? Yes, he was loathsome to all the rest of us, but from what I could tell all the rest of us were able to just chalk it off to a type of obnoxious fellow countryman. Rich, entitled, obtuse.

Jenna wasn't able to master her feelings for this guy who came leaping at her out of her past. But it felt significant that she wasn't confiding in any of us, either. "Hey, gang, wait'll you guys hear this about old Bob and me!" *Why not?* Why wouldn't she just offer it up over wine and *marinara con acciughe* as one of those fluky, "small world" things. Because, because . . . my fingers lifted the newspaper clippings . . . Jenna Bond had come to the Villa Orlandini with a private agenda. She had clipped and saved and carted all the way to Italy the published reports of key points in the Gramm and Bondi relationship. She had brought what for her were memento mori.

I had to find her.

And I knew I had to do it without putting out the general alarm. Much as I'd like to, I had no reason to overreact, yet. So I preferred to think Jenna was out stargazing somewhere, just enjoying the beautiful Tuscan night alone. Keep it small, I told myself. But once I located her, saw her back to the Puccini room with soft laughs and lots of *buona notte*s, in the morning I'd ream her out but good while she choked down some excellent coffee and biscotti. No solo midnight excursions. There are wild boars. (Well, somewhere.) Removing cutlery from the kitchen without Annamaria's okay is strictly forbidden. (Make it sound like I thought she wanted to do some private peach peeling.)

I replaced the clippings, framed photograph (had Bob Gramm himself taken that picture?), and Mass card. But I took the knife, wrapped in the napkin; I would sneak it back into the knife block in the kitchen before I began my Jenna hunt. Odds were good Annamaria herself would discover its magical reappearance when she set foot in the kitchen in the morning, and she'd assume we'd shamed the thief into giving it up. Let her. One less task for me.

With a quick look around, I turned off the light, left the room, and relocked the door. As I headed toward the main building, I realized Bob Gramm had turned off the light in his room. Maybe the best thing was to let him sleep. I decided to check for Jenna in the olive grove and the woods before spreading a wider net—where, I had no idea. Calling the neighbors made some sense. Vincenzo, our next-door-farmer who lived alone with Stella, his truffle-hunting Lagotto Romagnolo dog. Even Leo and Theresa Franchi at the winery. It was possible Jenna could have made her way there.

I entered quietly into Annamaria's kitchen, withdrew the utility knife from the cloth napkin, and shoved it noiselessly into the block at the back of the counter. Then I dropped the napkin into the laundry basket and left, which was when I noticed the line of light coming from under the door leading down to the wine cellar. I didn't think it was the overhead light that usually flooded the space, so it was from some other source—a phone flash, maybe?—which was what made me not want to announce myself.

The door itself was ajar. The wine cellar was enough

out of the way of general foot traffic, and led to a place with but a single purpose—to keep the wine collection at optimal temperature—that I felt cautious. Chef is never one to conceal his whereabouts. The man was pretty much his own brass band. Pete was in town babysitting the cooking students at the concert in the piazza. Annamaria virtually ran the entire place, so why would she go to pains to keep anyone from finding out she was down in what she probably considered her own wine cellar? Secret drinker? Who had time! My money was on one of the Bari sisters.

Slipping off my shoes to avoid the scratching they'd make on the old stone steps, I stole barefoot down the stairs, gripping the cool, rough walls for safety. Ordinarily, I could get creeped out at that moment, but I knew I could handle Rosa or Sofia. Reaching the bottom of the stairs, I glanced quickly at the racks of bottled wines in front of me, and noticed the light source bobbing from side to side around the corner into the alcove out of sight. Grimly, I walked silently around the corner, sucking in air for my big *J'accuse!* moment, and pulled up short when there, spread-eagled against a stone wall that held no racks, was . . . George Johnson.

10

Later, it occurred to me I should have mustered something memorable, like, "The '03 Montepulciano is in the next room," but in the moment all I could say to him was, "You!"

He whirled in a manly sort of way, not in the least nonplussed, and seemed to appreciate the humor in the situation. That made one of us. With my keen powers of observation, I identified the light source: He was wearing a headlamp. A nice red REI one. Definitely not an item on our checklist of What to Bring with You for Your Culinary Experience at the Villa Orlandini Cooking School. But maybe private detectives pack headlamps. Did he think we were going caving? He'd need to bring more than a headlamp if that's where I led him. For starters, oxygen, Xanax, and whatever he'd be wanting for himself.

I was feeling like I had wandered onto the set of a caper movie, but with my luck I was cast not as the heroine but as the Expendable Extra. The idiot who gets killed early on. Still, George Johnson was looking at me benignly, which I didn't trust a whit, but there we were, underground and alone in a place that had five hundred years of natural soundproofing. In a show of spirit, I flipped my hair. "Why aren't you in the piazza?" was my incisive tack.

He dusted off his hands and said almost apologetically, "I didn't like the music."

"So soon?"

"When you know, you know."

I squared my shoulders, which is pretty much what Expendable Extras do. Last. "And how did you get back to the villa?" As if I was catching him out in something unanswerable.

"Manny Manfredi dropped me off." His glance swung to the rough stones of the ceiling. "As a beloved guest, I had all my needs met."

"Well," I said with airy hauteur, "if that's what you—" I actually didn't know where I was going with that one. "I don't think," I said with some energy, "you can poke around anywhere you like at the villa. You can't just assume—"

He held up a hand. "I didn't. I cleared it with Chef."

"Chef," I said flatly. At first it felt odd to me that someone, well, went over my head. But why would I even think the head of Nell Valenti was at the top? Why was I feeling so . . . proprietary? The Villa Orlandini belonged to Chef. "He said it was okay for you to wander around? In spots that have nothing to do with cooking?"

George nodded, smiling. "Gave me a free hand, carte blanche . . ." He shrugged. "It was kind of a *mi casa–su casa* conversation."

I could just see it happening that way. I'd have to set Chef straight.

"Nell," said George Johnson, taking a step closer, his

casual hair attractively askew. "Don't you want to ask me what I'm doing down here?"

"I'm sure you have an answer all prepared." When I winced and folded my arms, with a quick movement he redirected the intense light.

"As a matter of fact," he said enthusiastically, "I do."

I sniffed. "Go on."

"I'm looking for the crypt."

Not at all sexy. "The crypt?" I believe my lip curled. "Can't you do that during the daytime?"

"And miss out on all this atmosphere?" He spread his hands, which, I noticed, were wearing blue nitrile gloves. "No."

Was there more to George Johnson's assignment here in Tuscany than merely keeping an eye on Dr. Val Valenti's daughter? What exactly was my father up to? I kept my arms folded, and said with a little less interest, "And you're looking for a crypt why?"

"It struck me during the wine cellar tour. A wine cellar is a more recent repurposing. Originally it had to be the crypt. Haven't you wondered where all those five-hundred-year-old Veronicans are buried?"

He might as well have been rhapsodizing about prehistoric Rodentia scat. I came up short. "No," I said flatly, reminding myself to snag a bottle of '10 Chianti on my way up. And one wineglass from the kitchen.

"The really interesting thing," the man went on, while he did a slow 360—"is, where is it? Look around you." I did an obligatory turn. *Ya do the hokey-pokey and ya turn yourself around.* No nuns. I was fine with that. George Johnson's voice dropped. "Where is it?" He ticked off two fingers on his blue-gloved hand. "And why?"

I played along. "Why can't we find it?"

He gave me a quick nod. "I think," he said as he scratched around the elastic of his headlamp, "it's been walled off."

After a moment deciding on an appropriate response to this theory, I hit on the perfect thing. "Well, there you go." Case closed, let's get the hell out of this creeporium.

George Johnson returned to the sprawling, blank, arched wall. While his body faced this stony expanse, and his blue-gloved hands ranged over the blankness, he looked back over his shoulder excitedly, reminding me of the way my high school algebra teacher demonstrated quadratic equations. "Doesn't it make you wonder why?"

Did it? I thought about it. "Not at all."

George was undaunted. "Is there no one left to mourn?" he asked, one arm outstretched toward me in a mute plea. I liked the Byronic pose, but the battery in his little headlamp couldn't last forever.

"Maybe they just needed the space." From a design point of view, I liked that explanation. "The . . ."—what?—"sealers of the crypt anticipated some greater need sometime down the—the—" I rotated my hand the way Annamaria had shown me to crank the mechanical pasta-making machine, and concluded, "long road." I glanced back toward the deep shadows of the wine cellar, where the racks were filling up. "More wine."

He studied his feet. "I suppose you're right."

I felt light-headed. "George," I said patiently, "let's go."

As we headed back to the main room of the wine cellar, he muttered, "I think they were hiding something." He sucked in air. "A body, a treasure, a document."

Leave it to a detective to settle on that possibility. I touched his arm, happy to get to the stairs. "We'll never know," I said ever so reasonably.

But George Johnson didn't answer. If I had left it alone

and just headed barefoot up the cold stone steps, his silence would have given me some concern. But in that fraction of a second, there in the dim light of a failing headlamp, we caught each other's eye. His were black, quick, and smart. And I had a very strong impression that George Johnson had been playing me.

Wordlessly, we parted company in the kitchen. George started hunting for an easy snack, and I stalked off to my office to hide behind officialdom. At my desk, I called the Franchis and got Leo, who hadn't seen Jenna Bond. But then, he said in pretty good English, had he ever? He left it that he'd ask Theresa and if she had any information, he'd call back. Second, I called Manny Manfredi, who, shouting over the music in the background, told me no, he hadn't seen Jenna Bond.

Then I called Vincenzo, Stella's owner. *"Pronto,"* he rasped, and once again I cobbled together enough Italian to tell him we were looking for our American student Jenna Bond. My heart picked up the pace when, based on my description of her, the sweet old farmer told me yes, he had, but not since two or three hours ago. *"Dov'è, Vincenzo?"* I just about shouted into the phone.

The best I could make out from what he went on to explain was that the little Americana had come across his property at dusk. He let her be, watched her sit by the edge of his pond. I could picture the sorrowful girl, sick to death of her grief, her loneliness, and Bob Gramm, staring into the darkening water. Vincenzo sent out Stella, who trotted across the back of the property, spied the newcomer, and made her way down to the pond, sniffing for new information as she went.

"And then what happened?"

To which he replied the girl and the dog sat there together for a while. *"Le piacciono tutti."* Stella likes everyone, he said, proudly dismissive. I gave a soft snort. He must have been referring to some other Stella.

I nearly dropped my phone. "Is the girl there now?" It would make my life so simple.

"No, no, no, she left when the man came for her."

Well, my internal organs were in freefall down to where my socks ought to be.

"Che uomo?" What man? Those two words felt so packed with disaster that I could hardly speak. I remembered when I announced to my parents over caviar and champagne that I had taken the job designing a cooking school in Tuscany. With no rehearsal, the two of them turned alarmed faces toward each other and uttered, *No good can come of it.*

Although I didn't catch every word, Vincenzo made it clear he didn't know what man, but you know the pond is close to the road, and a car she pull up and stop, and this man he greet the little Americana, he point to the car, and she go. Stella she watch her go and come inside. In the evenings, Stella like to—

"Vincenzo. Vincenzo. Describe this man who took Jenna."

At that moment, George Johnson stepped into the office, apparently recovered from his zeal over walled-up skeletal remains and quietly munching a hunk of cheese and small heel of ciabatta. The headlamp was gone. He was listening attentively. It struck me my father's new undercover hire might actually prove useful in this situation.

Vincenzo was sputtering, coming up empty in describing the man who had spirited Jenna away. I felt queasy.

When would I have to call the cops? All I managed to squeeze from the old farmer was that the man was tall, thin, long arms, loose pants. Take away the pants and it sounded like every hominid I'd ever laid eyes on. Well, you know what I mean. When I asked Vincenzo if he could tell me about the car, all he could offer was *"bianca."* Then he launched into a cough, which he finished up with what sounded like a quick, neighborly plea for me to please send some nuns to help with the truffle hunting. Hacking was keeping him down and he couldn't afford to miss the best of the season . . .

"Hai bisogno di aiuto." See? *You need help,* "I'll try."

With a grunt, he hung up.

I stood helplessly in the center of my office. I didn't know where to start. Shooting George Johnson a quick look, I suddenly didn't care about keeping cooking school problems under my chef's toque. I could address the stolen knife with Jenna privately (if I ever saw her again). Lifting my chin, I looked at George Johnson, whose mobile mouth was twisted sympathetically to the side.

"Someone snatch Jenna?" His voice was low.

There's something particularly horrible about hearing that kind of bald truth from someone else. "I have to find her," I managed to get out through a tightening throat.

"Of course."

"But how?" I let out a frustrated wail. "I can't go roaming around the countryside in the dark," I told him as though he had just that moment suggested something preposterous. "I don't know the countryside." I went on, my eyes wild. "I don't have a car."

"The Orlandinis have cars, Nell," murmured George.

Deep down I was glad there was no resident Italian there to see me lose it. They'd been waiting for it for a month. On the other hand, I swayed at the thought of *N.V. had hissy fit at 10:31 p.m.* entered into George Johnson's daily report sent to my father. Maybe I could persuade this crypt-hunting guy to gloss over it somehow. *N.V. considers automotive difficulties 10:31 p.m.*

"Well, let's go see what we've got in the way of vehicles." He actually sounded like he had something in mind.

I bucked up a bit. "What we've got"—I sounded aggressive—"is a three-wheeled Vespa and—"

"Oh, the Ape?" He was excited. The Y chromosome might just as well be a hood ornament.

"—and a '55 T-Bird."

He looked positively sanguine as we headed outside. "For a while my mother had a '55 T-Bird," he murmured, sliding me a quick side-eye. "One of her classics." In that moment I understood he was telling me she had let him drive it and he was offering to help me search.

If I let you drive it, will you forget about the hissy fit? I was just about ready to voice it. Nell Valenti, tough negotiator. As George Johnson and I started striding across the courtyard, I saw us in slo-mo, a new A Team. No long-armed Jenna snatcher in a white car could beat us.

For the life of me, though, I couldn't picture the A Team tooling around the Tuscan countryside in the Ape. If we found them, what were we going to do with them? There was barely enough room in the Ape for George and me.

On the other hand, if we tooled around the Tuscan countryside in the '55 T-Bird as broad in the beam as my aunt Charlene, we'd be able to sling half of the revelers in the piazza into the back seat, but we'd never get anywhere what with the T-Bird's terrible suspension, poor handling, and tight fit on the narrow country roads. I looked up at the stars. George, his hands in his pockets, had beat me there. "Milky Way," he commented, then slid his eyes toward me. "Just like home."

I appreciated what he was trying to do, but I couldn't buy it. "Only it isn't."

A beat. "Brooklyn and Jersey," he said suddenly, "they've got a lot in common."

"Both in the Milky Way." I smiled.

"Only not so far away."

I got into the crackpot spirit of whatever he was spinning. "Across a river."

"But not an ocean."

I sucked in air, then scored. "Bagels."

"Garbage strikes."

And then I realized the tack my father, his employer, had instructed him to take: Remind her of home. *Make her good and homesick and she'll come back to us.* I pressed my lips together, feeling sad beyond belief. Maybe like a Jenna Bond, but for different reasons. And not even with fathers at the root of it. I felt very vulnerable as I looked George Johnson, the Sam Spade simply assigned to me, square in the face.

After a moment, he asked, "Which car do we take?"

I was starting to feel chilled. "George, I thank you, really I do, but Jenna's disappearance isn't your problem. I've got to—" Figure it out? Call the police? What, exactly? "Vincenzo last saw her two hours ago. The guy in the white car has had her for two hours. He could be halfway to Switzerland."

"Or—or—" said George Johnson with a sweet vehemence that made me think the word "or" was all he had in mind, until he went on, "having a gelato in the piazza."

So that's what the guy really thought. Clearly he was the upbeat half of the A Team.

With a small laugh, I patted his arm. Dad sure can pick them. "Why," I asked reasonably, "would he be in the piazza?"

"Why would he be in Switzerland?"

We regarded each other uncomprehendingly. It was a stalemate. Finally, I turned to head for my office, where I could do the professional thing alone and seated. "I have to call the police," I told George, without moving. My phone trilled in my pocket. More bad news? Glynis drunk and stripping in the piazza? Chef demonstrating his bocce prowess? Zoe dazzled?

It was Pete, checking in. "Everyone's still having a good time." I heard a crowd and an electric guitar in the background. "Even Rosa and Sofia showed up."

Break it to him now? "That's nice," was all I could say.

"All we're missing is Bob Gramm—"

"He headed off to bed hurling threats." Among other things.

"—and George Johnson"—his voice slowed—"and you."

"He's right here counting the stars in the Milky Way."

"Ah."

I swallowed. Somehow, telling Pete made the problem—the crime?—of Jenna Bond's disappearance ghastly and real. "And Jenna. You're missing Jenna. Listen, Pete—"

"Who says? She's here."

I was flabbergasted. "Jenna Bond?"

"Of course."

I felt helpless. "What—what's she doing?" George looked at me quizzically. *Jenna,* I mouthed.

"Eating gelato." The Milky Way, I looked up later, contains billions of stars and planets, and gas and dust and dark matter, and measures hundreds of thousands of light-years across. I felt terribly fond of it. Pete went on,

"She came with Oswaldo," as if it was the most natural thing in the world. I hardly heard him while he explained that Oswaldo had spotted Jenna on Vincenzo's property and sweet-talked her into joining him for the music in the piazza.

I was still grappling with all the unlikelihoods. That Oswaldo noticed her by the pond. That Oswaldo described what he said to her as "sweet-talking." That it worked. That the peculiar, posturing Oswaldo gets dates. That the knife-stealing, grudge-bearing, gloomy Jenna was eating gelato like a normal person. That I didn't have to call the cops. "Say it again, please, Pete," I said, holding my phone up to George Johnson's ear. "About Jenna."

He obliged. "She's here eating gelato with Oswaldo."

Trying hard not to smile, George gave my shoulders a quick squeeze. *Not Switzerland,* he mouthed at me.

It was such good news I didn't know how to deal with it. George and I studied each other. "Nell?" came Pete's voice. I raised my phone to my ear just in time to hear him tell me that Chef wanted to know if La Della Nella was going to be the sole holdout against an evening of music and gelato and the line dancing Rosa was getting started. "Not the sole holdout," I answered. "Tell him there's Annamaria."

"Oh. Right. Annamaria." Pete gave her name to Chef. In a moment, he returned, and in his voice I heard more than I expected. "He says," said Pete sadly, "she never comes to these things."

That night the terrible events of the next few days were set in motion.

Despite the reassuring beauty of the Milky Way.

Despite the heartwarming similarities of Brooklyn and Jersey.

I slept through it all, after walking once around the villa courtyard in the breeze that wasn't quite warm and seemed to curl up at me from the cobblestones. I poured myself half a glass of wine in my room, put Sarah Vaughan's "You Go to My Head" on the Victrola, and sipped only as long as the Count Basie Band played. Then, I set down the empty glass, the closest light from the courtyard shining into my room just enough to make the glass glisten. Slowly, I set the arm of the Victrola back in its rest and clicked off the machine. *You go to my head.* Closing the blinds, I undressed in the dark that felt older than all the galaxies in George Johnson's Milky Way, and I slipped under the sheets. Tomorrow I'd call my father and ask him to call George off. Job well done and all that, Dad, sure. But my life was here now.

In the morning, though, when the news came, I had to wonder if my life was anywhere at all. It was Rosa who told me in a reverent hush that "Signor Grahm" was taken to Santa Margherita Hospital during the night. Glynis woke up Pierfranco, who drove them. Rosa had crossed in front of the '55 T-Bird, nearly getting herself and "Bub Grahm" killed as Pete swerved. *"Riso bianco con lim-one,"* white rice with lemon—Rosa kept shouting the old Italian home remedy after them. And that, she said with a shrug, was the last she'd seen of them.

Suddenly I felt bad for having breakfasted alone in the Abbess's room, door locked, shades drawn, pillows fluffed like cumulus clouds. I had plugged in my new gift to myself, a Keurig coffeemaker, which I had ordered and kept out of sight to be brought out only when I absolutely needed a secret guilty pleasure. Add two of the scones from the

Wolferman's Mix & Match package that a friend back home had bought, repackaged, and shipped to me since they no longer ship internationally. There are days I just want to hear the pop of the Keurig pod, days when I just want to rip at a cellophane wrapper encasing a bakery item that hasn't seen the inside of an oven since who knows when.

By the time I was ready to go to the office, it was 8:16 a.m., which was when Rosa intercepted me with the news about Signor Grahm. The light breeze from the night before was back, only now in the treetops, pushing at the high branches, caught in a rustling conversation that pretty much left people out of it. Which was when it struck me we were down three—Pete, Glynis, and Bob. "So who's around?" I put to the valiant Rosa.

"Chef, tutte le sorelle di Bari"—she reassured me of her sisters' reliability a little smugly—*"Giorgio, Chenna, e—"* She paused for effect. "The Zo-ee," she muttered, making a frilly gesture with her hand as though she was noting a hatching of mosquitoes. So, three students, down from five, and no translator for Chef. Rosa traipsed after me into the main building, telling me something else urgent about the day, but I was intent on avoiding the voices coming from the dining room. The Zo-ee's bright laugh rang out with her usual hand-clapping delight, which was followed immediately by the clatter and clang of pots and pans in the kitchen.

"Now, Rosa—?" I prompted my trusty lieutenant, softly pushing the door shut behind us.

Chef, she managed to convey to me, had decided to teach just one sauce today, the *sugo finto*.

The poor man's marinara. Now that he'd given the big finale, the *prima marinara*, no place of honor, I hardly cared what else he moved around. As long as it didn't make extra work for Annamaria. "What else?" I asked quietly.

Chef said Zoe and Annamaria would teach three kinds of pasta making.

"So Zoe will prep for Annamaria," I murmured, thinking it could work. Beforehand, nary a peep about home-made pasta making during the Marinara Misteriosa workshop, but hey.

Rosa corrected me. "No." Very clipped. "Annamaria prep for Zo-ee." Her steady eyes were expressionless. "He say"—she slid her glance to me without moving her head—"special treat."

My skin actually crawled, and I was nowhere near either the wine cellar or Oswaldo. *Special treat.* What, exactly? Watching the lovely outdoor education instructor from Chatham, New Jersey, bungle the dough? Watching the old goat Chef step up really, really close to help her with the cranking and stretching and cutting? Watching Annamaria step farther back into the shadows of a kitchen that was suddenly becoming a hostile environment?

When Rosa could tell I had digested the indigestibles in her report, she geared up for the final item. "Chef say La Bella Nella show off Stella."

A beat. "Stella the dog?"

"*Sì.*"

I was suspicious about what he meant by "show off." "What? Bring her over from Vincenzo's for some American admiration? Maybe Chef figured Stella was the closest Comfort Animal around for the crazy Americans (although personally I was wishing we had kept the porcupine). For Rosa's benefit I mimed petting and tossing of Liver Snaps.

Rosa shot me a sickly smile. "No." Again, clipped.

"You take Giorgio into woods"—not in itself a bad idea, but I stepped on my own toes to keep from developing that picture—"*e tutti gli altri*"—all the others, with another frilly wave of her hand—"and you show Stella hunt for *tartufi*."

Getting the disturbing picture, I took a step back.

Chef Claudio Orlandini was sending me on a field trip with what was left of the first class of Americans. I was taking a dog that really didn't even like me out into the woods to hunt truffles. Bob Gramm was sick in a local hospital, and Pete wasn't answering his phone.

11

The day's original culinary agenda:

- 9 a.m.: *marinara con olive*—Claudio Orlandini, Head Chef; Annamaria Bari, Sous-Chef (kitchen classroom)
- 11 a.m.: field trip, Silver Wind olive grove—Pele Orlandini, owner/grower
- 1 p.m.: *marinara alla pescatore*—Claudio Orlandini, Head Chef; Annamaria Bari, Sous-Chef (kitchen classroom)
- 3 p.m.: field trip, truffle hunting—Stella the Lagotto Romagnolo; Vincenzo Rossi, farmer/truffle hunter

The day's new culinary agenda thanks to Chef's wantonly monkeying around with it:

- Sometime in the morning and/or afternoon, three kinds of homemade pasta, whether we have the ingredients on hand or not, because who knew?—

Zoe Campion, Head Chef, apparently; Annamaria Bari, at-risk Sous-Chef with excellent knife skills (a routine pat-down might be wise)

- Sometime in whatever is left of the day, *sugo finto*, the poor man's marinara, whether we have the ingredients on hand or not, because who knew?—Claudio Orlandini, big pain Head Chef; Zoe Campion, suck-up Sous-Chef
- Whenever, wherever, truffle hunting to "show off" Stella the dog (as per big pain's half-witted demands)—Nell Valenti, truffle hunter substitute with no credentials whatsoever and better things to do with her time, such as booking flights home
- After dark, genuine Crypt Crawl in the wine cellar, "How many dead Veronicans does it take to fill a crypt?"—George Johnson, handsome snoop and horror enthusiast

In one of those gleeful, dangerous moods that tempt us every so often, I actually typed up the new agenda. Anyone can understand that. There is so much delight in indulging one's most scathing opinions by putting them on a page. The mistake I made was getting so caught up in the therapeutic moment that I hit the print button, no doubt because by then I was revved and running, contemplating the revolutionaries who had come before me and whether 9:03 a.m. was too early for wine.

Undecided, I patted neatly into a thin stack the ten copies that printed because that had been the last print run, deciding finally against the wine, and setting them on the communications table just inside my office door. No to the wine, but by all the saints in the crypt I was going to make myself a mocha with the espresso machine. A dollop of Kahlúa would definitely be welcome, although from what I could tell of the Orlandini stock, that dollop would have to stay imaginary.

Rather than having Rosa track down Jenna Bond and tell her to see me in the office, I decided it set a better tone for our "little talk" if I tried to pull off just casually running into her. It didn't take long. She was sitting alone in the pale sunlight on the lip of the fountain we were in the process of rebuilding. Only half done because the stone-mason took time away from us on a bigger job, the fountain had no jets of water, so the basin was empty. Still a long way to go. When I came up alongside her, Jenna was writing in her pink spiral notebook, but when she saw me, she pressed her lips together and closed up shop in a hurry. Oswaldo had probably been bending her ear about the unreasonable witch in the office. Or, maybe the girl who steals knives has a hefty hate on for Bob Gramm, and disappears without telling anyone where she's going has other choice tidbits to write in her pink diary.

"Morning, Jenna," said I with surprising warmth.

"Morning." I've heard nuns praying louder Rosaries.

"We were worried about you last night." Quiet, friendly, not at all the snarling, wingèd Fury I felt like letting loose. She frowned. Her strawberry blond hair hung in a single braid at the nape of her neck, and she was wearing a blue cotton dress with a floral print that passed her knees. The only defense against the cool October breeze was a thin cardigan. Ankle boots kept her feet warm, although socks would have helped. "We didn't know where you were."

"I'm not a minor." She pouted. "I can come and go as I please." For some reason, this assertion bucked her up, and she shot me a little look and smiled.

I inclined my head, heading straight for my default setting, which was one of Harry Potter's female wizarding profs. "That's as may be." I was still quiet and friendly, if tending toward stuffy, not adding the *you little twerp* that battered at the backs of my teeth, trying to get out. "But you're not back home—"

"I've noticed." Score.

I blew past the sarcasm.

"—and you're more likely to"—search for it, search for it—"fall afoul of . . . something."

I have to admit, had I been Jenna, sitting there in ankle boots with a pink spiral notebook, I would have let out a loud laugh at this point. *Fall afoul?* Seriously? Was this a Victorian potboiler? But to my surprise she looked kind of chastened. After a moment of studying the horizon, she turned her head to look me straight in the eyes. "I'm sorry," she said. "Next time I'll let you know." Her hand brushed awkwardly at absolutely nothing on her dress.

"Well, then," I said, surprised she'd capitulated with less stink than pecorino cheese. "That's great." Perfect. Just the right inflection, not a lot of crazy energy behind it.

But then she blurted, "It's just that I've been under a lot of—pressure lately."

This one was hard to get right. If I said something like *Do you want to tell me about it?* I would want to kick myself in the can for sounding like a campus shrink, even though in my book that was probably what she needed. In which case I would steeple my fingers and lead with: *Tell me about the knife.* However, growing up in the palace of psychodrama with Dr. Val Valenti, I had no taste for the role, and if I couldn't prevail over the likes of a wayward Chef on the matter of what happens in the kitchen, then I was pretty sure I couldn't provide shrinkage to this Baltimore girl on the edge. I felt my eyes narrow creatively. Perhaps I could talk Oswaldo into crooning to her, *Vuoi parlarmene?* Do you want to tell me about it?

Finally, I said, "Oh?" It came out a little lower and darker than I had hoped.

"I have some things to—take care of." Here the girl hugged her knees. For a minute she stared bug-eyed at nothing I could see. Then, with a lift of her head: "I can't talk about it."

"I'm sorry to hear that." I jumped in to add, "The pressure, I mean."

And she looked up with a weary little smile. "How old are you?" She was looking for clues based on my layered haircut, my cobalt blue wool jacket, my go-to black pants.

"Thirty on Thursday." The words didn't catch in my throat. "And you're twenty-four."

She nodded. I thought we were pretty close to done with being girlfriends for five minutes, but then she piped up, "I like that dog."

First I thought she meant the goofy, bounding Oswaldo, but then I remembered her moody pond-sit at Vincenzo's with Stella for company. Innocently, I inquired, "Dog?"

"Oh, last night," she breathed. "Not far from here."

I perked right up. At last, a course of action. "That's Stella. Today I'll be"—what's the right word for tramping through woods with a zigzagging, sniffing Lagotto Romagnolo?—"handling her." Suddenly we're the Westminster Dog Show. At Jenna's puzzled look, I added, "For a truffle-hunting field trip." Keep smiling.

I impressed myself, no denying.

She gasped. "You do that?" I was a person of interest, then, and not in a cop way.

How close to the truth could I come? "Vincenzo, her

owner, is out sick today"—fie, fie, Vincenzo—wait no,
fie, fie, Chef—"and I am filling in for the demonstration."
Jenna Bond actually smiled. If she liked the likes of Stella
the dog and Oswaldo the doggier, there was no help for
her. Now, at least, I could confidently say she did not have
a five-inch utility knife in her possession. "Tell you what!
Here's an idea." I licked my lips, it was so very much the
right thing. "Would you like to go to Vincenzo's farm and
pick Stella up?"

"Really?"

I could hardly believe I was actually having a Tom
Sawyer moment. But instead of whitewashing the fence, I
had offloaded my own Stella responsibilities on a willing
dog-fetcher. "Absolutely, Jenna," I said sincerely, "you'd
really be helping me out on this busy day. And while
you're at it, don't forget the *vanghetto*." Oddly, here I was
on sturdier ground than I was when I first found her mop-
ing at the fountain and I had to work to stay on the Nell
Valenti side of the professional line.

"What's that?"

Gripping her notebook, she started with me back up
the gentle hill toward the cloister walk, and I regaled her
with the scant information I had about the traditional
truffle-hunting tool. Considering I had only ever seen a
vanghetto once in my life, I had a lot to say about it. I
added to her list of retrievables: Stella, *vanghetto*, sack for
truffles, and treats for the estimable pooch. I was pretty
sure I had never used the word "pooch" in my life—
although I had a vague recollection of calling a college
boyfriend Poochie—but I was growing thrillingly fond of
Stella and all dogs everywhere, apparently.

When we stamped onto the cloister walk, both of us
were grinning; we quickly hugged ta-ta, and as she lightly

ran off to get her chef's apron for the kitchen madness, it struck me that those last few minutes had been the first time I had seen Jenna Bond happy. And it had nothing to do with Marinara Misteriosa. And nothing to do with working off a grudge on Bob "the Glam" Gramm.

Before I went inside, I checked the garage for the T-Bird. Not there.

Pete, Glynis, and Bob Gramm must still be at the hospital. I had a flutter of uneasiness, then, that had nothing at all to do with Chef himself. For that, I'd have to be in his presence. Suddenly, as I headed back across the cobblestones, it was as if I had invoked him. He and Zoe, their heads bent in what I could only hope was a Head Chef and Sous-Chef culinary conference, nearly ran into me. She was already suited up for the kitchen, but Claudio Orlandini carried his chef's duds slung over his bocce-playing shoulder in a swashbuckling way. "Sorry, Nell!" That was Zoe. Nothing from Chef himself, who was intently trying to make himself understood about exactly how much sweet potato purée gets blended into the pasta dough.

Well, I thought, grasping at some sort of bright side, at least they're on task.

I waited until they disappeared into the main building, heading, presumably, for the kitchen, and then I followed, but avoiding the lion's den and practically tiptoeing down the corridor to my office. I swear I could still smell lilies. At least for the morning I could hunker down at my desk and act busy. I pushed open my door, my eyes watering from either the anticipation of three uninterrupted hours in my hobbit hole or whatever lingered from the death lilies, and stopped short. "You!" I cried, wiping my eyes with the back of my sleeve.

Standing next to the communications table with a

stack of papers in his hands was George Johnson, dressed in jeans, a black T-shirt, and his chef's apron. All I could do in that moment was stammer, not in itself easy when your mouth is hanging open like a Venus flytrap, "Why are you always where I'm supposed to be?" His dark eyes slid sideways, considering the question. "Oh"—I piled it on—"and why are you always there two steps ahead of me? Huh?"

His lips made that little pondering side-pucker that I enjoyed watching. Then his expression was all about regret. "Well," he said, "if you're being honest, more like three."

"Three?" What was this man talking about? I pushed the door shut with my foot.

"Steps," he explained. "Three steps ahead of you." Then he amended, "Well, hard to say, really, I suppose."

I appealed to my ceiling for help. None came, although in just the right light I could tell a spider was rappelling her way down a thin thread. I sighed. Why does every other creature's job feel like the easy job, compared to mine? Gnawing on the inside of my cheek, I glared at him and asked, "What are you doing in here, George? This is my office."

His shoulders, just the right amount of broad, lifted. "Aren't you like the dean of students? Isn't your door always open?" He had me there.

"Not when it's closed," I barked.

"It's a figure of speech."

"I know what it is."

"Am I not supposed to come to you with my problems or concerns?" Oh, this guy was good.

As I directed him to the chair on the not-Nell side of my fancy desk, the one he had occupied the night he arrived, I said through gritted teeth as I headed around the desk, "Yes, George, of course. My pleasure. My duty. My job. Please do tell"—I folded my hands in a grip that had nowhere to go—"excuse me, *share*"—he tipped his head at my word choice—"your problems or concerns with me." My own spider thread was, at that moment, quite thin.

He obliged, as I knew he would. The man was comfortable everywhere. "Well, for starters, these." Very gently he laid the little stack of papers on my desk, and then sat back. When without even touching them I recognized the papers and was immobilized with horror, he pushed them just a little closer to me.

The day's new "agenda" I had typed and printed up in a snit. "What are you doing with these?" I managed.

"Wondering what I should wear for my Crypt Crawl. I've got an image to think about."

My eyes slipped like destiny down to the idiocy about *handsome snoop George Johnson*. Internally I got into a shouting match with myself. *What was I thinking?* The other side, which wasn't a different opinion at all, shouted, *Exactly when, Nell? When you took this godforsaken job? When you stayed? When you went into this business in the first place? When you said no to the easy landing your father held out to you after cooking school? What were you thinking exactly any of those times?*

With George Johnson, who was trying not to smile, all I could do was come clean. "Okay, you're good-looking. What of it?" I almost added "mister." I could have left it at that, or we could have done something kind of playful with it. Instead, I learned that when I'm embarrassed there's no accounting for my mouth. "I know your type. Your type's a dime a dozen."

He held up both hands. "It's okay, Nell. You really don't—"

The Dean of Students sat up plenty straight, having cornered the Cortona market in starch. "Now, I asked you a question, Mr. Johnson. What are you doing with these?" I noisily flipped the stack of incriminating papers.

His sigh said something along the lines of *Well, if that's how you want to go.* "Rosa gave me one."

"What!"

"You heard me, Ms. Valenti. She was handing out the new agenda—"

I kept shaking my head. "No, no, no—"

"But she saw me second, so I saw right away it was some kind of joke."

"—or full-blown idiocy," I put in.

He couldn't resist. "Except for the 'handsome snoop' part—"

"Still trying it on? Really?"

"If you have to ask"—he widened his eyes at me—"I guess you can't tell."

"Which should tell you something."

"About you."

"Ooh, clapback."

"Ooh, salty."

"This is getting us nowhere," I proclaimed. He lifted his eyebrows. I'd say, in agreement. Getting back on track, I couldn't help the squeak. "Rosa saw you second?"

With a nod, he went on, "So I took the agendas from her and hauled"—he altered his direction—"well, hurried back here—"

"Who was first?" Barely audible.

"—to bring the mistake to your attention." Who's Dean of Students now?

"Did you get the other one?"

Regret never looked so beautiful. "No. Sorry."

This was a desert slog. Collapse was just a matter of time. "Did Rosa say who got it? Please don't let it be Chef, please don't—"

A beat. "It was Sofia."

I bit my lip in thanks. Was there no end to the bath of good fortune sloshing over me? No end to my desperate metaphors? Bob Gramm would get better and go home. Chef's bocce team would make it to the semifinals and he'd give up this misbegotten cooking school for good. There was a TAP Air Portugal flight on Tuesday from Florence to JFK at 7:10 p.m. I could even get a ride back to Florence with Manny Manfredi in the Cucinavan. I'd ask Dad to meet me with a big bouquet of lilies. "But," he went on, still offering a life raft of regret on his dime-a-dozen face, "she had passed hers on to Annamaria."

I sat back in my chair in quasi-defeat and closed my eyes. Annamaria. Not so bad as Chef, I supposed. In terms of whose command of English was worse, hers or Chef's, it was pretty definitely a toss-up. She might very well not understand what things like "at-risk" or "put down" mean. I thought there was an atom-sized possibility that she might forgive me. But I'd better go and make things okay or she could land me in a vortex of *malocchi* before I'd even get out of Cortona. I needed a nap. Maybe even a coma.

At that moment, the door boomed open. It was Annamaria, wearing her apron and her fiercest face. In her hand was the copy of the new agenda. I stood, my heart pounding, stepped out from behind my desk, and faced her. At 9:32, it was High Noon. *"Hai scritto questo?"* Did you write this? Her voice was steely.

Take it like the Dean of Students. *"Sì. L'ho scritto io."*

George leaned out of the line of fiery curses.

Suddenly, Annamaria pursed her lips until they disappeared off her face. Then she tossed back her fine head. "La Bellissima Nella," she cried. Sensing this reaction might be better than I'd hoped for, I waited her out. She marched right on over to me, all smiles, with arms outstretched. *"Mille grazie!"* she roared, flinging her arms around me.

In lesser hands, that embrace would have been the tepid but acceptable thing you'd come across at family reunions, but that woman had been kneading dough for sixty years. I was good and clasped, in a love clinch of death. George Johnson, unfolding himself from his chair, pointed himself in the direction of the kitchen and left, but not before I shot him a small, grateful smile. "'Big pain Head Chef,'" laughed Annamaria, which she then topped with "'suck-up Sous-Chef.'" We laughed together until she wiped her large, lovely eyes and judged, "Better than a *malocchio*."

Maybe in the short run, I felt like telling her.

But for the long run, you can't beat boils.

O ver the rest of the morning, three kinds of pasta—spinach, sweet potato, and gluten-free—got cranked out surprisingly expertly by Jenna, Zoe, and Mr. Johnson. The kitchen was a miasma of flour. Annamaria whistled through her teeth and kept sharpening her knives. After lunch, Jenna brought around Stella the dog on a leash, who, of course, ignored me and the shankbone I offered (I say when it comes to bribes, go large), and off we set toward what I refer to in my own head as the truffle woods.

Waving one weak hand palm-up like a panhandler, I uttered the basics of finding the prized fungus, and Jenna caught on quickly and took charge, beaming from ear to ear when the redoubtable Stella came up with the goods. Wags, treats, praise passed among the Core Four of us— Jenna, Zoe, Mr. Johnson, and me—and Jenna actually managed to twirl the *vanghetto* like a baton. I found it hard to believe she'd ever been quite this delighted to serve up a grande caramel macchiato back home.

Later, while the three students left were learning *sugo finto*, the poor man's marinara, from Chef, I popped in, stunned at the mess. Maybe I was wrong. Maybe Italians still did big things in the big picture. Stacks of dishes, pots, pans, cutting boards, knives, slotted spoons, manual pasta-making machines, covered every work surface. Including what looked like a woman's top and a man's pair of socks. Hadn't Rosa promised to clean up last night's dinner dishes? My eyes swept over the wreckage— nothing had been cleaned up after the morning's session of making three kinds of pasta, and nothing had been cleaned up from yesterday's Big Reveal of Chef's *prima marinara* sauce, and the boisterous dinner preparations that followed. What, what, what were these people using? Was any cookware still clean?

This was a colossal mess of a full twenty-four hours' duration.

It was so out of the ordinary that my mind landed on the only possible explanation. There was a mind at work here. Glancing swiftly at Annamaria, who I think had been restored to her forty-year role of sous-chef to Chef himself, not the cheerful American, well, nobody, I suddenly saw it. She was serene. Either she had spun such a whirlwind of a *malocchio* that the cursed kitchen had exploded . . . or she had quietly instructed Rosa and Sofia to do nothing in the way of cleanup. Let it stand. Let *her* stand. After all this time, the indispensable Annamaria Bari might have just rewritten her job description. If the health inspector dropped by for a peek, we'd be shut down as fast as you could say "revenge."

Was it even possible that Annamaria was angling to phone the inspector?

It was such a beautiful setup. I could see at least half a dozen broken rules.

Could she really sink that low? Or, depending on how you looked at it, aim that high?

In truth, I shook my head as I headed back to my office, I didn't know her well enough to say.

Quietly closing the door to my office, I sank into my chair, then half-heartedly pushed some papers around on my desk. I, Nell Valenti, was going to go into hiding.

12

(decorative flourish)

At 4:48 that afternoon, a text came in from Pete. *Where are you?*

My thumbs got busy. *Off my feet in my room. Where are you? How's Bob?*

No reply. The knock, when it came, was so soft I hardly heard it. Rosa? I wondered. Some question about exactly when and where to serve the antipasti? I pushed off the bed and sprang to the door. Wrenching it open, I discovered Pete standing there, just shaking his head. "Pete?" A quick scan of the property, the cloister walk, anything part of the villa grounds I could see, turned up nobody. I pulled him into the room, and waited.

When he lifted his head and looked me square in the eyes, it was an expression on his fine face that I had never seen in the month I had known him. "Turn for the worse?" was all I could say, softer, even, than his knocks at my door.

A few slow nods. "You might say." His eyes narrowed at the sauce stain on my best white blouse. "He died."

I gasped. "Died?" I was incredulous. It was as if he had told me Bob Gramm of Naples, Florida, was off skydiving somewhere. Just then I felt like joining him. "Died?" Apparently it was the only word I had at my disposal. I couldn't catch a breath. "What happened?"

"Nell," said Pete, his voice choked, "it was awful. I wouldn't have wished that kind of end even on Bob Gramm."

I looked around, as if somehow I had missed her. "Where's Glynis?"

"Still there." The effort to speak was getting too hard for him. "In shock."

I swallowed. "What time did it—?"

"Three thirty, maybe?" He sounded drugged with details he couldn't remember—or see even what earthly purpose they served. "Finally, I left her sitting with him. Said I had to tell the others and I'd be back to get her. I don't know what she heard."

"Oh, Pete," I said, grabbing him tight. He clung to me with his broad shoulders shaking. Letting go of him, all I could think to do was get him over to the bed, where he fell back with a sigh so vast it could have been the first breath of Creation. Flinging his arm over his head, he stared at the ceiling. Not knowing what else to do, I staggered to the bathroom, grabbed my toothbrush cup, and filled it halfway with Grand Marnier from the bottle that Oswaldo Orlandini had given me by way of thanks for the hire. "Here, Pete." I held the cup for him while he wadded one of my pillows behind his head and pulled himself only as upright as he could safely take swigs. He frowned, then shivered, but it didn't stop him.

I sat down on the edge of the bed and just waited.

"Well," he managed finally, gazing hopelessly into the

cup, "I guess I got to forty before seeing the worst thing in my life." I said nothing, let him take his time. His eyes squeezed shut. "He got so sick so fast, Nell, and there was no help for him." Pete turned his face to mine, and passed me the toothbrush cup. I took a sip. "The convulsions." He just kept shaking his head. We both let that sit for maybe a minute, then I set the empty cup on the floor. "The coma seemed like a blessing."

For no more than a minute he sketched medical chaos—*what did he drink? what did he eat? what time? when!*—IVs, blood tests, monitors. The rushing, the yelling. Glynis, gripping one of his hands, which she could hardly hang on to. Everything she had known—the boy who had loved fast, beautiful cars and fast, beautiful her—unspooling right before her eyes on tormented, stained sheets in a room in a hospital she couldn't even name on a hilltop town in Tuscany.

I started to shake my head. "No one, Pete," I started, "no one is that gluten-free. I don't believe it." He started to say something, but I went on, "Bob Gramm had to have some kind of" —my hand grasped at the air over us—"of—preexisting condition. How could we have known?" I ached. "How could anyone have known?"

He pushed out his lips, his eyes bright. "Oh, it wasn't the pasta, Nell." He let out a short, bleary laugh. "That didn't do him any harm."

"Then what?" I had a flash, remembering a comment Bob Gramm had made just two nights ago. "You remember he said at dinner he was just getting over hepatitis."

"From what I heard," said Pete softly, "that probably contributed. No." He sounded weary, suddenly all the lovely effects of the Grand Marnier fading. "Nell." To my ears, that word was the most forlorn sound in the world.

Something was about to happen. Would I ever forget the precise look of the light—just words and dreams—there in the Abbess's room when Pete spoke? "Bob Gramm died of an amatoxin."

"Amatoxin? Are you saying something poisoned him?" His nod was nearly imperceptible. "What? How?"

"Death cap mushrooms."

And there it was. And there it would stay.

I went very still.

They all gathered in the common room, including Chef, Annamaria, and whatever other Bari sisters were on hand. There was no mention of building a fire. Before we asked Rosa to find everyone and announce a meeting, Pete and I holed up in my office, looking for our game faces. "Depending on the final pathology report, Nell," said Pete quietly, looking out the window at a landscape that held no joy, "I think we may be done." Refund the fees and let them go home early? I wanted to know. His smile was grim. "No, done. For good." One shoulder lifted. "How can the villa cooking school survive this, Nell?" We agreed to wait and see. We agreed he'd fill them in on Bob Gramm and then return to Santa Margherita Hospital to fetch Glynis and pretty much take her wherever she wanted, short of across the Atlantic Ocean. *Keep it simple,* I had told him about informing the Americans, Chef, and all the Bari sisters. *For now, answer only what they want to know.*

We stood in front of the cold fireplace and looked at the expectant, upturned faces. Two fewer than yesterday. Chef was stretching his back, leaning this way and that, and suddenly swiped his toque from his head in a familiar gesture. Happy with the day's culinary progress, he was whistling a passable version of "Take the A Train," gazing up at the ceiling. Annamaria sat next to him on one side, Zoe on the other. Jenna turned up in a tight little grouping of Baris, a bit like finding E.T. in the closet.

Sitting slightly off from the others, leaning forward with his clasped hands between his open knees, was George Johnson, his black hair falling in three different directions. His head was turned toward Pete and me. If I had to guess, from the looks of him I'd bet George was the only one who sniffed a whiff of bad news. No capers for tomorrow's marinara? Truffle-hunting dog discover a schedule conflict? He was brilliant at the game of fitting in.

Pete cleared his throat. "Bob Gramm has died," he said.

"Take the A Train" turned into a long whistle of alarm.

Every single Bari stabbed the sign of the cross.

Someone titched. Maybe Annamaria. Someone tutted. Maybe Zoe, who patted Chef's knee sympathetically, as though she was mistaking him for Glynis and all the grief was his. Annamaria went stony. From the middle of the safety net of Bari bodies came Jenna Bond's voice. "Died?" She seemed to be choking on the very idea of it. In that moment, she sounded like me, hearing the news from Pete.

Rosa stroked her strawberry blond hair, murmuring in Italian Jenna couldn't understand something along the lines of *He wasn't a very nice man*. Then, on second thought, she added, *God rest his soul*. Sofia, Lisa, and Laura nodded sagely. *Not nice, but God rest*. Blinking, Jenna turned, looking—with her hands at her throat—for escape. Finding none, before even the Bari sisters could stop her, she fainted clean away, disappearing onto the warm wool pile of geometric golds and whites.

I left them all fussing over Jenna. Work on that front was proceeding slowly, because the group was horrified to learn about the death cap mushrooms. "Bummer," said Zoe, feelingly. Annamaria flung wide her arms in a gesture that implied there was nothing she could do about idiots who don't listen when she shows what to pick, what to leave. Even Chef could tell this judgment seemed a bit harsh. He countered eloquently with, *"Ch, ch, ch, ch, ch."* Some carried Jenna toward the couch, some dashed for pillows, others loped off to brew some basil tea, and one applied light taps to Jenna's chalky cheeks. This was Laura, and I felt calmed at her gentleness.

The rest of the Bari sister act went to the Billy Joel source with "Slow down, you crazy child," which seemed to me about as helpful as anything else. When Pete's phone trilled, George, suddenly looking like he was poaching a deer, almost dropped the passed-out Jenna. Pete listened silently to the caller, thumbed off the phone pretty quickly, and slid it back into his pocket. But not before mentioning that he didn't have to retrieve poor Glynis Gramm from the hospital. The cops were happy to bring her back when they came.

I could say I sprang into action with that bit of news, but in truth it was more accurate to describe it as sliding off into action. Murmuring to Pete that I'd be in the barn, I backed out of the common room, thinking hard, and then turned and dashed down the corridor to my office. There I grabbed what I thought of as my jailer key ring, which held master keys to every likely spot in the villa—including the renovated barn apartment occupied by the Gramms. Then I ducked into the kitchen, where Sofia was waiting on the teakettle, and snagged a pair of latex gloves from the closest box.

I had no idea, I had no plan, but having just come off a murder investigation a month ago, I saw this next half hour as what might be my only opportunity to get ahead of the game. If the Gramms had anything in their room that would implicate one of the Orlandinis in the murder, I wanted desperately to see it first. Bad enough the dead man was dosed with death cap mushrooms while on our watch—I couldn't even begin to consider how this crime would affect the cooking school. I could hear the whispers already: *What the hell are they serving up at the villa?* If that's what happened, more than Bob Gramm would never recover. Forget the cooking school. Reputations, trust, and . . . home.

I couldn't let it happen. I wouldn't disturb any evidence. But I couldn't let it happen.

I full-out ran diagonally across the deserted courtyard and down to the barn. With shaking hands, I managed the lock and let myself in, and although there was still enough afternoon sunlight, I switched on a couple of lamps. There can never really be enough light. Then I tugged the chef gloves over my hands and looked around. The bathroom, converted from the old tack room, smelled from the sickness that had hit Bob Gramm less than a day ago. Vomiting, diarrhea, cramps. If wailing had a stink, this was it. Stained pajamas lay heaped in the bathtub. Some used tissues had made it into the trash can; some hadn't. Soap sat in the sink. All I saw here was terrible sickness.

I hurried through the rest of the finest guest accommodation the villa had to offer. By the far side of the queen-sized bed was a pail Glynis must have found in the shed section of the barn. It had been used. While the rest of us were off snoozing and dreaming in our beds, the Gramms were dealing with all of this, mistaking it for . . .

what? A stomach virus? A twenty-four-hour bug? Some godforsaken gluten that had gotten past the annoying Bob's defenses? I felt myself sag right where I stood, swamped by the sad realization that it must have looked like something familiar, something they could handle—until it didn't. At what exact point did it become too late for Bob Gramm to recover? How could those two ever have guessed he had been poisoned by death cap mushrooms?

Their roller bags stood together in a corner. I remembered Bob's was black, so in a swift gesture, I swung that one up and onto the bed, where covers were strewn in the haste to get help. Flinging back the top, I was looking at an empty interior, but just to be sure, I let my hands rove across and inside all the surfaces. Nothing. Zipping it shut, I set it back in the corner, next to Glynis's Louis Vuitton bag. Shaking out the bedclothes, I hit pay dirt.

A phone clattered to the finished floor of the Orlandini barn. Dead. This phone in its rubbery case had to be Bob's—I remembered Glynis handling hers, encased in metallic gold. I heaved a sigh, then found the charger cord on the floor, the other end plugged in. What I wanted from this device was Bob's contact list and calendar and email. Maybe some photos. Maybe some documents. But I had no time. Not enough time. Even if I charged it, all I'd get would be his lock screen. Glynis must know the passcode, but why would she help me, instead of, say, the cops?

Stumped, I decided to keep searching. As I set the frustrating phone on Bob's nightstand, my eye caught something solid at the bottom of the gunk in the used bedside pail. I debated going outside and finding a stick to fish it out of the disgusting brew. No time. So my gloved hands tipped the pail far enough to the side that the object came into view. A wet, dark clump of—something. Something that had been stewed in toxic vomit now. I stared. And then I recognized it, the blue velvet drawstring bag I had seen Bob tuck into his jacket pocket as he headed out of Tesori della Toscana two days ago. I studied it as gravity finally took over and the mess started to slide slowly back into the contents of the pail. From the rounded contours of the destroyed pouch, I could tell the gold bangle bracelet the cheating Bob had bought for someone named Joanne was still inside.

This was Glynis's to explain to the police, if it came to that.

I couldn't help hoping they took the whole pail, contents and all, to the crime lab.

And with that thought, I sat back on my haunches. The crime lab.

So there it is.

I left my gloved hands dangling off my bent knees as I quickly rejected the idea of accidental death. Because how could an accident have happened? Not by his hand, no, I couldn't see it. In a sudden rush, I dashed to the kitchenette side of the lodgings. Clean as a whistle. The Gramms hadn't so much as made themselves a cup of coffee here since their arrival.

That figured. Bob Gramm, always braying about the villa's charges for the four days of Marinara Misteriosa, was paying strict attention to getting his money's worth. I could hear him complaining to Glynis before he fell asleep that "they" could damn well provide coffee on demand, eh? So, if they hadn't struck up their kitchenette facilities, how would the diet fusspot Bob have accidentally whipped up anything with slices of the death cap mushrooms that had now killed him? I just didn't buy it.

And suicide?

Him? That possibility, on our brief acquaintance with the Lamborghini dealer, seemed more far-fetched than accidental death. Very nearly comical. But I forced myself to consider it, casting my mind back over his comments, his attitudes. What would make a philandering egotist (I'd better not be called on to eulogize this guy) kill himself? A mean and domineering bully, he perversely seemed to be enjoying himself during the time so far in Orlandini Land. He didn't care for cooking, but he sure relished every single opportunity for cruel jabs, and for insisting on class "rights." "Oh, Boy, carry my bag by the side handle."

He was always poised to catch a glimpse of what he could deem inferior or inadequate, people included. This was the kind of guy who could possibly be driven to self-destruction if his business life was threatened beyond repair, but from scraps of conversations I was remembering, Gramm's Lams had passed through hard times, made adjustments, survived, thrived. He strutted; he preened. And from what I could tell, no devastating information had derailed him in the last couple of days.

No accident.

No suicide.

That left murder. I drew in a sigh. On some level, I think I had jumped right to that conclusion from the moment Pete told me about the death cap mushrooms. Bob Gramm of Naples, Florida, owner of Gramm's Lams, what a killable guy. What had taken someone so long? I could imagine his Florida high school yearbook entry. Robert E. Lee Gramm, Future Homicide Victims of America, Most Likely to Be Murdered, Homegoing King. Had it really been just a matter of time? And was it our

Orlandini-Bari-Valenti bad luck to have it happen here? I licked my dry lips, feeling my snooping time was winding down, and stood up from my crouch.

I felt through every coat, shirt, and pants pocket of Bob Gramm's hanging in the closet. And there, slipped over a hanger of its own, was a beige travel money belt—the last thing on the poor guy's mind when all he wanted was to get to the closest hospital. I could almost hear him complaining about how none of these godforsaken Italians speak English, as they wheeled him on the gurney to the emergency room. I zipped open the money belt and found Bob's passport, couple of credit cards, several twenties in U.S. currency, a fistful of what he had termed "so-called euros," and a folded piece of paper. A crude, handwritten spreadsheet with a series of numbers. I'd need a closer look and more time to figure it out. This, this, I could easily swipe with no one's necessarily missing it. Swipe, study, slip back into its place—or, if the cops took charge of the money belt, some new place.

Tucking the folded paper into my pocket, I rezipped the money belt, smoothed it next to a pair of dress pants, and returned the closet door to its half-closed position, the way I had found it. Last up: Bob Gramm's nightstand, where a cord snaked out. I tugged open the drawer and fingered through the objects inside: a dirty book, a Kindle (for his more private readings, apparently), a pack of Airborne, a pack of Emergen-C, a pack of Viagra, a pack of Tums—well, Bob, sad to say, but those wouldn't have done diddly to help you in your extremity—and small bottles of Beano, Lactaid, and something labeled Dynamic Man Virility Formula. The cord was charging the Kindle. Worth snapping up? Here again, I'd run smack into a possible wall of Glynis. Why would she help me and not the cops? I surely didn't want to make off with anything she would miss right away, or anything that would be hard to explain. That especially.

My phone dinged.

Pete, texting. *Get the hell out of there, Nell. The cops are pulling in.*

I swung a quick, nervous look around the room Bob and Glynis Gramm had shared. Had I done enough? Would I get a second chance? I knew I couldn't count on Glynis's sticking around here, where her dead husband had been poisoned. Once she absorbed the truth that Bob had been murdered, why should she? It had happened here. Here. At the Villa Orlandini Cooking School, where it seemed she had dragged him for a cooking course, against years of his protests. Holding aside the sheer window curtain just far enough to scope out the courtyard, I decided my chances of avoiding the cops' notice were better if I slunk away now, as they headed up the driveway, than if I waited until they were parking.

When their car disappeared for one moment in the curve of the driveway, I slipped out, relocked the door, and dashed around the tree-shielded corner of the barn where Bob Gramm had been dying, only he didn't know it. Heading for the woods behind the villa property, so I could make my way to the Abbess's room under greater cover, I passed the sagging, rancid arbors and blankets of lily extravagances my parents had sent me two days ago, now adorning the compost pile. With the terrible news about Bob Gramm, funeral lilies seemed to fit right in.

I heard the distant slam of car doors. Then, high voices raised in welcome. Overhead, the sky had started to change, gray stripes of clouds appearing, shifting, obscuring what was left of the day's blue. A strong breeze stayed high in the trees, and whatever else was earthbound went unmolested. I trudged up the hill past Silver Wind Olives to my left, then Pete's cottage, and past the broken fountain with the figure of St. Veronica. I could slip unnoticed into my room, and stretch out for ten minutes, maybe just five. Even five would do. The voices I heard from the courtyard were Pete's, Chef's, and Joe Batta's—the phlegmatic investigating officer from the *carabinieri*. I remembered him from last time. Nowhere could I make out Glynis Gramm's voice. But she had to be there.

I slipped into my room, where I breathed in the cool, pleasant air. I smelled my perfume. No time to put up my feet; in this short run, I had a school to run. But I teased the folded paper I had swiped from Bob Gramm's money belt out of my pants pocket and started to study it.

Ding. Another text from Pete. *Join us?*

Me: *Coming.*

Pete: *Useful?*

Me: *Yes. Drinks later?*

Pete: *The bad news, likely much later.*

I frowned, and sighed. We were in for it.

Pete again: *But, yes.*

With a small smile, I pulled off the chef gloves, and just as I was about to drop them into my waste can, I reconsidered. From a cop's point of view, why would Nell Valenti have chef gloves in her bedroom? Unlike the Gramms, I didn't even have a kitchenette. I could plausibly explain the tossing of the used gloves, but I didn't want to give Joe Batta anything to think about in my direction, so I balled up the gloves and stuffed them in the breast pocket of my jacket. With just a moment alone in the villa's kitchen, I could get rid of them. There were plenty of others from the day's culinary class to keep mine company.

Hidden in plain sight was a concept I always enjoyed.

13

I found Police Detective Giovanni Battista Onetto, Joe Batta for short, casting his eyes around the courtyard without moving his bald head. He then proceeded to unwrap a hard candy. I swear if he dropped the wrapper I'd make a citizen's arrest for littering. Instead, he rolled the cellophane into the size of a grain of rice and slid it into his pocket. Popping the round sugar blast into his wide mouth, he managed a ghastly smile at Chef, who was standing with him. Nina, the translator, dressed in a red skirt and white blouse with a deep-cut V-neck, oozed up alongside her boss. A plainclothes subordinate who drove made the threesome.

Some Italian etiquette about murder scenes followed. Murmurs, head bobbles, brays. That done, Chef made a grand gesture with his free left arm, swinging wide in the direction of the kitchen, and stepped back. The four of them headed toward the main building, all but Chef Claudio Orlandini striding as though they wouldn't be wandering off for a nap anytime soon. In the late afternoon light, the red skirt swayed with a certain amount of snap.

A second car disgorged two more *carabinieri*, flanking Glynis Gramm, who had aged about twenty years in twenty-four hours. If George Johnson wanted a gander at skeletal remains, Glynis might be his best bet. Her cop companions were questioning her, but she seemed dazed and unhelpful. My cue. As I loped over to them, Pete appeared at my right. In a low voice, he said, "I'll show them the barn. You done in there?"

A tight little nod was all I could muster as I pulled up next to Glynis Gramm, not knowing quite what to expect. She was here, back at the place where widowhood began. If she had dissolved into hysteria or launched into accusations, I really think I would have understood. But then we locked eyes. It was rather touching that she appeared to remember me, and I slid an arm around her shoulders, quietly telling the others, "I'll take care of Glynis." Grateful, Pete signaled for the two cops to follow him to the barn, where the Gramms had been staying.

With nothing better to suggest, I placed my hands on Glynis's shoulders, then found myself telling her there's a nice, unoccupied room in the dormitory where she could lie down. For the first time since she'd arrived at the villa, she had no opinion. On anything. And that wry, cheerful personality was nowhere in the vicinity. Her backbone appeared to have lost a few vertebrae, her rumpled clothes were looking dingy, and she couldn't quite hold her lips together. As I headed toward the dormitory, steering Glynis as far as possible from the barn, Rosa and Sofia hovered, and peppered me with some ideas in such rapid Italian that I didn't have a chance of catching it. But they seemed satisfied with their plan and darted toward the main building. All of a sudden, Rosa stopped short and called after me, "Vinci?"

"Vinci," I called back. Up the steps to the second floor we trudged, Glynis propelling herself forward with some combination of hand railing and sheer grit. With my master key, I unlocked the unoccupied Vinci room and showed her inside. No sooner had I turned on the table lamp and the ceiling fan, on low speed, just enough to clear the air, than Glynis Gramm of Naples, Florida, sank sitting onto the side of the single bed with the white quilted coverlet. With dead eyes that had about as much life in them as Bob Gramm's, she slowly looked around. The decorator from Cassina's had redone this room in what they thought was a seaside cottage style, although what that vision had to do with Leonardo da Vinci, I was still scratching my head over. The walls were light gray with glossy white wood-work, one wall was beadboard with an antique gilt-edged mirror and metal-framed photos of button-up ancestors nobody could claim, and on the windowsill was a gray planter with an indestructible snake plant. On the floor was a fluffy, whimsical rug that looked like a skinned sheepdog. I was sure the nuns never had it so good.

"This is a nice room," said Glynis.

"It is." I waited to see where she'd go.

With a curious glance at her hands, as though she didn't recognize them and didn't care, Glynis set them with infinite care on her knees. "The mirror's a little too rococo for the beach."

When I agreed, she said she wanted to sleep.

I blurted, "I'm desperately sorry, Glynis."

"I guess," she managed with a hint of her old drawl, "I'm desperately sorry"—she took in a jerky breath—"that I'm not desperately sorry." She narrowed her eyes just a bit and searched mine, looking to see if she had offended me.

I had nothing to offer. "Rosa and Sofia will bring some things. Don't stay up. They can be very quiet. Bathroom's down the hall. Tomorrow"—I blinked once—"we can take you wherever you want to go. There's a hotel in Cortona you might—" I stopped at the word "enjoy," since as words went at that moment in time, "enjoy" seemed particularly preposterous.

"I'm not going anywhere, Nell. This room is perfect."

Perfect felt along the lines of *enjoy.* "Well, after what happened, Glynis, we thought—"

"Nell." She closed her eyes delicately, the lids just shutting with no muscle effort. "You don't understand." At that, the woman so recently widowed with the murder of her impossible husband, let herself fall over gently onto her side. She clasped her hands together with no show of tension. "I'm not going anywhere," she said from behind her closed eyes. With barely moving lips, Glynis Gramm added with a faint smile, "I'm their chief suspect."

*A*fter he perused the chaotic kitchen while Annamaria stood by serenely, Joe Batta had made his first request: "Everyone please to come . . ." He eyed Nina the translator briefly, who gave the go-ahead to his halting English, and then he raised his voice, which to me always sounded like it emanated from the crypt George Johnson was so keen to explore. "To . . ." A bold statement, so bold he chewed his lip in the fleeting agony of linguistic uncertainty. "To common room."

When Nina inclined her head in mute approval, deciding not to address the absence of the definite article "the,"

Detective Joe Batta stood up straighter. The instruction to meet in the common room was followed by his chomping through what was left of the hard candy and his insistence that the kitchen not be entered. For quick clarification, he turned to Annamaria. "How long is this filth?"

Troubled, Nina leaned into him, whispering. He corrected himself: "This dirt?" This time Nina leaned in more closely and whispered something, if I could gauge just from her gestures, about connotations and fine distinctions. His mood flattening, Joe Batta muttered to her in frustration, *"Dammi la parola!"*—Give me the word. As she complied, he slung a cadaverous smile at all of us. Finally, as Nina dropped back, he sang out to Annamaria with equanimity, "How long is this mess?" He whipped one hand in the direction of the kitchen.

We were all looking at Annamaria with varying degrees of horror. She was wearing her *malocchio* face, although it might not be familiar to Joe Batta. Next to her were her henchmen in the noncleaning of the sacred villa kitchen she was being fast-tracked to lose, Ronn and Sofia, who were smiling shyly, hands folded at their waists. Who needs the evil eye when what you've got is a colossal mess of passive-aggressive origins that might now serve the interest of justice? Annamaria licked her lips (was that lipstick she was wearing?) and blared, *"Trentadue ore e mezza."* Thirty-two and a half hours. Chef was staring at her as though a duck-billed platypus had wandered into the company.

While Joe Batta, Nina, and Annamaria conferred in a tight little scrum, for more details about the filth, Chef looked on and seemed sincerely perplexed at his exclusion. His villa, his crime scene, his filth. Sensing his discomfort, Annamaria turned only half toward him and shot him a look of fake sympathy. I could tell the guy could see the sympathy, but not the fake. In his early seventies, the poor famous celebrity chef could stand to be a bit more savvy about human feelings.

It was one of those instances when supreme talent is in no way matched by other great personal attributes. The man could cook. Aside from bocce, maybe that was all. How had this emotional numbskull raised such a great son as Pete? And if Chef Claudio Orlandini couldn't read Annamaria Bari, his kitchen and (once in the mists of yore) bedroom intimate for over forty years, any better than that, could he possibly get an accurate take on Zoe Campion—whatever her agenda—after only two days?

Pete and George Johnson had moved one of the stainless steel worktables from the classroom side of the expansive room to the space in front of the wall sporting the William Morris–style hanging banner and the gold-leaf-painted sprawling brand of the Villa Orlandini Cooking School—what Chef would call "broth is everything." During that team-building exercise, Pete kept a cool look on George Johnson, and George Johnson kept a speculative look on Pete. The table got placed in its new spot with infinite precision. Bored, Joe Batta was now cracking his knuckles and perusing his fingernails.

Pete started to carry over two chairs. George had one to start, but when he saw Pete hauling two, he grabbed another. In the meantime, all the rest of us were deploying ourselves rather haphazardly on the couch, the love seat, and the upholstered chairs. After the manly little table-and-chair-moving demonstration, Joe Batta didn't seat himself behind it. Instead, he stood in front of it, leaning. So did Nina, who went on to translate his official remarks.

The deceased, Robert Gramm, expired at 3:28 this afternoon at Santa Margherita Hospital. Preliminary lab reports show cause of death was the ingestion of amatoxins in the form of *Amanita phalloides*, the death cap mushroom, approximately twenty-one hours ago. He is given to understand—I slid a look at Pete, never putting much faith in the phrase "given to understand," which always sounds like someone's put one over on you but you haven't quite realized it yet—yesterday included a trip to the woods for a lesson in mushroom identification, which included *Amanita phalloides*. Is that correct, Signorina Bari? She inclined her head.

This was not news to any of us, so I wagered we were wondering just why she looked so terribly pleased with Joe Batta. He continued, which meant so did Nina, announcing that his first order of business was to determine whether the deceased's ingestion of poison was—he paused for effect, sucking in air through clogged nasal passages—accidental, or—a purred whisper—intentional. Interviews with each of those present will aid in that determination. To the best of your knowledge, Signorina Bari, is every one of the mushroom pickers in this room now?

Annamaria narrowed her eyes and gave the room an elegant scan. *"Non il signor Gramm,"* she reported silkily, *"ovviamente."*

"Ovviamente," concurred Joe Batta.

"Anche non la signora Gramm."

I piped up. "She's resting."

Intending to be more colorful, then, Rosa, Sofia, Laura, and Lisa added what Nina translated as collapsed, prostrate, contemplating self-destruction, and asking for a few cookies. Joe Batta met these details with a simple statement that he had already conducted his first interview with la signora Gramm at Santa Margherita, at which the

rest of us exchanged wide-eyed glances that communicated something along the lines of *Poor Glynis is in for
it now.*

Zoe elbowed George. "She wouldn't do it," she said
with proper Jersey girl scorn. "Sure, they bickered, but
lots of couples do. It's what jazzes them, right?" Nina
could hand off the Italian version of those thoughts to Joe
Batta, but there was no way she could match the attitude.
Instead of watching the attempt, I couldn't get past the
word "bickered." Recalling the fight Rosa and I overheard
in the barn room that first night, Glynis and Bob Gramm
were doing more than bickering. It was raw and vicious
and full of pain. And no, I wouldn't say it jazzed them. I
realized, then, that I was on the spot. In any interview
with Joe Batta, whether we talked our way over to that
incident or not, I had knowledge I would have to reveal.

Still . . . why would Glynis Gramm, if she had murder
in her heart, wait until getting to her longed-for cooking
class in Tuscany to kill off her husband? To me, it seemed
so risky, waiting to do the deed in a foreign, unfamiliar
environment, and you can't count on having at hand either
a serviceable weapon or any other reasonable suspects.
Glynis was a successful businesswoman. It was Glynis
who had bailed out Gramm's Lams a good couple of
times when it looked like it would go belly up. From the
little I knew her, I thought that woman most definitely had
game, enjoying everything we could throw at her in terms
of new recipes, new culinary tips and habits, related field
trips . . . For one, Mushroom Picking/Avoiding 101. It was
hard to imagine why a woman like that would feel some
pressing need to do away with her husband.

I tried gazing into my memory of that recent trip to the
woods with Annamaria and the others, carrying our

sacks, our harvesting knives—in Jenna's case, her pink notebook and clickable pen. I couldn't pull up any image of Glynis Gramm harvesting mushrooms—safe, edible mushrooms, let alone a surreptitious slice at a death cap. All I could dredge up from the memory locker was Annamaria standing there like a high priestess intoning something along the lines of *Behold, Death!* We fell into a semicircle like some kind of awed, mushroom-worshipping coven, and listened to her lesson on *Amanita phalloides.*

I hadn't harvested any edibles myself (perhaps the only thing I could point to as something in common with Bob Gramm); I just overlooked the scene. Glynis had harvested, and so had Zoe and George and Annamaria herself. After she had properly freaked us all out about the death cap, to my recollection we all just stepped away from the spot, as if any second the fatal fungus would hurl itself at us. Annamaria had led the way home, and I had brought up the rear of the little class, lost in my own never-ending mental script about how well everything was going, where we could improve, and so on, I *had* brought up the rear, hadn't I? Had any of the others lingered without my being aware of it? Lingered long enough to take a slice from the *Amanita phalloides*?

A t first, the questioning was general, and I could tell that Joe Batta was trying to determine mealtimes over the past two days. To help with this effort, Annamaria contributed some inconsequential information and made the point—with a critical look at Chef—what with the change in kitchen routine, school life had become disorganized. Chef gasped. Annamaria lifted an eyebrow. Joe

Batta checked his phone to see if it was indeed recording. Then, he swung around the table, noisily took his seat, and addressed us. According to Nina, he was attempting to establish *esattamente quando*—exactly when—the death cap mushroom had been introduced into Signor Gramm's food.

Everyone in the common room appeared to have a theory. No two were alike. It could have been the gelato in the piazza. It could have been the melon and prosciutto before dinner. It could have been the chocolate drops he kept in his pants pocket and popped in midafternoon. It could have been the last of the caprese salad he had for lunch even though Jenna had expressed a prior interest in it. It could have been the gluten-free linguine he ate for dinner. Or it could have been the *prima marinara* sauce atop the gluten-free linguine he ate for dinner. At the end of this barrage of theories, Joe Batta was scowling. Then, very slowly, in soft-spoken Italian, he asked a key question.

Adjusting her red skirt, Nina translated. "When did Signor Gramm first express not feeling well?"

A fresh barrage of conflicting reports peppered the air. As Rosa appeared through the door to the courtyard with a rolling cart filled with carafes, cream, a sugar bowl, and snacks, the tension in the room slackened. When Pete stepped over to help her, I recognized these things from his cottage. If the villa kitchen was temporarily off-limits as a probable crime scene, no reason we had to go without. The mood mellowed, and various reminiscences about exactly when Bob Gramm had expressed a bad tummy abounded. The fact that the information ranged from about four in the afternoon to nine at night pretty much clinched it for me that the guy was a chronic complainer.

Something was always wrong, especially if it had to do with his health.

"Well," added Zoe contemplatively, "I think the four o'clock complaint was more about his knees than his stomach, right? I think maybe what you overheard, George, was Bob moaning a suspicion that the whole gluten-free thing was worsening his arthritis."

"Ah." George wisely left it at that.

"Technically," she made her point, "not his stomach."

We all seemed to come to the same conclusion at once.

"Poi," intoned Joe Batta, elevating his index finger, *"è stata . . . la cena."*

It was the dinner.

14

I think so," said Zoe, folding her arms. Chef was beaming as though these proceedings had nothing to do with
him. "By the time the rest of us left for the piazza, his
stomach was already off."

None of us quite knew what to feel about this zeroing
in on the culprit meal. On the one hand, it focused Joe
Batta's attention—which meant a breather for any of us
on the scene those other times. But on the other hand, all
I could picture of *la cena* was an orgy of pasta pots and
sauté pans and swaths of handmade noodles and steam
and dirty dishes left over from every other meal of the
day. Annamaria's plot to complicate Chef's kitchen managed to hand the cops a whopper of a crime scene to examine. But—but—it also held the possibility of identifying
amatoxin residue on a plate or plates. If the kitchen had
been up to its normal sanitary standards would any clues
remain? Would amatoxin on Bob Gramm's plate survive
the 160-degree wash water of a commercial dishwasher?

This was a break for them.

But for us, as long as the villa kitchen remained off-limits, Pete and Annamaria and I could figure out how to feed our little Orlandini family out of Pete's cottage kitchen. But how could we run the final two days of Marinara Misteriosa? The answer was we couldn't. But even beyond that, why—in good taste, after the murder—would we even want to?

All of a sudden, Detective Giovanni Battista Onetto was wired for action. He sprang up, filling me at the same time with both hope and dread, and strode toward the kitchen, his Italian coming so fast it sounded like water trying to swirl down a clogged drain. Nina turned to us as her boss disappeared through the door to the corridor, and told us, "He and crime scene techs descend on the kitchen now, which you will remember is off-limits. He will see each of you privately as time permits. That is all. Go about your business."

At a wide-eyed glance from Annamaria, Pete spoke up. "Our business is the kitchen."

Nina shrugged. "You can cook, Signor Orlandini," she made it plain, "you just can't do it there." To no one in particular, she added, "I will be making calls in the car, if I'm needed." Grabbing a hot pink bouclé jacket that was surprisingly smart with her red skirt, she half ran out the door, and that left all the rest of us. A dispirited group, if ever. Jenna sat softly crying by the fireplace where there were only ashes for cold comfort. Laura saw a need and trudged over to build a fire. George and Pete glared at each other for having failed at cave care. Annamaria stared inscrutably at the hand-painted Orlandini brand, TUTTO FA BRODO.

It was Chef who actually started flipping channels, pausing happily at a mountain biking event. Rosa, Sofia, and Lisa started swiping with cloths at the classroom tables, although they didn't need cleaning. Sitting near me, Zoe seemed restless. When Chef tired of the biking, Rosa took the remote gently from his left hand and stepped up closer to the wall-mounted TV. One click got her to the channel usually the home of her fantasy squeeze, Stealth Chef, but just in time for a commercial break from a green building reality TV show featuring straw bale houses. She howled when the canned voice announced Stealth Chef reruns until next week when Stealthy returns with Recipes for All.

George laughed. *"Rosa,"* he called to her from across the room, *"ti piace quello?"* You like that?

She seemed judicious. *"Stealthy è un bravo chef."*

"Or *brava*," George said pointedly.

Rosa snorted her disagreement.

"What a gimmick." He sighed and shook his head. "At Fraîche Take Bistro, we feed real people real food." When Zoe suppressed a laugh, he shot her a look. I sensed that those of us who knew Rosa Bari deemed it unwise to suggest to a fan girl that TV cooking was pretty much staged with not too much accountability. Beyond our walls there in the common room, regardless of whether Marinara Misteriosa had ground sickeningly to a halt, or whether none of us sitting around on the stylish Cassina rentals had anything more than a fire to warm ourselves by, events out in the corridor were noisy. All that stood between the ten of us sad and quiet in the common room and the "official business" bumping and hauling and squawking and shouting just thirty feet away was a door.

Out of nothing, not even thin air, I came up with a couple of useful ideas. The first I whispered to Pete, who seemed grateful to have something to do. Wordlessly, he left us to take my advice and do two things: get his cottage ready for dinner guests and call the pizza delivery place just down the road in Cortona. Dinner was set, and I hardly cared how it tasted. When he had gone, I called Jenna, George, and Zoe over to the love seats by the fire. I spread my hands. "Here's the way I see it." All three were watching me closely. "We're all suspects, so for the next couple of days at least"—I looked at each of them in turn—"you're not going anywhere."

"Agreed," said George. Zoe nodded. Jenna, at least, did not dispute it.

"So here is my question," I went on, "for you." I paused, partly because I really wanted their attention and partly because I was hoping I wasn't being crass. "Do you want to continue?"

"Continue?" That was Jenna, and I could tell her mind was filling in a whole lot of wrong blanks. Continue stealing knives, running away, hunting truffles with Stella, living. For the moment, I decided to hold off on adding, "Sprinkling *Amanita phalloides* over anybody's pasta."

I cleared it up for her. "Continue cooking. Continue with the second half of Marinara Misteriosa."

After a dramatic intake of breath, Zoe blinked and said, "I do." Having decided, she even smiled. "I came to learn from the world's greatest chef"—at that she and the old culinary scoundrel twiddled fingers at each other—"and I want all of it." She beamed.

Oh, well, you, I found myself thinking as I looked at her neutrally.

Annamaria covered a snort with a delicate cough.

Clasping her hands around her knees, Zoe rocked a little. "I'm in." Then, as if she hadn't already made the point: "Still so much to learn."

Chef ambled over, trying to look as macho as a man could who had an arthritic knee, one palsied eyelid, and now his arm in a sling. We looked at him expectantly. But once he planted his huarache-clad tootsies in our midst, he couldn't find anything to say. I turned to George Johnson and lifted my eyebrows at him. "Count me in," was all he said. "I guess just how is the question."

For her part, Jenna Bond nodded mutely, hugging herself tightly.

What was I going to do with that girl? And why did I keep thinking of her as a girl when she was only five years younger than I was? I stood. George seemed interested. So did, of all people, Annamaria. Raising my arms, I beckoned over the Bari sisters, wishing with all my might that Nina the handy-dandy translator would reappear. "Tomorrow," I announced, "we continue."

Rosa lifted her gray-clad shoulders expectantly. *"Più scuola?"* More school?

I gave her a hug for making it so simple—and for being someone who would hug me back at the moment, when I was too professional—so I would tell myself to try George Johnson. "Yes, Rosa." We stepped into the hug. "More school." I had hoped the clapping would have been lustier, but so be it. Then I turned to Chef and the Bari sisters, and ticked off a short list of tasks for tomorrow, our third day of Marinara Misteriosa classes.

Make a shopping list of all necessary ingredients, including a few easy meals for Glynis, who would probably not be wanting to consume any pasta with marinara sauce anytime soon. (Chef and Zoe both raised their hands. I chose Chef, who made subtle gestures to include Zoe in list making, which I ignored.)

Call Oswaldo for an emergency delivery of whatever

produce we need. (I gave this job to Chef, who did not raise his hand to volunteer. Let the guy work.)

Help Oswaldo with the delivery. (Jenna. Consider sending bodyguard. For Oswaldo.)

Go to market in town for the herbs and spices. (Rosa would bike there.)

Call the closest kitchen supply place for cookware, knives (I slid a glance at Jenna), utensils, plates. (Zoe and Annamaria both volunteered. When I chose Zoe, Annamaria shot me an alarmed look, which I tamped down with one hand, because . . .)

Set up and prep in the makeshift kitchen for the day's lessons. (Annamaria.)

"That leaves a stove, a fridge, a sink—" counted George.

"No worries," I positively sang out, heading toward the crowded corridor. "All under control." From whence this optimism? "A few phone calls and we're golden." Someone whistled. I believe it was the always surprising Sofia.

"Wait!" called George. "What's my job, Nell?"

"You, George?" Think fast, Valenti. "You set it all up."

"Set what up?"

"The stove, the fridge, the sink." You want 'em, you got 'em, buster. What I thought was a coup got demoted when I noticed he sat back, hiding his delight at scoring probably the biggest job of all. "Find a good place for our culinary classes and set it all up." Really, from his expression you would think I had just presented the boy in him the Millennium Falcon Lego set.

"Anywhere?" he asked inscrutably.

Now I was worried. "Anywhere."

Even great-looking guys are capable of reptilian smiles. "I'll look around."

"Remember," I improvised wildly, wanting to pile it on, "you'll need to move some worktables. And stools."

"Ooh," he said teasingly. "Stools. Such a lot for me to do."

I went prim. "You must own your education." Where did I come up with that bit of swill?

With his hands in his pockets, George Johnson came up right beside me, his mobile mouth not two inches from my left ear. "So must you."

I raised my voice, saying, "I have calls to make." But it was lost on George, who was already studying the make-shift kitchen possibilities, heading toward the chapel dining room. "Oh, George," I called out, going all Dame Maggie Smith. "Please choose four bottles of wine from the wine cellar for tonight's dinner." Then I added wickedly, "You know the way." He threw me a salute without turning around, and his laugh followed him out of sight.

I whispered to Rosa to please go check on Signora Gramm, but be careful not to disturb her. And as I headed in the direction of my office, I called back to staff and students needing to fill the time in ways that didn't include local law enforcement, "Dinner in thirty minutes in Pete's cottage." I registered some gasps of delight—from whom, exactly, it did not bear thinking.

"But, but—" tried Rosa, always tracking everyone, "*Giorgio non lo sa.*" George doesn't know. She craned her neck to see if he was in earshot and had caught the plan.

I wrinkled my nose at her. "He'll find us."

Or not.

In the meantime, before pizza showed up, I had calls to make.

* * *

*E*arly the next morning, ten of us reconvened to salvage what we could of Marinara Misteriosa. Annamaria reported to me with hands that were too tired to wring for maximum effect that she was deeply mourning the temporary loss of the kitchen. She went on to make me understand that the *carabinieri* had busied themselves until just after two a.m. From the way she said it, you would think Annamaria was waiting to hear a loved one was out of brain surgery. Her other key piece of information was that Joe Batta had made his way through the four younger Bari sisters, which may not be the best way to put it, leaving Annamaria herself for sometime after midnight when they were both *quasi morti*—almost dead—and he would return this morning to interview the Orlandinis, the students, and—she winced apologetically—me.

Before the pizza party last night, I arranged for the delivery of the temporary kitchen equipment we'd be needing, spending in about ten minutes' worth of phone time about €2,600. Roughly half what, say, George Johnson had paid for four days of instruction at the Villa Orlandini, not including airfare. That meant in those frenetic ten minutes I had spent one-tenth of our income from Marinara Misteriosa. First, I shuddered. Then, I determined to put my spendthrift ways behind me to chow down some pizza and knock back a couple of glasses of wine.

I wasn't the life of the party. Nobody was, really, although George and Zoe made some efforts in that direction. On her third glass of an unassuming little Chianti (really, George; ask a man to do an errand . . .), Zoe regaled us with a tale about an outbreak of poison ivy during Senior Citizen Camp week at the outdoor education center, and

George was minimally entertaining with stories about celebrities he'd served, such as Anthony Bourdain and Toni Morrison. Jenna was wearing jeans and a pale pink T-shirt, quietly sipping the half glass of wine she had asked for, which she had topped off with some ginger ale. Rosa, Sofia, Laura, and Lisa seemed happy to be there—only Annamaria had begged off.

Pete took care of everyone. We all sat separately, separate love seats, separate chairs, separate floor cushions, looking like a random assortment of strangers. I guess that was really the truth. Chef stretched out on his side, aiming for youthful, and managed to down two slices. I watched with detachment to see whether he'd choke, but no. We'd have to content ourselves with stories about celebrities at Fraîche Take Bistro.

But no amount of margherita pizza and passable red wine and amusing stories could erase the possibility that one of us could have poisoned Bob Gramm. I sat back, dabbing my lips with a cloth napkin. We could be sitting in our solitary seats, listening to an endless loop of Sarah Vaughan that never goes wrong, the days ahead uncertain, but at least there were cloth napkins. It was a kind of comfort. Pete caught my smile. I knew I should stay to help him clean up, but I was Dead Nell Walking at that point in the day. Without a word, I communicated with Pete, who nodded, holding up a dismissive hand. With a quick good night to the others as a group, I headed to the door and slipped out.

So my surprise was vast when, the next morning, I showered, poured coffee, and got some work done in my room, half-aware of distant rumblings in the courtyard and delicate raindrops on the roof. Equipment being delivered? At 8:43 a.m.? I didn't intend to unlock the door, raise the shade, and leave my precious room until I finished my list, a hodgepodge of sleuthing tasks and business nightmares. The business list had two entries: turn over my office to Joe Batta for the duration (better to keep the common room and chapel open to the students staying on, and better to keep official police investigation in a confined space); and do the math for partial refunds to Glynis for the unused portions of the Gramms' registrations (discuss full refunds with Pete).

The other, sleuthing list would be more time-consuming, and I'd have to see what I could reasonably turf to Pete and the Baris to free me up a bit today: study the spreadsheet with all the numbers that I'd discovered in Bob Gramm's money belt (ask Glynis? risky?); dig into the backgrounds of the five Americans, see what bubbled up that didn't make it onto their applications for Marinara Misteriosa; review the events of the day Bob Gramm took ill. New item for new list, nothing to do with business or sleuthing: consider own tendency to use euphemism (e.g., "took ill"). Q. for self: Any point in asking Dad to call off George Johnson when whole awful ugly workshop murder/sexual tension thing ends in two days? Dr. Val Valenti has probably gotten an earful from his man in the field over the last couple of days. So . . . why hasn't he called me? Was Dad growing up? Or . . . was I, that it hadn't even occurred to me until now?

Stepping into my high-rise flare pants and tugging my green cropped sweater over my head, I slipped my lists into my laptop sleeve, then hesitated on the threshold for just a minute as deliverymen passed by, their two-wheelers stacked with boxed equipment. They kept on the manicured path until it ended, then gamely wheeled their goods across the wet grass toward Pete's cottage. Oh, no.

No. George wasn't setting up our makeshift kitchen in Pete's cottage, was he? I'd wring his appealing neck. Maybe I'd place that call to Dad after all. Then I stopped in my tracks. If the murder of Bob Gramm spun out, resistant to easy solutions, did that mean I'd have Zoe Campion, George Johnson, and Jenna Bond on my hands for the foreseeable future?

So be it. My eyes narrowed. Maybe I could talk them into staying at the inn in town. On our dime. Which was just about what we'd have left to spend for three rooms for however long. Still, I could play Lady Bountiful, why not? I bet it was all the same to Joe Batta, here, there, wherever, those three. As soon as he cleared any of them of suspicion, off Manny Manfredi would whisk them. For that matter, why pay Manny Manfredi to drive them to the Florence airport? I'd do it for free. I'd even speed.

I hoofed it to the courtyard, where Laura was directing traffic implacably: restaurant equipment delivery vans to the right, *carabinieri* to the left. Rosa was pedaling down the driveway with her socks rubber-banded over her loose pants leg, and the worn out panniers flopping from a missing strap. Chef, buttoning up his shirt, peppered the madness with laughing comments.

Pete and Annamaria escorted the boxed deliveries down toward Pete's cottage. "What's going on?" I grabbed his sleeve. For the first time since I'd arrived at the Villa Orlandini, Pete wasn't tracking me. My location, my mood, my activities. When he looked at me, he seemed surprised to find me there.

"Your pal George Johnson made his choice."

"He's not my pal."

"Oh, Nell," said Pete softly. "He's something." When the delivery guy cleared his throat—no translation necessary—Pete started to walk with him, calling back with no inflection in his voice, "We'll be cooking in the oil production space." Without another word, he continued on his way.

I didn't know what to make of it. "Well," I yelled, sounding a lot like my father at his shrinkiest, "how does that make you feel?"

Pete Orlandini, my first—maybe my only—friend at the Villa Orlandini Cooking School, heard me and pulled up short, just long enough to turn around. "The way I figure it," he yelled back, shoving his fists on his hips, "it might as well be used for something." With that, he turned away angrily. "At least I managed to pay for all the equipment."

15

I wanted to charge after him, buck him up about the oil production space. It was only for the duration of Marinara Misteriosa, I wanted to remind him. That's all. Beyond that, we were under no obligation to provide any more kitchen instruction, not for these four remaining students. And the next workshop was a whole month down the road. If ever, considering there were as yet no registrations. Two days, Pete, just two days. Then back all the rented kitchen equipment could go, and he could store the harvested olives there again, and press what we needed at the villa, take the rest to market—no changes. I watched him disappear with the deliveryman and the two-wheeler around the far side of his cottage.

But I understood.

No matter how much sense I could make to Pete Orlandini, the dream was being invaded, by philistines, no less. A Brooklyn waiter, a Jersey girl—all right, all right, make that two, since at the moment he was none too happy with me for giving the Brooklyn waiter a free hand—and a gloomy Baltimore barista. Even the Bari sisters, full of bustling competence and Billy Joel. The oil production space was the dream incubator for Pete, a private space. I should have been more sensitive to it and told George Johnson he could set up our makeshift kitchen anywhere but there. No explanations needed. There are just some spaces that need to be safe from intrusion. Just a few weeks ago, Pete had spoken softly of saving money to enlarge the business.

I didn't know him very well then, but I was excited for him, for his vision.

Maybe I just identified with that kind of soft, shy love of an idea. It was what landed me in cooking school design. I could bring better cooking to millions. Or maybe just thousands. Or a couple hundred. As raindrops spattered noisily on the path, I watched Nina heading my way under an umbrella sporting poor Van Gogh's *Starry Night*. Face it, Valenti. Given these last few days, you can't even bring better cooking to five. One's dead from poison, one's putting Annamaria out of a job, one's working undercover for your domineering daddy, one's spreading sunshine all over the place, one's out a spouse, and one's doing very unacceptable things with mushrooms.

Nina informed me Detective Batta awaited me in the common room.

Oswaldo picked that moment to arrive in his farm truck. Losing no time, he made his awkward way across the grass and asked where to put the produce if the kitchen was out of bounds, and when he might expect payment.

Annamaria stared past me in a stained apron and asked if we'd be needing her.

Rosa asked for the day's agenda. I smacked my forehead. The agenda.

Jenna, with Stella on a leash, asked if she could keep Stella in her room. (Stella averted her eyes from me, showing plainly she didn't give a pig's foot what I thought.) Vincenzo was still sick and if she hunted *tartufi* with Stella (she actually said *tartufi* as though it was her first word after "mama") Vincenzo would share profits with her.

Chef had no actual questions. Instead, as he tucked in his shirt, zipped his pants, and groped his baldness, he let me know we needed to add bocce lessons to the day's agenda back there—he gestured vaguely—somewhere.

I meted out my answers.

To Nina: "I will speak with Signor Batta at eleven, when I am free. Go."

To Oswaldo: "Find Pierfranco. Ask him. Find me and I'll pay you cash. Then go. No, wait. The commissario might want you." Our farmer hailed Jenna, and patted Stella.

To Annamaria: (mad and with plenty of gestures) "You are the sous-chef! Of course we need you!"

To Rosa: (with wide eyes and my most demonic smile) "No agenda. Let's just see what happens, shall we?"

To Jenna: "Yes." (When might we expect you to buy the villa with your truffle profits?)

To Chef I made a speedy change of course. I nearly said *Over my dead body*, but I didn't want any one of these possibly homicidal people to take that for an invitation. So I told him, instead, *"Qualunque cosa, Chef."*—Best I could do in Italian for "Whatever." I added, since I was in a banishing mood, "Now go." Bocce lessons, for all I knew, might well be a better, more lucrative choice for the Orlandinis than a benighted cooking school that invites homicide. Maybe, when it came right down to it, a bocce school was more a dream for this unmanageable chef than a cooking school. Pete had his olive dreams. Chef may well have dreams very different from what had brought the likes of Nell Valenti to Tuscany.

Why had he hired me?

Why had I accepted?

Suddenly, the last two months of my life seemed baffling.

Ordinarily, I would have taken Chef aside out of earshot of the others and quietly schooled him in being fully dressed before leaving his apartment because—oh, we could argue it back and forth—doing so would make a better impression. And we could have a big old laugh together about old stick-in-the-Tuscan-mud Ornella Valenti. But today I stepped out farther into the misty rain and didn't particularly care about governing the ungovernable. I was young enough not to be very attuned to when I was wasting my time.

Maybe by the time I hit Chef Claudio Orlandini's age, the signs of disinterest were writ large across the side of the barn where Bob Gramm had been locked in a death struggle with *Amanita phalloides*. Maybe I'd still be quacking to well-paying customers about the need for high-end cooking schools, all the while really just wondering when my sky blue inkpad kit would turn up for my latest scrapbooking project.

They dashed off in different directions, Stella receiving pats and ruffles from everyone she passed. I'd have to work on her. Or myself. Unleashing the truffle-hunting Lagotto, who promptly tore off in the direction of the woods—I let out an evil little laugh—Jenna grabbed the sack and the *vanghetto* and ran full-out after her. It was the most energy I had seen from our resident grudge-bearer that had nothing to do with making off with cutlery or yelling over the roadside into Cortona. Just then George and Zoe came along, effortlessly carrying one of the stainless steel worktables between them, like old hands, George walking forward, Zoe backward.

"Buongiorno!" piped Giorgio.

I muttered.

Zoe was bright-eyed even at a distance of twenty feet. "Have you seen Chef?"

"Yes," I said helpfully. "He was just zipping up." I drilled her searchingly.

"What a character," she roared. "Best part of the whole Tuscan experience." She wasn't naming the murder, I saw. Then, all business: "Your turn, George." Then she did a 180-degree turn, leaving George the backward half of the trip to the makeshift kitchen.

He was unfazed. "Oh," he called to me, "I took the liberty of ordering a couple of Genesis Basecamp cooking systems, Nell. I figured you probably just want electric on some hot plates, right?"

I stood mute, goggling at him. That he had guessed correctly and gone over my head and was so disarming about it. Then: "Basecamp cooking system?" I said it like we were talking about an unpleasant discharge. Jersey girls are very clear on this sort of thing.

His smile made a lovely arc from twenty feet away. "You'll love it. It's propane." As he kissed his fingertips, the table angled toward the ground and Zoe yelled, "Oops!"

Still trying to get the picture, I said, "Like . . ." I didn't even know the right word. "Backpacking equipment?"

"You bet. You'll love it."

Zoe piped up with a grin, "They're coming sometime this morning."

"Who?" I pictured Everest guides.

They went merry on me. "The Basecamp cooking systems," called George.

Zoe added fondly, "Silly!"

"Until then," explained the Brooklyn waiter who might just as well have dumped wine and lit candles in my lap, "we'll carry on with the little, well, hot plates you got." He wrinkled his nose at me. "Stop by later."

"We're in with the olives," shouted Zoe over her shoulder.

"Owning our education," added George, and I could swear he winked.

Backpacking, Mr. Johnson? You don't know what you're up against. I had half a mind to go and make him as humanly miserable as I could. As Zoe started guiding him around little hills and divots on the way to Pete's sacred olive oil production room, I shot him a sickly smile. I watched until they grew smaller and smaller, and then I caught sight of something amazing. Coming toward me, slowly, unbothered by the light rain, was Glynis Gramm.

I went to meet her. From what I could tell, her face was scrubbed, but her usual artful makeup was nowhere to be seen, and she was wearing what looked like some of Sofia's clothes—the closest Bari sister in size to Glynis herself. Gray pants, a long-sleeved heather crewneck, a green rain jacket, unzipped. "Nell," said the new widow carefully, "can you spare some hair clips"—she rotated one hand—"or something."

I rubbed her shoulders. The neoprene jacket actually rasped. "Come on." While I tried to come to some "best practices" determination about how to handle this poor woman, I jerked my head toward the Abbess's room. "I've got something."

"Also," she added softly, "some lipstick would be nice."

"Can do, Glynis." I pushed open my door and let her pass me inside. As she stood still and blinked, turning a little, I asked, "Barn room off-limits?" No doubt she had left all her things in there when she and Pete dashed off with Bob in the middle of the night, not expecting the worst. And why should they have expected the worst? A big dose of wheat flour was about as bad as it got in any-one's imagination. No need for makeup or prescription meds or clean underwear. Or toothbrush.

Glynis lowered her head. "No," she told me. "I just can't go back in there." She pressed her lips together.

As I moved her gently toward the bathroom, she glanced around. "Oh!" she exclaimed. "The birdcage!" She walked right up to it and peered inside, her fingers lightly on the gilded bars. "All those feathers." I explained how it had belonged to Pete's mother, Caterina, who had died. My room pleased her so much that I heard her hum-ming. In the bathroom, I opened the medicine cabinet and handed Glynis a new freebie toothbrush I had brought with me from home. Leaning over the sink, wearing So-fia's clothes, she brushed her teeth as though it was an unfamiliar task, and I felt terrible for her.

I brought in a small plastic case with an assortment of hair clips, bobby pins, and scrunchies. "When you're ready," I told her. "I found these in a drawer. More stuff from Pete's mom."

She lifted her head and eyed me, then herself, in the mirror. "The toilette of the dead."

I leaned against the doorframe. I was itching to ask her about Bob's mysterious spreadsheet, but I could tell it was too soon. "Glynis," I told her, "everything at the villa is such a jumble"—I watched her widen her eyes and shake her head, left to her own thoughts—"I'll be out of my room all day. Would you like to hang out in here? I can get Rosa to bring you your meals, and—" I stopped because I didn't know what more to add.

"Kind of you, Nell, I'm sure," she said with strength, pulling herself up straight and wiping her lips with the hand towel I held out, "but I've got plans." Hire a lawyer, file a whopping lawsuit against the Villa Orlandini Cooking School, pack for home? I held my breath as she spoke through the slicking of a cherry red lipstick I passed to her.

"Plans?" was all I could get out.

"I've got cooking classes."

My grilling by Detective Joe Batta was so bland it made me nervous. I thought the guy must be hatching something, stringing me along until he could pounce. He seemed pleased when I turned over my office to the *carabinieri*. I could tell it felt like more familiar surroundings to this candy-sucking Italian cop, more accustomed to a desk, a couple of chairs, a file cabinet, and—maybe— even a tampon lamp than what he encountered in the villa common room, what with all its Orlandini branding flung about. It felt downright peculiar for me to be sitting on the non-Nell side of the fancy desk from Cassina's, which Nina stroked appreciatively, but I sucked it all up and answered his questions.

Resting his chin stubble on his hands, he asked for my account of the day of the murder. In Italian, he leered something, looking like the Cheshire cat preparing to disgorge a hairball, which Nina translated as "You were so very helpful just three weeks ago." I decided to overlook his suggestion that I was running a show that somehow whisked up homicide on a regular basis. So I described the mushroom-picking trip to the woods, and pretty much stated that to the best of my recollection, nobody dallied to collect a fine specimen of a death cap. With Annamaria at the head of the group and me at the rear, any of the five would have had to pull some pretty fancy footwork to harvest the poison.

Then I did my best to get the idea across about the kitchen chaos later in the day.

"Chi era presente?" Who was there, asked Joe Batta in a mundane voice. Even though the voice memo on his phone was recording us, he watched his pen with some manufactured interest as he listed the names, sliding the paper to the side to check it against another list. I felt lulled, I have to admit. It was odd trying to describe chaos in an office atmosphere of supreme humdrum.

I cast my mind back. "Oh, Chef, Annamaria, Rosa, Oswaldo, Theresa, Glynis—" I named whoever crossed my mind, but I felt disorganized, and then I pulled up short. "People," I explained, wincing, "were in and out." His head whipped around to Nina inquisitively. *"Dentro e fuori,"* she told him, thumbing through some tweets on her phone. "Ah!" he exclaimed, suddenly clear about something, chopping his hands to the left of him, *"Dentro e fuori,"* and then to the right of him, *"presente tutto il tempo."* He raised his sparse eyebrows to regard me. *"Capisce?"*

At that moment, Nina let out a squeal and held up her phone to show me the video of the meerkat in math class.

I asked him, "You want me to separate who was in and out and who was there the whole time?" Nina didn't help, but he seemed to understand.

"Il meglio che puoi," rumbled the detective, acting as casual as he could stand.

The best I could do. I heaved a sigh. At the end of my recital, the only ones I had put in the kitchen the whole time were Annamaria, Chef, Rosa, and Zoe. But I couldn't say whether it implicated them more or less in the eyes of Joe Batta. On the in-and-out side of the ledger: George, Pete, Bob, Glynis, Sofia, Pete, and me.

"Oswaldo Orlandini?" He rippled an accusatory eyebrow at me.

So that's what the cops had in mind? Oswaldo of all people? I doubted he could farm, let alone plot a murder. I had forgotten our new produce purveyor was on the premises the day Bob Gramm "took ill." I decided to keep it simple. *"Dentro e fuori."* I shrugged. "He brought vegetables."

Nina translated.

"E"—he consulted another list—*"Theresa Franchi?"*

Theresa? Another flitter I had forgotten in the high-spirited chaos of the late afternoon in the kitchen. *"Dentro e fuori,"* I said dismissively, adding a "fft." Another shrug. "She brought wine."

Nina translated.

From another stack of papers, Joe Batta drew out a hand-drawn diagram and passed it over to me. Someone had sketched the villa kitchen with just enough detail to show all the cabinets, major appliances, windows, doors, workspaces—and their proximity to each other. No lighting fixtures, no dimensions, no stools. It was a good job. Setting his fingertips on the diagram, Joe Batta said something in Italian and then clasped his hands. Nina explained he wanted me to indicate where exactly the gluten-free plate was. It was an interesting question, and

I wondered how many versions he'd gotten in the way of answers.

While I considered, he moved his fingers across separate areas of the paper, with every stop, looking at me inquiringly. Back here next to the stove? Here on the worktable? On the counter by the door? *"Dove?"* He added to the question, and Nina translated his need to understand whether Bob Gramm's plate was standing alone, or side by side with all the others, requiring an expert to tell them apart.

Could, in other words, someone have made a mistake?

I felt a sudden chill.

He didn't come right out and ask it, but there it was. Was the intended victim someone else? Not—I thought as I saw the kitchen clearly and pointed to the diagram—when someone as hateful as Bob Gramm was around. *"Separato,"* I told him, adding: *"Qui."* Here. On the counter by the door. While he digested that, I saw the implications. The poisoner didn't have to be someone present in the kitchen the entire time—although it gave him or her more opportunities to sprinkle death cap, which might blend in with the freshly grated Parmesan.

I shuddered. If the plate was set out separate from the others, just to keep the gluten-free fare apart, no mistaking one for the other, even someone *dentro e fuori*—in and out—could have managed, with enough nerve and coolheadedness. Not to mention a pretty sure knowledge by sight of what gluten-free pasta looks like, cooked. Could I myself tell the difference? Not sure.

We took a break without stretching any legs while Nina checked her watch and then plunked a few big gumdrops in her boss's hand. He sat back in my chair, chewing, and Nina adjusted her blouse, her skirt, and her attitude. Scowling at her phone, she muttered, *"Un troll terrible,"* and clucked her tongue. All I could do was wait. At last, Joe Batta inquired about Bob and Glynis Gramm's relationship. Any, oh, and then he shadowboxed to Nina's delight.

So he already knew about the argument, either from Rosa or Glynis herself. I gave him the bare bones, a bracelet bought for another woman by a man with an apparent history of womanizing. Then came the final question: *"Raccontami"*—he leaned back in my chair as though he was going to impound it as evidence and make off with it, chuckling—*"il coltello, per favore."*

Tell me about the knife.

For that, I didn't even need Nina.

Ah, Jenna, Jenna. The knife returns to slash you in the keister.

And I had hoped that my simply returning it surreptitiously to the knife block—no harm, no foul—would end the matter. She had stolen a knife the day of the mushroom identification field trip. Later, Bob Gramm got sick and died horribly. But not from stab wounds. In a way, as I watched the famous police detective press all the flavored sugar from his mouthful of gumdrops, the more interesting question was . . . how had Joe Batta gotten to me? One of the Bari sisters had to have noted the return of the stolen knife. That stood to reason. But how had I been brought into the picture?

When I eyed Joe Batta, what I saw was humor. *Lucky guess,* was what his look was telling me. And a little of *You Americani are outfoxed by high-level police work.* Annoyed, I gave him the slimmed-down truth. Worried about the missing Jenna, I had looked in her room for some clue as to where she might be, and I discovered the knife Annamaria had reported stolen. It was my situation to handle (although even as I said it I found myself wondering why), and—I smiled sweetly at Joe and Nina—since I believed we had nothing to fear from Jenna Bond, I thanked my stars for letting me come across the knife, which I cleaned, returned to the block, and moved on.

What about you? I felt like asking, but didn't.

Instead, standing up with as much poise as I could muster, I tugged at my sleeves and addressed them. "If we're done here, Signor Investigatore, I have work to do."

Joe Batta purred something complacent in Italian, and Nina gave him a wooden look. Turning to me, she said, "Go right ahead. We all have work to do. And we will be making an arrest soon."

The walk to my office door had never seemed so long.

16

[decorative leaf ornament]

I was stewing.

No, I was brooding. With stewing, something gets done. A stew. And that morning, as I aimlessly wandered the villa property, I felt trapped in a smoky room inside my head. Tramping close to Vincenzo's land, I ambled among a field of beautiful yellow crocuses in full autumn bloom. Was it Glynis? Or Jenna? Who would be leaving with Joe Batta? And . . . how much time did I have? I felt sad for what could only be the fate of the cooking school at the Villa Orlandini.

Chef and Pete had spent a lot of money to pay me to develop this school with a free hand, and now not only wouldn't they profit from it, I couldn't see how they'd recoup what had swirled right on down the drain. Nell Valenti could just go on home, maybe get a restaurant job, maybe join the Dr. Val empire after all. But Chef and Pete were home. And the villa would resume its slow crumble into decrepitude, and Chef would return to bocce and obscurity, and Pete would press some delicious Moraiolo olives that would never make it into a bigger market. But I would get to go home.

My shoes were wet through from the meadow walk after a rain shower. But I found myself jogging back to the Orlandinis', skidding now and then through the grass and a sudden clarity of mind. I needed more information from the Americans. I had taken them two days too long at face value. Who were these people? One thing I knew for sure: I couldn't imagine why Glynis Gramm would bring her ill-fated husband all the way to Tuscany just to kill him.

She could have done that back in Naples, Florida, back in an environment where the odious guy had a whole warehouse of enemies. Not here, not in a place he had never been, among people he had never known. No, I had to believe a homicidal Glynis would have brought her business talents to bear on the problem of eliminating Bob. Where was the best and biggest market? Home. Where he had built a business with periods of greater and lesser success, lopping off who knew how many heads in the process, cheating how many customers, smearing how many competitors.

As I reached the courtyard, registering the sight of Rosa and Sofia in a two-woman huddle near the dormitory, I thought no, Glynis Gramm would never put herself through anything more dire than a messy divorce. She might leave herself open to alimony, but not to a murder charge. Still, I had to know for sure. Rounding the corner of Pete's cottage, I pulled up short at the outbuilding that two hundred years ago had been built as the convent's guesthouse.

One of the double doors stood open, and I slipped inside. I always loved the high windows and ceiling in this space that was Pete's small-batch oil production facility, built onto the side of his cottage. The stone walls were whitewashed, and the woodwork was left natural. At eight hundred pounds, his olive press—which could process sixty-five pounds of olives an hour—wasn't pushed off into a corner to accommodate the makeshift kitchen.

Shouts of "Nell!" came at me, but it was only Pete who came over, leaving the others clustered around one of the worktables Zoe and George had moved from the common room, where Chef was being oratorical about *marinara alla pescatore*—the "original" marinara sauce, generally attributed to sailors. I gave the transformed space a quick once-over. Pasta pots were steaming away on George's camp stoves lined up on the worktable. Glynis didn't seem dazed, but she did seem flat. Annamaria stood dressed in her best apron, her black toque, her hands folded mildly in front of her, her head turned away from the action. Zoe was sampling the sauce simmering in one of the large sauté pans, and George was stirring his way into everyone's heart, pinkie finger extended, as he said the other day, "for balance." I could never tell when this private dick was joking.

As Pete drew up alongside me, his look was more one of curiosity. "Come to join in the fun?" I guess I couldn't tell when he was joking, either.

"How's it going?"

"See for yourself. It's a hit."

I pressed my lips together. "Well," I told him quietly, "it's about to get bad."

We stepped aside, closer to the entrance, and away from the class. "It's already bad," he said, looking off into a corner where his bushels of olives stood.

"You just said it was a hit."

"It's a hit. And it's bad. They're not mutually exclusive things, Nell."

"What's the matter?"

He flashed me a quick look. "It doesn't matter," said Pete, his expression closed; and then he added, "enough."

"What do you mean?"

"This isn't the time."

"No," I said quietly, "I think it is the time. Listen"—I took in a big breath—"I know things feel kind of out of control—"

Pete moved closer to me. I'd never seen him look so intense. "Not things, Nell. You."

"Me?"

It would have been easier if he had exploded in some grand Italian operatic way—easier to dismiss, at any rate—but I watched a change come over him. When he spoke, I heard a depth of feeling that confused me. "You haven't been playing by your own rules, Nell. You've been"—he shot a quick look around the room—"fraternizing."

"'Fraternizing'?" I looked at him wide-eyed. At first I nearly laughed, but then I suddenly felt stricken. "Exactly what are you accusing me of, Pete?" The wronged female.

"Do I have to spell it out?" The wronged male.

I gave him a long look. We were doing Jane Austen on a bad day. Tugging at his arm, I pulled Pete outside. "If this is about George," I said, as the door slammed behind us, "I understand completely. It's okay if I fraternize with you, but not with him."

He gasped. "That's not what I—"

"It is. And by the way, Pete," I told him through my teeth, "your conversation used to be a whole lot better."

He rallied. "I could say the same about your profes-sionalism."

I gasped. "Thin ice, mister."

"You're on it, too," he blustered.

I waved my arms around. "The ice?"

"Yes, the ice."

"We're on the same thin ice, is that what you mean?"

After a moment, he blurted, "I guess."

We stood silent for about a minute, in a shared huff on thin ice, apparently. Finally, Pete looked past me. "I think you're right. I think my conversation used to be better." He leaned against the door to his oil production center.

I scuffed at a stone. "Mine, too," I said. "I'm sorry."

"So am I."

In that moment something really good could have hap-pened. A hug that felt new, more exploratory, different from the kind you give a beloved friend. A kiss that felt slow and surprised. But as we stood just inches apart, our eyes on each other, all I could see was fatigue. So I crossed my arms and managed to crawl off the thin ice. "Pete," I said, "Joe Batta's about to make an arrest."

His breath came out in a soft whistle. "Who is it?"

"I don't know, but I'm guessing Glynis or Jenna." I looked over at them. "Toss-up."

"Well . . ." was all he could say. Then: "The whole villa—" he said softly.

"—Is on thin ice. I don't have much time, Pete, and I've got to talk with them."

He nodded quickly. "I'll send them out."

"Thanks," I said, and we gave each other a small smile as he ducked back inside.

What had happened to us?

There's a moment when a sauce goes sour. It's so

subtle, so nearly imperceptible, that you can't avoid it and you can't fix it and for sure you can't go right ahead and enjoy it. It tastes like acid, and burn, and inexperience. And maybe that was me, too. Acid and burn and inexperience.

"Nell?" It was Jenna.

When Glynis drew up, the slick of my lipstick just a memory on her lips, we left.

There was no ideal place for the Talk. Any indoor place I considered had either vomit in a bucket (whose job was that?) or Joe Batta. I wasn't sure which was worse. Anywhere in the main building was too open to interruption. Anywhere in town was too far away. So in we went, as a last resort, to the Abbess's room, and I was happy I had made up my bed. They stood uncertainly just over the threshold, totally in the way when I drew the door shut. I elbowed both women farther into the room and pulled over the two lightweight café chairs, part of the set I had found in a secondhand shop off the main piazza in Cortona when I decided I needed a small table near the window.

I sat on the trunk at the foot of the bed. We looked at each other for a minute, Jenna flushed with new purpose as Stella's day-care provider, Glynis gaunt with some cross between despair and crazy-headed resolve. As for me, I picked at my cuticles. I thought we looked like the day not too many people showed up for the Traveler's Aid support group. My meeting, my agenda, so I began, cleared my throat, and began again. "Joe Batta is about to make an arrest." When neither of them asked the obvious question, I blundered along. "Let's clear the air."

I turned first to the widow. "Glynis, they know about the argument you and Bob had that first night." I steeled myself, prepared to elaborate that although Rosa and I had been passing by the barn room at the time, our chance passing (leave out the ten minutes we stood still to eavesdrop effectively) certainly did not preclude (use of big word lends credibility to the story) the possibility of others' overhearing as well; after all, it was nighttime. I didn't want to point the finger at Rosa, but since I knew I hadn't told Joe Batta about the fight yet, that left her. Rosa had scooped me.

"I know," said Glynis matter-of-factly. "I told him."

"You—"

She shrugged, but Sofia's clothing was just enough too big for her that Glynis's shoulders bumped up against the inside of the dress's fabric. "Believe it or not, I didn't kill my husband." Her gaze narrowed in the direction of the empty Victorian birdcage. "I kind of liked the bum, you know. His sins were all so petty." She let out a short, soft laugh. "Lying, cheating. Such small time dreams in such fancy designer shoes." I noticed Jenna was breathing faster and the flush of happy dog care was getting bleached clean out of her.

But Glynis went on, "Or . . . maybe he just found small-time ways of soothing himself about the big-time dreams that never went anywhere." Suddenly, she looked directly at me. "No, I didn't have to kill him. I didn't even have to leave him." Her voice went soft as it caught in her throat. "Even so," she said philosophically, "I'll understand if that cop arrests me. I'm probably the best candidate. Wronged wife, and all that. It's just so easy. Not to worry, Nell, not to worry. I don't hold you or the Orlandinis responsible. The cops will figure it out."

Glynis Gramm: not a Jersey girl.

I gaped at her, not at all sure that if they could make a case against the widow they'd keep right on digging just to see what else turned up. I had a sudden question. "Why did he come with you, Glynis? Why this time? Sounds like you'd tried before, but these travel cooking adventures weren't Bob's thing."

She nodded, running her tongue along her teeth. "Not at all. No, this time was different. Everything came together so quickly I just took him at face value and signed us both up. Over the past three or four years he's been on a kind of upswing, like the business was picking up and he was feeling good about things. The poor sap always felt competitive with me, so I never asked for any details. Especially now, when luxury cars seemed to be doing well and Bob had some dough to spread around, and he liked being a man of mystery about his daily operations. All he ever wanted me to see were the dazzling results. Sleight of hand, no hard work, no scrambling with the nitty-gritty, win some, lose some."

In the short silence, my own mind went to the key question that Glynis had overlooked: *So, what had changed for Bob Gramm in the last three years?* "What's your guess, Glynis? Why now, why here?"

She made a face. "From past experience? I'd say he had an angle he wanted to work. Lamborghini HQ's in Bologna. How far is that from here?"

I squinted, trying to visualize the map. "Two hours, maybe."

"I'm guessing he was going to make time for a side trip there and pitch something to the top brass. Not that they'd listen. Not that he'd get past Reception."

Nodding, I pulled a folded piece of paper from my pocket. As I unfolded it, I said, "This was tucked into Bob's money belt, Glynis. Do you have any idea what it is?"

She took it from me, with not so much as a question about how I got my mitts on it. With a puzzled look, she checked out what had seemed to me to be a spreadsheet. "It's Bob's writing, a kind of log, I'd say."

"Something from Gramm's Lams?"

She winced thoughtfully. "Nah, he's got a bookkeeping service for the business, and they use QuickBooks. I use the same people for the boutique, that's how I know."

"So, something off the books," I ventured.

"And he brought it with him on this trip."

"Could he have been taking it to show someone at HQ in Bologna?"

"Maybe." She handed it back to me. "I just don't know."

I tried, "Let's say he had a line on something. Some malfeasance?"

"And this was his record of it? His proof?"

"Record, maybe. Not enough for proof. Just dates and figures."

Glynis shook her head sadly. "In another age, my husband would have been wearing shiny checkered coats and smoking cheap cigars." She jutted her chin at the paper I still held. "He wouldn't know big trouble if it was sprinkling poisonous mushrooms on his pasta." I bit my lip. Then: "While he sat there watching."

"I get it. If it"—I waved the paper—"was something big, he couldn't pull it off."

Glynis raised a hand. "But he wouldn't know he couldn't pull it off."

Which struck me as the kind of shortsightedness that could get you killed.

She pressed her lips together in a tight, sad smile. "I knew Bob so very long. All I felt was . . . sorry for him."

Jenna erupted. "Well, I didn't. He killed my father."

And it was going so nicely. Where was a really good therapist when you needed one?

Glynis reared back and jerked around to face her. "What?"

"Take it from me, not all his sins were petty, Glynis." Hunching over, all Jenna could do was rock back and forth. I waited for her to explain, but she seemed overwhelmed at her own outburst. Personally, I would have prescribed more frequent outbursts, twice daily until symptoms subside, but then the girl started keening. Alarmed, Glynis tried patting her on the back, but poor wretched Jenna twitched her off.

So I told my story about searching Jenna's room for clues when, two nights ago, she went missing. That opening salvo was met with tearful indignation. "You searched my room?" Jenna shouted. You would think I had just confessed I'd taken Stella to the pound.

I was done handling. "Oh, grow up," was the best I could do. "You . . . were . . . missing. Within reason, we have a responsibility to our guests. You don't know the area at all"—at that, she shrank back—"and in not telling anyone here of your plans to go off and sulk, you behaved immaturely. So, yes." I scooted my trunk closer to her. "I searched your room." She clamped her arms around herself and stared moodily at her shoes. No protests. I went on to describe the two key things I found. "First . . ." I held up a finger, careful in my choice of which. "The five-inch utility knife you stole the day of the mushroom"—I circled my hand, trying to catch the right word—"field trip."

Jenna gasped.

Glynis gasped. "You?"

Since I was way past gasping, or so I thought, I hurtled on. "Second . . ." I toned it down because I was nearing the heart of things for the Baltimore barista. "All the material about your dad's death." I could tell from her stony expression that she had just seen me, Nell Valenti, for what I really was: a desecrator of shrines. For some odd reason, this new understanding of a Jersey girl posing as a cooking school designer made her actually, for the first time, look her age. "Tony Bondi." I uttered the name, let it sit there in the air for a moment. "Tony Bondi was your dad."

Glynis peered at her. "Tony Bondi? I remember Tony. Bob's partner, the guy he . . ." her voice slowed as she realized the possibilities. Then her face lit up. "You're Tony's kid?" Jenna muttered something that Glynis wheeled right over. "I remember you," she said happily, snapping her fingers as an aid to name retrieval. "Little—little—Jennifer. You used to drag around a Scooby-Doo purse." Dogs, I thought, sharp sleuth that I am, even then.

"Bob Gramm fired my dad—"

Glynis corrected her with a manicured hand on little Jennifer's arm. "No, no, honey," she said in a way she probably thought would make everything all right, "Bob forced him out." All cleared up, so much better. "They were partners. Fifty-fifty. But then came the crash of—what?— '08, and it was a nail biter for Bob, I can tell you."

"For us, too." Jenna made the point.

"One day Tony Bondi was just, *fft*, gone. Tony and little Jennifer."

"We went to Baltimore," was all Jenna breathed. "My grandma was there."

Glynis went skeptical. "All Bob ever told me was that he bought Tony out." She snorted. "But, bought him out with what? He didn't have the dough to cover Tony's half. I figured Bob had to have finagled something, something to make Tony look bad, ruin his rep in the luxury car business. Fudging EPA records on Tony's inventory. Something. Then all Bob had to do to force Tony out was to pay him off just enough to get him to sign over his half of the works and promise to go away."

Jenna lunged kind of ineffectively. "Then why didn't you—"

Glynis widened her eyes at both of us. "I'm just guessing, Jenna. Like I say, at the time all Bob told me was Tony and the kid wanted to move north, so he bought him out."

Jenna's voice was cold. "That's not quite what happened."

Glynis cast around to say the right thing. "How's your dad?"

"He killed himself."

"Over Gramm's Lams?" She was incredulous.

It was Jenna's turn to make corrections. "Gramm's Lams was his life. It may not have been yours. Or even your husband's. But it was his. He got a job at Home Depot in Baltimore, selling sinks and toilets." Until, she wound down finally, he couldn't. Without lifting her eyes, Jenna described what it felt like just three weeks ago when she had driven down to Englewood, Florida, to visit her grandma now living in a trailer just three blocks from the beach, and a commercial came on TV. It was Bob "the

Glam" Gramm crowing about his end-of-year sale on current models, and how he and his beautiful wife were heading off to sunny Italy to increase their culinary skills at the villa of Chef Claudio Orlandini.

There he was, getting to be middle-aged and well dressed and heading off to Italy with a beautiful wife to take cooking classes. "And I knew two things," ended Jenna. "My dad, sweet and gentle Tony Bondi, killed himself without ever having any of those things. That was one." She shot a quick half smile. "And the second thing was that I was going to kill that man. I sold my car and borrowed some money from my gram, who was so pleased I was furthering my education with some cooking classes." Jenna laughed the kind of laugh that's hard to tell apart from a sob.

I put in, "So you stole the knife."

"And wrapped it and kept it safe. I told myself I wanted to choose my own time."

"And somebody beat you to it." That was Glynis.

But Jenna shook her head and seemed to buck up. "Oh, no. No, even after the first day, I didn't think I could do it. Hiding the knife gave me options. Gave me a way to make it all right. In a way, seeing him in person day in and day out, hearing how stupid and cruel he was, made me realize I couldn't do it." She slid Glynis an apologetic look. "Bob Gramm just wasn't worth it."

"Not at all," agreed the widow. They had found something in common.

Jenna stood up, shaking her head. "Here I spent all that damn money to get up close and personal with the monster who had destroyed my father, and I couldn't do it." She smiled. "He has no friends."

Glynis seemed almost merry. "None at all."

"Or a dog," added Jenna hopefully.

"No dog. No, sirree."

"All right"—Jenna had to accept a point—"he had some cars—"

"Status symbols way over his head." Glynis brushed it all away.

"—and I sold my old beater."

"So you did."

"But right now . . ." She took a deep breath just as the pounding on my door began. "Right now I'd say I've got my money's worth." Even without her shot at homicide. The three of us looked at each other. Maybe the Traveler's Aid support group had managed a stellar meeting. "Even," added Jenna, straightening her shoulders, "if I get arrested."

More pounding.

"Coming!" I made it to the door and wrenched it open.

There stood Rosa and Sofia, wringing their hands, crying in Italian so headlong I had no chance of understanding them. They clawed at me, pulling me outside, until I stumbled and that became grist for more tears and chagrin. Lifting my head, I caught sight of the cars in the driveway. I could account for the Orlandinis' two, the Ape and the '55 ocean green T-Bird. After the early deliveries from the camping and kitchen supply stores, all that was left were the dark blue official wheels of the *carabinieri*.

Standing at the open rear door of the SUV turned to face the bottom of the driveway, its engine running, was Detective Joe Batta. I got my footing and was pulled along with Rosa and Sofia, who were wailing. Being helped into the back seat by a black-uninformed cop in a black beret, was Annamaria Bari. For me, standing there gaping, the worst had finally happened. The cops had wrenched the cornerstone out of the villa's foundation and were driving it away with no concern for the soft rumbling I swear I could hear behind me.

17

🌿

I stood in my office now empty of the sugar-loving Joe Batta and his blond sidekick Nina, and for the first time in my life I considered calling in an exorcist. Or ordering some online smudge supplies. Since time was short, I opted for opening the window all the way and positioning a diffuser loaded with thyme sticks on my desk. That, I was pretty sure, would cancel out the smell of his sweat and her perfume.

It was a core group I had assembled for the OMG WTF meeting following Annamaria's arrest for the murder of Bob Gramm. Pete paced. Chef moved from corner to corner, shifting his weight and glowering. The four remaining Bari sisters stood in a huddle that left any inclination to break into some Billy Joel outside my office door. Zoe Campion actually tried for a spot in the room, claiming she could take over Annamaria's sous-chef duties for what was left of Marinara Misteriosa.

"No, thank you, Zoe," I said quickly, pushing her back.

"Or . . ." She tried further. "I could even pinch-hit for

Chef himself"—was she out of her mind?—"since he'll be busy in town at the jail, if he'd care to share the true and complete recipe for the final marinara—"

"No, thank you, Zoe," I said again, this time succeeding in getting her over the sill, and shutting the door in her face.

From out in the hall she raised her pleasant voice. "But, what should we all be—"

"Doing?" I answered with my lips close to the blessed wood that kept our core group from the interfering Americans. "Have Jenna take Stella and the rest of you out truffle hunting." Just then I had something less than a perfect brainstorm: "I will call Manny Manfredi to transport you all—including Stella—to Oswaldo Orlandini's farm. He'll show you around. Give you tips." Here I was just making it up as I went. "Say, two o'clock?"

"Great! I'll go tell . . ." And the rest of whatever Zoe had to say was lost as she hurried off down the corridor.

"You do that." So much for pleasantries, as I whirled to the group, wringing my hands.

Pete was reduced to stating the obvious. "This is a disaster."

I was suddenly tired to death of Italian vagaries. "Be specific, Pete, okay? What's the disaster—the school, these people, the murder, Annamaria's arrest—what?"

Chef swelled. *"Tutto."*

Pete nodded vigorously.

"Be that as it may," I said as I took my seat, swiping it clean of Joe Batta's bottom, channeling Lady Macbeth— *Will this seat never be clean?* "We need to come up with a game plan."

Pete stopped pacing. "I'll set things up with Oswaldo.

And I'll call Manny Manfredi and arrange for the van." Just to punctuate his comments, he added helpfully, "This is a disaster."

"No, Pete, let's have Sofia call Oswaldo and Manny. I need you here to translate."

He gave me a very long look I couldn't read. Then, with a nearly imperceptible nod to Sofia, Pete resumed pacing, and Sofia sprang out of the Bari scrum and swiftly opened the office door. Peering out at a corridor empty of undesirables, she disappeared, softly shutting the door as she went. Chef, still wearing his chef's jacket and toque, faced the wall in one corner with his face buried in his forearm, like he was playing hide-and-seek.

I couldn't read him, but since he wasn't high up on my list of people I'd shelter during a storm, I let him be. Unfairly, I supposed, I held him accountable for this fresh hell. He was doing well with the dental bridgework in place daily before turning up to dazzle rich Americans, but he stank like swamp gas when it came to maintaining a professional distance from the dazzled rich Americans. Let him stew.

I turned. "Rosa?" My second-in-command stepped forward like she was volunteering to go over the top. How to put this nicely? "What have they got on Annamaria?"

Easy one, her tight, tiny nod seemed to say. Rosa reported—thanks to Pete's murmured translation—that the cops were coming up short on motive, although they'd learned that Annamaria knew that Bub Grahm was threatening to report Chef as a fraud on Yelp. One might therefore say (Rosa went oratorical) that Annamaria was protecting Chef. At this point in Pete's translation, there came from the corner a shudder and a sigh. But—resumed

Rosa—on means and opportunity, *mamma mia*, they had her dead to rights. So to speak. A key piece of evidence had turned up in one of Annamaria's kitchen junk drawers.

"Namely?"

Rosa settled back into her report. Apparently, a small plastic bag—"zip," she enunciated clearly, "lock"—the kind that holds yeast, was nearly empty. Except—Rosa held her thumb and forefinger very close together—for a powdered residue of . . . dramatic pause . . . death cap mushroom. This information she received through the kindness of a Bari second cousin who is married to a lab technician named Santini whose oldest child is the godson of Annamaria. At that, Lisa, Laura, and I all murmured our understanding of how things worked.

Rosa stepped back into the Bari scrum. Kisses flew all around.

I certainly liked having this insider information.

But I didn't like anything else about it, and I resolved to dig into it. I turned to Pete, who looked troubled. Chef, who must have heard Rosa's report, had turned to face into the room. From his contrite expression, I think all he heard of what Rosa related was that Annamaria killed Bob Gramm in order to protect Chef. "Pete," I said slowly, "Rosa called it Annamaria's kitchen junk drawer. Does anyone else use it?"

What followed was a big reaction.

From all of the Bari sisters and even Chef. It was a chorus of "No!" across two octaves and several tempos. I got the picture. It was common knowledge it was Annamaria's exclusive drawer. I found myself wondering, what better place to implicate the long-standing sous-chef at the villa? I had only been with the Orlandinis for not quite a month, but in that short time I knew one thing for certain: Annamaria Bari wouldn't commit murder—not even for the heartbreaking Chef—but if she did, she certainly wouldn't shove such a hot piece of evidence in a kitchen drawer. Everything in that kitchen kingdom of hers was sacred.

For the next few hours, the Americans were occupied. But beyond that? "While they're gone," I said to what was left of what I'd call staff at the Villa Orlandini, "we need to plan. What's the program for tomorrow, the final day? And let's divvy up the inquiry into Bob Gramm's murder, which seems to me the best we can do for Annamaria, right?" And then I began making assignments. "Chef, why don't you—"

Very slowly, Pete held up a hand. "Stop," he said. Closing his eyes just briefly, he went on, "Right now. Stop." He motioned to the Bari sisters, who joined him over in the corner where Chef swung around, dazed. In rapid Italian that wasn't taking into account my failure to keep up, Pete was dispensing opinions and tasks that met with a lot of relief from Rosa and the others. With sympathetic smiles at me, the sisters headed out of the office. As for Chef, I might as well have been back in New Jersey, I went so completely invisible to him. It was with a certain amount of perplexity that I watched him ease out of his chef's jacket, drape it on a wall hook, and—exchanging a few final words with his son—leave. Not a word to me.

Pete shut the door behind his father, then turned to me. "Nell," he said plainly, "you need to take a few steps back. Annamaria's arrest changes everything."

"What do you mean?"

He managed a smile. "The cooking school is closed until we get through this."

I blinked at him, then spread my hands. "A unilateral decision?"

"That's right."

"Pete, you hired me to—"

When he sighed, I could tell he had been sighing already in private for quite some time now. With some spirit he said, "We hired you to design a cooking school—"

"That's what I'm—"

He overrode me. "—not run the villa." All I could do was stare at him. "Thank you for your help. We've needed it." Tugging at his hair, he did a slow turn, trying to say clearly just what he meant. "You've done a good job."

Why was he placating me? "I can't believe what I'm hearing, Pete."

"Well," he said with a flash, "at least you're hearing something."

It was a day, I guessed, for gasping. I was in an exit interview and I didn't even know it. "Are you firing me?" I was incredulous.

He blinked. "If you can't lay off what isn't your concern, then yes, I guess I am."

My cheeks burned. "Why do you say it isn't my concern? If Annamaria's arrested, then—"

He exploded. "You just don't get it! This is family!" And there it was. The invisible wall that's high and wide and unscalable, that's easy to pretend isn't there, doesn't matter, until it does. "And you're not."

It was all so plain.

I felt like a fool. "You made your point," I said coldly, pushing past him to the door. Then, fumbling in my pocket, I pulled out the keys and tossed them at the desk, and missed. He left them where they fell on the rug. "This is the school office. Yours or whatever Orlandini runs the joint. I can finish up the design job from the Abbess's room. Now that I won't have to run interference on the daily decrepitude of your family and the family pile, I can finish out my contract much more quickly." I will always remember my parting shot. "Good luck with the olives, Pete, which, by the way," I yelled back at him as I headed down the corridor, "don't fall very far from the tree. You goddamn jealous hypocrite."

They all seemed to leave at once. I watched from behind my mostly drawn shade as the distinctive shrill horn of the Cucinavan tooted its arrival. Either truffle hunting got axed or it moved to after the farm tour. I was so angry at Pete and his whole aggravating family that I briefly considered jumping on the van with the other Americans. While Manny Manfredi spoke his usual encouragements to Zoe, George, Glynis, and Jenna, I felt like I had been flung back to my childhood, watching every group of kids go off without me.

What followed was always my mother's and father's reliably dismissive observations that only isolated me that much more. You don't need those dumb old pony ride birthday parties, Nell. You don't need that field hockey team trip to Asbury Park, Nell. You don't need those sleepovers, movie dates, mall crawls, and proms. It felt so familiar to me, watching from behind a blind as peers went off and had fun. Last up the step to Manny Manfredi's Cucinavan was Jenna, coaxing Stella with happy tugs on the leash.

No sooner did they spurt down the driveway, through

the puddles that spattered as they passed, off to wherever Oswaldo Orlandini's farm might be, than Chef, Pete, and the four Bari sisters marched into the courtyard and clambered into the Ape and the T-Bird, and I realized they were all going as a family into Cortona to visit Annamaria in jail. Orlandinis and Baris. It flitted through my furious mind that Bari and Orlandini were two separate families, weren't they? Then why did the Orlandinis get to go with Rosa and the others? I shook my head. There was probably some shared ancestor from back in the days of the convent or the plague that centuries later still made them "family."

I set the two café chairs back at the table, sat down, and booted up my Mac. Clicking on the folder for the Villa Orlandini Cooking School, I browsed all the files without so much as a whiff of sentiment. What was left of this job? The chapel dining room was fine, the culinary classroom half of the common room was up and running, and the "student center" half of the common room was up and running except for the pending delivery of two computer workstations and desktops. I highlighted that item. Four single-occupancy dormitory rooms were renovated and housing three students, now plus the widow (note: as yet no complaints and no suggestions). The double-occupancy barn room was renovated and at present a disgusting wreck. I highlighted that item. The Orlandinis could hire a cleaning service.

The biggest pending feature of my design was the expansion of the kitchen itself to bring it in line with others drawing up to a minimum of a dozen students per workshop. My sketch included breaking through the existing kitchen wall to the largely unused adjacent storeroom. The Orlandinis were looking at an easy hundred grand to execute this part of the design, what with the construction, addition of windows, venting, plumbing, wiring, lighting, commercial-grade appliances, worktables, stools.

Since I had no taste for wasting any more of my time on this godforsaken project in a place where it was made clear to me that I'd never be accepted as an equal, I opened Word and fashioned two fast choices on how to proceed. One, they could go ahead with the design as it was envisioned and had been provided; see sketches, blueprints, order form. Price tag: neighborhood of $100,000. Sarcastic footnote: To save money, consider asking George Johnson for the permanent contibution of the camping stoves. Then I redlined that suggestion and added magnanimously, *Never mind, I'll take care of that myself one of these nights*. Other choice, disregard the expansion and run a school out of the existing spaces (*as per Marinara Misteriosa*), for six students/workshop. This was half the original concept but would at least work given adequate help from (underlined, bolded) trusted extended family members.

And then I realized there was even a third choice I could point out in this final report, so I did: close the cooking school ASAP, shut down the website, return all furnishings, pay all accounts receivable (including final check for Nell Valenti, address herewith), list the villa with Airbnb, and just plain go to hell. I saved the final report to the cloud, then attached it to an email to Pete, subject line "Final Report," and sent it. A toothless Chef would be happily playing bocce again before the week was out, and his awful son could press olives in small batches until his treacherous heart gave out. The Baris would become a Billy Joel tribute band. Jenna would marry Oswaldo and if there was any justice in the world sell enough vegetables they could boot their cousins off the villa property and turn it into an agricultural education center. Or dog kennel, better yet.

All that left . . .

All that left was Annamaria. In the Italian equivalent of the hoosegow.

Where did I see her, the stately queen of the kitchen, and Chef's Muse?

Where did I see her? Back in the convent of St. Veronica of the Veil, with her sisters?

Somewhere altogether else, that's where. Put these faithless and impossible Orlandini men well behind her. Don't even waste a perfectly good *malocchio* on them. Just go. But . . . how? All she had was half a dozen of them visiting her behind bars, no help whatsoever. Eyeing her pitifully. Accepting poor Annamaria's plight with that robust fatalism I've seen Italians like my father leap to as fast as a tarantella. And I wouldn't allow my mind to go to that dark and obscure dreadfulness.

No, I told myself as I took out Bob Gramm's handwritten spreadsheet, unfolded it on the table, and smoothed out the creases. I was done designing a cooking school for this family. They could read my final report, and by then, if I was lucky, I'd be halfway over the Atlantic Ocean, at peace in the night cabin, sipping wine nowhere near as good as anything in the Orlandinis' wine cellar. And it would be delicious in the moment. But until that deep blissful flight home, I would solve this murder and free Annamaria.

* * *

*A*fter studying the spreadsheet, and fixing myself a cup of Twinings white tea I had come across at a shop in Cortona, I pushed back from the table. I came to one conclusion pretty quickly. Bob Gramm was spending money at a rate of $5,000 a month, and keeping track of the bloodletting on this His Eyes Only sheet torn from a notebook. Glynis wasn't able to explain it. So where was the money going? Gambling debt? Would $60,000 a year seem like an insupportable loss to a Lamborghini dealer? Maybe not. But to a marginally successful Lamborghini dealer? The amounts were so regular, so clockwork, that I wasn't happy putting it down to gambling debts, where a wide swing in "outgo" would make sense.

So Bob Gramm was making these regular payments for what? Child support? Mistress maintenance? A double life? Knowing the guy for only a few days, I found it hard to believe he could manage one life, let alone two. Could it be payback for even honorable debts, but to make good some claim he wanted to keep secret from Glynis and the business bookkeepers? Clearly, it wasn't the Lamborghini dealership. And if it was some kind of blood money paid to the Bondis, Jenna would have known. Instead, she suffered. Her dad worked a retail job and then killed himself.

No.

Glynis had said that Bob had seemed on the upswing over the last three or four years. No questions asked. The dates on the spreadsheet ranged from November 2017 to just this past May. Then, nothing over the entire summer and into the fall. Debts paid? Mistress bounced? Was the gold bangle bracelet a lovely parting gift? Maybe. But how would an outlay of that kind of money every month for almost four years lead to an "upswing" for Bob? Glynis had said his sins were petty—lying, cheating.

Sometimes there's nothing at all petty about lying and cheating, but from Glynis I got the idea that Bob Gramm pretty much worked at the level of glib lies about his whereabouts and cheating at a weekly poker game with buddies who were totally on to him but let him get away with it. Maybe, then—I slowly drew the sheet of paper close to me—maybe this secret activity was Bob Gramm's big score.

I lifted my head. And I knew the truth.

This was a record of his under-the-table income.

Was Bob Gramm a blackmailer? But who? And how? How had someone so self-absorbed as this fancy car salesman come across the kind of flammable information he could hold over some poor sap, to the exorbitant tune of $200,000 over three and a half years? What strange set of circumstances had led to Bob's second income? Did it have anything at all to do with the Lamborghinis? Possibly—otherwise, why would he have been so uncharacteristically willing to come to Tuscany for cooking classes with Glynis? Why? The HQ was just two hours away. Had it been an opportunity to put a bigger squeeze on the mark? Without access to any online records from Gramm's Lams, how would I ever be able to figure it out?

At just that tangled moment, I realized what I needed: a detective.

The mere thought—plus the image of Marinara Misteriosa's own undercover George Johnson—handed me a laugh. But the truth had gone unspoken between the two of us, up until now. I needed help, the kind of help that detectives commonly have in terms of connections and resources, and I'd pay George extra to add a Nell line to his job for the Dr. Val shrinkage empire. But I wouldn't approach him blindly. Do women and men in that line of work have areas of expertise? Or was what I needed a generalist? Since I didn't want to tackle George uninformed, I knew what I had to do, odd as it felt. I'd check him out with his current employer, same as if the name Dr. Val Valenti was on George's CV as a reference.

And then, dear Mr. Johnson, time for the unmasking.

Picking up my phone, I smiled at the screen for face recognition ID, and when it didn't recognize a smiling Nell Valenti, I tapped in my passcode, hit contacts, hit Dad, and waited for his voice mail. "Dad," I announced, "it's me. Call me soonest, old bean, okay? I need to talk about your detective."

Whenever I called him old bean, Dr. Val knew he had nothing to fear.

We weren't at the end of the day's surprises. Not just yet.

Ending the call, I laughed out loud. Great final word, detective. I could hear my father sputtering already. What a day: getting fired, quitting, a sudden nonemployment standoff. A lighter workload, for sure, what with not "running the villa," as Pete Orlandini put it. Reviewing the paperwork on the Villa Orlandini Cooking School project, then writing up the final report. Still approving the last bit of professional advice, namely, "Go to hell." I didn't even care if the same unseen family lawyer in Florence who had hired me for this gig—that I knew now was less about cooking school design than about wrangling these impossible Orlandini family members—gets instructed to go right ahead and hire another goopy-eyed simpleton.

Midafternoon was a trifle early to celebrate my new unemployment, so I poured half a glass of Franchi Estate Winery's '08 Chianti and topped it off with seltzer water. A red wine spritzer. It felt good to lift my glass alone, and to punctuate the new plan by folding two articles of clothing, in between refreshing sips, and lay them in my open suitcase. I took five minutes off from packing, from sipping, from picturing my sandbagged father when he realized four thousand miles away that little Nell was on to him. I made a brand-new To Do list:

1. Move the Gramms' belongings to the Vinci room. (strike-through)
2. Ask Rosa and Sofia to move the Gramms' belongings to the Vinci room.
3. Confront George Johnson.
4. Hire George Johnson.
5. Quit thinking about George Johnson.
6. Solve murder.
7. Present Chef with formal letter of resignation.
8. Visit Annamaria before leaving.
9. Call Manny Manfredi re transportation to airport.
10. Book flight home.

Book flight home.

When my phone trilled just as I was failing spectacularly at #5, the screen gave me a heads-up. I pulled it to my ear. "Hi, Dad." I gave it the kind of crackbrained heartiness he cajoles from his studio patients.

"Hey, Little Red Corvette!"

So he was in that kind of mood. My Corvette nickname came out when—believe it or not—Dr. Val Valenti believed he was showing the kind of cultural sensitivity that steered him to safe ground in the split second before calling me "Sugar Pie Honey Bunch." I knew how his mind worked. Cute car, convertible, red, vroom vroom. I mean, how did the Gidgets and Moondoggies get to the beach for spring break, right?

"Dad," I said in my best nonjudgmental voice, "you know the song is about casual sex, don't you?"

A tiny sputter. "No, it isn't, Nell."

"'Girl, you got an ass like I never seen'?"

He was aghast. "That?" he squeaked. "From the Beach Boys?"

"Prince."

In the four-thousand-mile space between us, I knew he wasn't entirely sure who Prince was, so he needed to divert. "Well," he declared like we were both just sitting around the old cracker barrel, "I can't be expected to know everything, Nell." His tone implied he came really close, so he could afford to let this one exception just lift right off his hand like dandelion fluff.

"So true, Dad. But I'll ask you something I know you've got down cold."

"Like what?" The man was a champion staller.

"Like tell me about this detective you hired."

"What detective?" I heard him suck in air between his teeth. "Now, if you're talking about Hal from last month, you were right, I was wrong, and we had it out. I was worried sick. Do we really want to revisit that time?" To hear him tell it, when creatures were climbing out of the primordial mud.

"I'm not talking about Hal, Dad."

A beat. "Then what are you talking about?"

"Undercover detective number two. George Johnson."

His voice dropped. I could tell he was thinking it over, like maybe hiring George Johnson to keep an eye on me, guard me against the uglier eventualities, whatever they may be, and submit daily reports to my father, had slipped his mind. "George Johnson." And one more time, from a place of befuddlement: "George Johnson."

"It's a common enough name," I threw in.

"Maybe so," declared my father, "but I've never heard it."

"Really, Dad." I gave him the withering tone.

He pulled up the dregs of the old Valenti fighting spirit. "Exactly what do you think I've done, sweetie?"

"You hired this detective"—I suddenly put him on speaker phone so I could flail my hands freely—"George Johnson—to get in close and dog me. You really upped your game, Dad. This one's great."

Dad mumbled affably, "I'm glad you like him, Nell, but he's not my hire."

It was out before I knew it. "Then whose hire is he?"

Dr. Val Valenti had one of those favorite sitting-around-the-cracker-barrel suggestions that made audiences swoon. Considering Val Valenti grew up in Bayonne, New Jersey, where there isn't a cracker barrel within five hundred miles, he came up with it all by himself. "Maybe"—which came out pretty close to *mebbe*—"maybe he's nobody's?" If we'd had a studio audience, there would be claps and whistles.

Nobody's hire. "A free agent, you mean?"

"Why would somebody dog you for free, Nell?"

He had a point, strictly from a business perspective, but I felt vaguely insulted. Just as I was starting to miss the Little Red Corvette years, I piped up, "Then why's he here?"

Dad was back on the kind of firm ground that made him the Afternoon Delight of television-watching millions. "Maybe he wanted to learn some Italian cooking?"

The *call me crazy* went unspoken.

18

I had no alternative, really, but to take my slippery father at his word.

However, I did make him swear. About the so-called George Johnson, I pretty much wanted to swear as well, but for different reasons. I made Dr. Val Valenti swear he had not hired a detective named George Johnson, pretty much ever in this lifetime. That left the commonsense answer to the problem: *Maybe he wanted to learn some Italian cooking.* Or maybe the guy was exactly who he said he was, George Johnson, a waiter at Fraîche Take Bistro in Brooklyn.

Why couldn't I buy it?

Why couldn't I just get through the rest of Marinara Misteriosa, wave them all goodbye, and get on with my own packing? And then I uttered the great question that had been the anthem of Italians since Michelangelo perused the ceiling and responded to the Pope's offer: *How hard can it be?* I felt my eyes narrow, and then I told myself, "No, there's something. There's something, and

I'm going to find it." I went on to protest that in the interest of the murder that had overturned the villa and all the people in it, I needed to get to the bottom of—as Pete had put it—my "pal" George, who may very well have signed on for more than cooking lessons. Had he known Bob Gramm was coming? And had he just been biding his murderous time?

I had a plan. A small plan, a starter plan, but it felt right to me.

Jersey girl investigates Brooklyn boy. And she had to go all the way to Tuscany to do it.

Around four p.m., I taped a hand-lettered sign on the outside of my door:

NON DISTURBARE * * * DO NOT DISTURB

* * *

FOR ALL QUESTIONS, COMMENTS, AND COMPLAINTS,
CONTACT AN ORLANDINI

* * *

ENJOY THE EVENING!

I was unsatisfied with this notice, but when I agreed with myself that it achieved its purpose of keeping everybody off my doorstep and my design role completely separate from everything else, I taped it up and went back inside. If I spent so much as one minute more on it, trying to make it clever and attractive, then I was doing pro bono work that would go unappreciated. So, no. I had just Googled Fraîche Take Bistro to start my investigation of

George Johnson, when I heard noise out in the courtyard. One finger moved the shade half an inch. The Ape and the T-Bird were easing back into their parking spaces. It surprised me how heavy my heart felt. Maybe the simple truth was that, to me, Orlandinis and Baris were interesting people, but too much work.

Was I too provincial to work this far outside the metro New York area?

Could I still lead a happy life?

Maybe I could take over the catering part of Dr. Val's empire. Was there a catering part? Better yet. The first pictures that came to mind were all food trucks—call them Chez Nell—at Chelsea Piers, where Dad's studio and offices were. Give me three months' run-up and I could develop some intriguing new recipes that'll keep customers guessing. Asian Fusion? What about a Mediterranean Fusion, call it Medi-Fuse—no, sounds too medical—what about *Riviera Fusion*, blending the traditional foods of that crescent seacoast. Throw a few delicious curveballs from Sardinia.

I had just Googled Fraîche Take Bistro, where the so-called George Johnson worked, when somebody chose to ignore my Keep Away sign. A quick peek between the shade and the window showed me Rosa, back from visiting her jailed sister. And she looked like a woman with a purpose. "Rosa?" I spoke through the door. *"Può aspettare?"* Can it wait? *"Sto lavorando."* I'm working. She of all people understood that.

"No."

I was glad to have put the chain bolt in place earlier. Now all I had to do was open the door and discuss through a two-inch opening. Half expecting the formidable Rosa Bari to roll her eyes at the precautions, I was surprised when the limited access to me didn't even seem to register. *"Che cos'è?"*

Standing there in her loose brown wool coat, she locked eyes with me and kept it as simple as she could. "Annamaria say not possible." When I made an encouraging gesture, Rosa went on. "She no put empty bag *nel cassetto.*"

Cassetto. Drawer. "But it was a yeast bag," I pointed out. At the sight of her perplexed mug, I explained, "Yeast. *Il lievito.*"

"But empty." Rosa filled her cheeks with air. "Why she keep *nel cassetto*? Is for—" At that, she whistled and jabbed a thumb over her shoulder.

"Garbage."

Rosa frowned in approval. "Also, why she keep *i funghi velenosi*"—here she clapped a hand around her neck, miming strangulation, poisonous mushrooms—"in little bag?"

"For that matter, why would she keep them anywhere?"

"Sì, sì, sì!" Rosa seemed to get the general idea.

I was silent for a minute while I thought. "Did Annamaria see"—here I circled my eyes with my hands—"the bag?"

"No." She was emphatic. *"Joe Batta l'ha descritto."* Joe Batta described it.

"And—?"

Rosa let out a groan. "Yes, is her yeast bag." Rosa hung her head and added: *"Uno."*

I was coping with a stir of interest, the kind that had made me say yes to this job at this villa, sight unseen, brain unconsulted. "Rosa," I said, "where does Annamaria keep them?"

Bright eyes. "You want?"

I temporized. *"Alcune."* A few. Before I could even add a please, she ran off. Through the narrow gap, I saw

Pete and Chef waiting to welcome the Cucinavan as it pulled in. As Chef moved closer, mugging something to the Americans' delight as though he was being sucked under the wheels—*there's a good idea* was what wandered through my mind with no emotion whatsoever—Pete half turned in my direction. Just in time to see me slam the door shut. True, the whole slamming effect wasn't much, considering there's was just a two-inch gap to navigate. But he's got sharp eyesight. Nice to have some good quality, I sniffed.

I settled back into my seat and stretched my fingers in readiness as I glanced at the Fraîche Take Bistro listing: 137 Atlantic Ave., Brooklyn Heights. Links to reviews on *HuffPost*, *Gothamist*, and the *Times*. All right, not shabby. Candlelit photos of exposed brick walls and twigs in umbrella stands and cozy couples. Days and hours of operation. A phone number. Clearing my throat, hoping somebody would pick up, I pressed in the number, feeling pang after pang. Of being part of a couple. Being in New York. Being served something that didn't necessarily feature Roma tomatoes. "Yello?" came the distant voice.

Not in the mood for niceties. "George Johnson, please?"

"Johnson?"

"One of your employees."

"Hang on." Hang on? Is it possible George was just what he said he was? "Not here," the voice came back a full five minutes later.

So now I was trying to pull together what I was hearing. "When will he be back, do you know?"

A transatlantic snicker. "No time soon. Johnson doesn't work here anymore."

Anymore. "Ah," I breathed, oddly pleased. "Fire him, didja?"

"Nah. Hear he quit three years ago. Chef's the only one here remembers him."

Think fast, Nell. "Do you know where he went?"

"Nope. Chef says Johnson hasn't been heard from since."

"So, he . . . was one of your servers and left, no forwarding address."

"Servers?" A hoot. "I don't think so. Chef says GJ—that's what he calls him—GJ was one of the greats."

Well, now I was lost. "One of the great whats?"

"Chefs."

D evils get invoked at the drop of a hat, apparently. No sooner had I ended the call to Fraîche Take Bistro than a slip of paper was slid under my door. I had a swift moment's hope that it was tear-stained with an apology from Pete. Standing still, ignoring it and staring at it, just to give the note writer time to disappear, I finally heaved a sigh. Whatever it was, whoever it was, it spelled work for Nell. That much I knew. Chef wondering who was preparing the dinner ahead of us, as if he himself wasn't capable of making it. Jenna wondering if Oswaldo and Stella could stay for dinner. Glynis wondering if I knew just how long the cops would keep the gold bangle bracelet as evidence. Zoe asking if I knew just how long the kitchen would continue to be off-limits, and if for the foreseeable future, should she just take over Annamaria's role.

I picked up the note. *Come have a drink with me? Meet just outside gate. GJ.*

Well, I thought, the timing couldn't be more perfect: 5:02 p.m. A designer's workday is over, thus spake Nell

Valenti. And I felt myself stand up straighter and did a little tap time-step when I realized I have no responsibilities whatsoever with anyone at the villa at this point. Time to make George Johnson come clean. As I slipped into my square-necked olive green T-shirt dress that really emphasized my broad shoulders, I pictured worming the truth out of my unsuspecting companion. As I added a glossy lipstick, a spritz of Chanel, and enough mascara to shine the shoes of the Fourth Infantry, I pictured leveling my companion with the far-reaching consequences of my investigation.

At last we'd get to the bottom of things, this undercover guy and I. As I grabbed keys, phone, and Sherpa coat, the little voice inside was cautioning me that my father could have pulled the washable wool over my eyes, George Johnson could be playing a deeper game than I knew, possibly including the murder of Bob Gramm, and I should avoid any appetizer with broccoli or cauliflower.

I was halfway across the courtyard when Rosa accosted me, pushing a few little bags into my hand. *"Eccoli, Nella."* As she charged back to the main building, she called over her shoulder, "I make *lu cena* tonight, no worries, you go have the fun, *capisci? Sei bellissima." You look beautiful.* If I were staying, I'd insist on giving Rosa a raise.

"Be sure Pierfranco helps."

She waved. *"Oh, Pierfranco ba-boom nella cucina con le pentole."* She shook her head, laughing. Apparently he was banging around in the kitchen. And he thought olives were work . . .

So now four plastic bags with 2¼ teaspoons of bread yeast apiece were going with me on a date—rather, the next step in my laser-like investigation—and I stuffed them into the pocket of my coat. Instead of full-out running down the driveway in pursuit, of course, of truth and justice, I forced myself to walk out the gate at a professional-but-slightly-bored pace. And sure enough, not twenty feet down the road, leaning against a black Audi, was "one of the greats," George Johnson. I guess a day down on the farm with Oswaldo didn't destroy his spirit, because he was wearing a Baltic blue Italian wool suit and white shirt. A car? A suit? What explains anything of this?

I couldn't help it. "You're dressed like you knew I would come," I said as I held out a hand.

We shook. It was strangely nice. I wasn't passing him a whisk, he wasn't passing me a gnocchi board with flour on his hands, I wasn't handing off a small bowl for the sautéed garlic and onions. Always something between the hands, keeping them apart. Suddenly I felt a little exposed. But then he topped me.

"No," said George Johnson, "I'm dressed like I hoped you would come."

I took it in. "You always have a good answer."

We gave each other a long look, then we started around to the passenger side. "Nice to hear," he said as he held open the door.

"I'm thinking," I said languidly, as I settled into the leather seat and looked straight ahead, "of when I surprised you in the wine cellar." As he started the Audi we shot each other a glance. "The crypt. Dead nuns. Quick thinking. You're good on your feet." As if in the disappearing daylight we understood we'd wait for drinks to move into what was promising to be a frank conversation, George Johnson and I sat companionably on a fast ride into town, without another word. On the Via Nazionale, we found a parking space a few doors up from the Bottega Baracchi, and George nodded us in that direction.

Inside it reminded me of the villa's wine cellar, so I figured GJ must be feeling right at home. The Roman arches, exposed stone walls throughout, terra-cotta–tiled floors. At our table for two, a server appeared and when the man of mystery gestured to me, I ordered a medium dry martini, straight up, stirred, with an onion, and he ordered a double Lagavulin on the rocks. When I asked him about the Audi, he told me he rented it for these final couple of days at the Villa Orlandini, as well as a room at the Hotel Italia since his back has been acting up due to the mattress in the Dante room. When he asked me about the Keep Off the Grass note on my door, I told him I had been fired and didn't want to see much of anybody. At the mention of the word "fired," GJ widened his very dark eyes and ran a forefinger over his mobile mouth. We sat, both of us musing, wondering whether these were developments of any consequence.

Finally, I asked him. "I hope the hotel room isn't for me."

"If I tell you it's not, would you believe me?"

"Since you're such a liar?" It came out without thinking.

"I'm not a liar, Nell," George said plainly. "But I am a pretender."

It seemed a big admission somehow. I forgot all about the hotel room.

The drinks arrived, and we lifted glasses. "Here's to full disclosure." I eyed him. With a dip of his chin, we clinked and sipped. "My father," I began, "tells me you're not his private detective." I extended my glass.

Without missing a beat, George Johnson said, "And my friend Pierre Moreau, the chef at Fraîche Take, tells me you called." I sat back, embarrassed. My surprise—

that I called my father and found out GJ was not working undercover to keep an eye on me—was pretty good, but his was exponentially better. "You go first," George proposed, extending his glass. "Why did you think I was your father's private eye?"

I hadn't had a martini in a very long time, and it was such a nice change from Chianti. George's question was a good one, and as I pondered, I held my glass up to the light and watched it glow through the gin and vermouth. "Because he's done it before," I told him finally.

"Dr. Val Valenti."

I put down my glass as George picked up the menu. "You know him?"

"Seen him around."

"Are you investigating him?" For what, exactly, wasn't anything I wanted to explore.

George actually laughed. "So am I following the daughter," he managed, "or the father?"

"Well?" I said softly.

"The answer," said George, examining the menu, "is neither. How about we share the calamari?"

A tight shake of my head. "I feel bad for the squid."

"Okay." His eyes ran down the *aperitivi*. "That lets out the octopus, the clams, and the oysters. Do you feel bad for tomatoes?"

I thought about it. "No."

"Let's see what Bottega Baracchi does with that old standard, bruschetta." He signaled the server and placed the order in surprisingly flawless Italian, then shot me an innocent look.

"I repeat"—I smiled at him—"well?"

"Neither. Not you, not your dad." With that, he opened his hands wide. "I have zero investigative skills."

"True."

"When it comes to people," he added as a throwaway. Then he leaned toward me, and I found I wanted him to keep right on coming. "The crypt," he reminded me.

"Well"—I sat there defending him suddenly—"it's an excellent idea, really. You never know what you might find."

"Besides dead nuns. My thought exactly." His eyes were twinkling.

I got into the spirit of things and leaned toward him, looked right and left, and whispered, "Treasure."

"Of one sort or another."

"Ah, cryptic."

George smacked his forehead. "Ouch."

"Sorry," I said, wincing. Then I inhaled and sat back. "I accept your answer. You are not following me—"

"Not that it's a bad idea."

"—and you're not investigating my father. Fine." I pulled off the cocktail onion with my teeth and chewed reflectively. "So you're not undercover."

I almost missed it when he said, "Ah, I didn't say that."

Suddenly the lighting was turned down and soft jazz was turned up, just a keyboard and percussion. "Why do I feel I know you?" I said finally.

"Past lives?"

"Try again."

"Mutual friends?"

"We turn up at the same parties, that sort of thing?"

"Right."

"Wrong." I would have remembered him. I would have made it a point to meet him. "I avoid parties like—like—"

"Calamari."

The bruschetta arrived, and I watched George examine the dish closely. "Very exciting, Nell. It's got pumpkin puréed with the garlic. And . . ." From his unfolded black linen napkin, he pulled his fork and lightly tapped a couple of what looked like small cylindrical spears of rosemary leaves. *"Elicrisio."* In real delight, he widened his eyes at me. "Helichrysum. It's an evergreen. I don't see it used much, so this is"—he breathed—"wonderful. Tastes like curry, but not exactly. Ah, what a bold bruschetta we have here, Nell."

I chose a toasted oval of rustic bread topped with the old familiars of bruschetta—the tomato, the fresh basil, the oil and balsamic, the garlic—and nibbled. It was sensational. The pumpkin-garlic mash spread as the underlayer was a creative stroke, but the helichrysum made this bruschetta something altogether new and exciting. As George savored his first bite, his left hand made rapid little circles as he tried to find just the right words to describe it. I decided to add to his difficulties, and uttered two words: "Pierre Moreau."

"Pierre Moreau. Let's get some wine."

"He called you one of the great chefs."

He gave a little grunt. "Well, it was bound to happen. Sometimes he can't help himself. But that's what makes his cooking so special."

"Evasive maneuvers," I scolded him. Then I went on, "You left the bistro three years ago." Nodding as if this was old, old ground that held no buried mines whatsoever, George ordered a bottle of the Antinori Tignanello—a Super Tuscan, he explained to me. I picked up my point. "And no one's heard from you since."

He toggled his fine head, that black, black hair shifting. "Well, there's Pierre," he corrected, "and, of course, my mother."

What happened next was one of those moments that seem both infinitesimally small and catastrophically big, and when it happens you are left feeling everything makes sense all of a sudden and nothing will ever make sense again. There is thrill and dismay. And at the two-top table in the Bottega Baracchi in Cortona, Italy, at that particular moment, I felt a tectonic plate inside my chest shift. George lifted the heavy black triangle of his linen napkin and held it up to his lips with both hands. But the fold rose up over his nose so that all that was visible were those sharp, active black eyes.

"Stop," I cried. "Don't move."

"What is it?"

His signature stirring in the villa kitchen that first day, pinkie raised. In two steps I crouched next to George Johnson and pressed the napkin to his cheeks. The famous black bandana obscured his identity, but there were those eyes. "George," I said, then set my mouth next to his ear and whispered, "you're Stealth Chef." No wonder all Rosa found this week were reruns—Stealth Chef was here at the Villa Orlandini for Marinara Misteriosa.

19

George eased an arm around my shoulder. "Nell," he said, his lips so close to my own ear that each word had a shape. "Here's the wine." He pressed the small of my back, and set down the telltale bandana napkin. The server uncorked, George sampled and nodded, and when our glasses were filled, George seemed to lose his appetite, his eyes cast down at some thread on the tablecloth. I, on the other hand, helped myself with great relish to more pumpkin-helichrysum bruschetta. I felt an undertow of sadness about George, that he didn't know me well enough to know his job was safe. Very carefully, I lifted what looked like the best of the bruschetta and set it down on his plate. "George," I said, then again, "George, please talk."

When he looked at me, his eyes were unguarded. "Maybe it's time it's over."

"But maybe it's not. Have some bruschetta."

"Thanks."

A beat. "Full disclosure."

He tried a smile. "You go first."

"Oh, no." I shook at finger at him. "I went first last time. Your turn."

Sitting back, swirling his wine just once, George Johnson eyed me. "How much?"

"Start small, like Chef teaches. With a marinara, first sauté the garlic."

"Small is all the time we have." There was that. So George Johnson, professionally known—or not—as Stealth Chef, told me it was the promise of the recipe for Chef Claudio Orlandini's *prima marinara* that got him here. And Zoe, his sous-chef. They thought there was a chance it was on the level and that the great Chef O would indeed "unlock his recipe vault," and all George and Zoe had to do was show up to come away after four days with a secret that had been guarded for fifty years. It was George's job to look around for—don't laugh—an actual vault—maybe Chef O's "recipe vault" was literal. It was Zoe's job to cook with Chef as closely as possible to see if he'd confide in her or just plain let something slip.

"She wasn't angling for Annamaria's job?"

He looked a bit horrified. "No."

"Or her . . . man?" How else to put it?

He looked a bit more horrified. "Chef?"

"They had a fling forty years ago." I made a limp two-handed gesture that in Italian means *Make of it what you will.*

"That's all it takes?" When I shrugged, George went on, "I think Brett might complain."

"Who's Brett?"

"Zoe's husband." We savored the wine wordlessly, then George picked up the story. It became clear Chef was holding out on one final secret ingredient that fifty years ago had put all other perfectly nice marinaras to shame. Citron wasn't the whole story. I mentioned overhearing them talk, George and Zoe, that day. *Something was missing.* No vaults in crypts, with either recipes or dead nuns, were turning up. No inadvertent dropping of secret ingredients in the heat of the culinary moment. They had reached an impasse. *Chef's a sweet old guy,* Zoe had concluded, *let him keep his secrets.* And that was pretty much where they stood.

"What would you have done," I asked, rather afraid of the truth, "if you had found it?"

After a minute, he answered. "You and I," he said, giving me a long look. "We don't know each other."

I shook my head sadly. "You don't know I wouldn't out you."

"You don't know what I'd do if I came across his recipe."

"You'll just have to take my word for it, George."

"Then," he said, that beautiful mobile mouth making wry little moves, "I will."

But something was left unsaid. "What would you have done?" My voice was soft.

"If I had found it?"

I nodded slowly, hardly breathing. "Yes."

"Well . . ." George Johnson refilled my glass. "I did."

"You did? You found it?"

"Better than that. Cleaner than that. I figured it out."

I could hardly believe it. So I joked, "After all, you are one of the greats."

"Pierre's a deluded sweetheart. I'll introduce you sometime." No, George explained, what gave away Chef Claudio Orlandini's fifty-year-old secret recipe for the *prima marinara* that catapulted him into the culinary stratosphere was the murder of Bob Gramm. When Joe Batta was interviewing George, he shook a bag of gumdrops into a glass dish and motioned to George to help himself. And that was that. Paying no attention to his choice, he picked up a gumdrop and popped it into his mouth, which was the moment he, George Johnson, raided the recipe vault of taste and imagination, and knew.

He was chewing a licorice gumdrop and identified the closely guarded secret ingredient of Chef's *prima marinara* sauce. Licorice. He said nothing, not even to Zoe Campion. Did Chef distill pure licorice root? Cheat with a dram of Sambuca? Boil down licorice sticks? As yet to be determined.

"Only," finished George, "I won't."

The Bottega Baracchi was filling up, the room sounding like a happy, muted hive. "Why not?"

"I'm not going to use it." One Baltic blue shoulder lifted. "I'm not going to make it. Anywhere. On the show. At home. Not anywhere."

"Why not?"

He widened his eyes and glanced past me as he tried to explain it. "Recipes aren't for all. Maybe most are, but then there are a few—" He gave me a look I'll never forget. "Some things deserve to be mysterious."

"Even you?" I challenged.

"For a little while longer." He added, "*Prima marinara* is as delicious as it is because we don't know what's in it."

"And because it was the creation of one of the great chefs of the last century. And he's old."

"It means more this way."

I looked at my hands. "I like meaning." We said nothing else, just companionably enjoyed the last of the bruschetta, the last of the wine, the last of the shimmering lights, and what felt like the first of each other. George paid the bill and we walked arm in arm to the Audi. "Thanks for not telling," I said.

We tightened our jackets around us. George leaned in. "Thanks for not telling."

"Well, I'd say we're even." I slipped into the seat, losing myself in the fresh dark of the day, that always feels original, like there's never been a star or a moon or a bat. *Prima marinara, prima* everything. That time when you can see inside lighted houses and trattorias, where we live our lives. In no time at all, we parked outside the villa gate and walked into the main building, shuddering with the warmth, and found our way into the common room.

With Annamaria in jail, it was no night for games or songs, but the Baris were teaching Jenna Italian. Oswaldo was discussing eggplants with Chef. Glynis had gone to bed, yes, already. And Rosa informed us that Pierfranco and Zoe were in the school office planning the final day's agenda. Stella, stretched out by the fire, lifted her head, lost interest when she saw it was me, and went back to dreaming.

After a few minutes, and a bit of chatter that went nowhere at all, George winked at me and took his leave. Oswaldo's farm, said Jenna, blushing furiously, was the best thing ever. Oswaldo thrust out his chest and said what must have been a flurry of modest things in Italian. Chef flung his good arm around me and proclaimed, "I miss you!" Then, trying to understand the new world order, he gave me a sideways glance and pointed at me like a scold. "Just . . . *la disegnatore, è vero?*" I'm just the designer, right? I smiled. He wasn't scolding me for overstepping, he was just trying to understand my role. He wanted to get it right.

So did I.

An hour passed—enough time to claim sleepiness and pull a Glynis and go off to bed. The hard part came when I walked down the kitchen corridor to what had been my office, where the door stood open. There, bent over papers on my old desk, tampon lamp on its high setting, sat Pete and Zoe. Pete's sleeves were rolled up, and he looked drawn and more like fifty than forty.

It was Zoe who heard me first, looking up with a smile. It's not that I was seeing her in a new light, it's that the old light wasn't a true one, and I felt oddly happy knowing she was Stealth Chef's faithful sous-chef, that she had a husband named Brett, and that she still hadn't cracked the recipe for Chef's *prima marinara*. "Hey," she said with a wave. "Did you have a good time?" I said I had, and felt sad at how unreadable Pete's expression was.

"Off to bed," I told them. "Just wanted to wish you two *buona notte*."

Pete seemed too tired to speak. He just lifted a hand. And that was about all we could manage, I guess. How quickly, totally, and invisibly some things can break. And how resistant to repair. *"Ciao!"* called Zoe and went back to the papers as I moved down the corridor and out of the main building. At the door to the Abbess's room, I left what George had called my Keep Off the Grass sign in place. Inside, I stood alone in the dark room, turning slowly to capture glimpses of moonlight on small things. No moon, not yet. I stilled my mind and just let my feelings roam. At one point, I heard footsteps—Pete's, I knew the sound well—slow on the path, stop for maybe five seconds in front of my door, and my heart pounded. I refused to read the signs. Then I heard him move on into the night.

He had hesitated. And he had made a choice.

No matter how I turned it around in my mind, nothing about it felt good.

With just two days left in my third decade of life, I did something impulsive. I fumbled for my flashlight, let myself out of the room, locked the door, and found my way, with only dim squares of light from a dormitory room, down to the side of the barn that stood in complete darkness. Strapping the flashlight to the handlebars, the way I had seen Rosa do, I borrowed the bike, wheeling it outside the villa gate. I unbuttoned my Sherpa coat, hitched up my dress, and set off single-mindedly down the road into town, every part of me lifted by the breeze I could swear was a tailwind, speeding me, Nell Valenti, on my way.

In the Piazza della Repubblica, the night was just beginning, and teen clusters ducked and laughed in and out of bars with music. I passed other dogs than Stella, other dignified elderly than Chef, and, in one of these buildings, Annamaria, who lay on her proud back, staring into the darkness at the ceiling. I biked quickly to the Hotel Italia on the Via Ghibellina, when I realized I had forgotten a bike lock. So I carried the bike into the lobby of the hotel, got the night clerk's assurance she would keep it in the luggage room, and gave me the room number. When the elevator took too long, I bounded two flights up the stairs to #230.

Catching my breath, I stared motionlessly at the door. For quite some time. Taking in the crenellations in the woodwork, the scratches on the keypad, the tiny burn on the carpet. When I started counting the crosshatches in the wallpaper, I quit. I remembered Pete, hesitating outside the door to my room. And I understood in that moment there could be so many explanations for it, because we had been good friends. But here, now, with my hand frozen in a position all set to knock until George let me in, I stood. Was this night what I wanted? Could I be very sure I wasn't acting out of anger at Pete?

No one would know I had come.

No one would know I had gone away.

It meant more to me, then, to turn aside from room #230 and slip unnoticed back down the stairs than anything would have meant had I stayed.

As I retrieved the bike, I realized with a smile that I was ready to turn thirty.

I took my time on the ride home.

S leep well?" It was Rosa outside my door at the Abbess's room, trying out her English, just about half an hour after I made it back to the villa on Rosa's bike before dawn.

"Sì, Rosa, ho dormito molto bene, grazie."

She thrust a plate of pastries and a small insulated coffee carafe at me, then reported: *"Primo, nella nuova cucina"*—she jerked her head in the direction of the oil production center past Pete's cottage, which meant the kitchen in the main building wasn't restored to order and stripped of its crime scene status—*"Marinara Misteriosa per tutti!* Everybody make *una grande sorpresa.* Make their own *ricetta e allora, un gioco d'ipotesi."*

I believed I could have been standing there in my underwear and Rosa wouldn't have noticed, she was just that thrilled at the morning's plan. Apparently Jenna, Zoe, Giorgio, and Glynis would each make their very own sauce and everyone had to guess. *Un gioco d'ipotesi. E allora—e allora*—breathed Rosa, we choose *il vincitore!* The winner. There was such a madcap competition to the plan that I got a whiff of reality TV, which had to mean Zoe's hand at work.

"What does the winner"—I eyed her—"win?"

With her eyes wide, Rosa pressed her lips together. *"Una lezione gratuita."* A free class? Potentially a registration of thousands of dollars lost to the school coffers just to award a tasty, off-the-cuff sauce? Oh, Pete, Pete, I whistled low, this is the road to business perdition.

When I asked Rosa what about the afternoon, she said matter-of-factly, "Picnic. Cucinavan take us to Lago Trasimeno. Oswaldo provide. Very fun," she said in kind of a cyborg voice.

"Dinner?" The last meal at the Villa Orlandini.

"Here, very fancy. Oswaldo shop. Chef and Giorgio cook."

I explained I had some work to do here in my room, but I'd catch up with everyone later. Rosa patted my arm, but as she turned to go, suddenly mindful of the time—"we pray for Annamaria's *innocenza*"—she asked if the yeast bags were helpful. I felt guilty that I hadn't worked on the investigation, so I promised her I'd have something to report later. Off she went, with a lighthearted skip, and I shut the door quietly against the dawning day and whatever it might bring.

It was just day two of both my unemployment and my lack of control over the workings of what somebody was probably still calling the Villa Orlandini Cooking School.

Surely there was something I could be expected to do. But I was grooming the line in the sand that separated school design tasks from general operations. With Annamaria in the clink, Chef playing the star as usual, and Rosa and Sofia unqualified to run things, daily operations were now Pete's job.

And he was welcome to them.

Villa and school operations were the exclusive property of the Orlandini family? He'd soon discover he'd have to loosen up that idea or fail miserably. The villa was too large and decrepit, the grounds too sprawling, the demands of vanloads of high-paying students too never-ending for Pierfranco Orlandini to handle it all himself, as—what?—"scion" of the family name. All of it still didn't sound like Pete, but that's what he said and that's what he was stuck with unless—after I went—he could dig up some hitherto unknown and out-of-work Orlandini cousins. Not my problem, not my worry, not my job.

Would that leave him any time for small-batch olive oil production? Now that the harvest was ending, how long could he wait before processing? One thing I knew for sure: It wasn't my problem. In the lambent glow of a Tuscan sunrise on the last full godforsaken day of Marinara Misteriosa, all I wanted to do was honor the letter and the spirit of my contract to develop a world-class farm-to-table cooking school at the villa. As the legal language read, *to the satisfaction of the Orlandinis*. I ignored a flutter of unease, stripped, and stepped into the shower.

S omeday I'd have to raise the shades. But I couldn't quite bring myself to do it. This room was now my office for the remaining time on my Orlandini contract, and I just didn't want to seem approachable for anything beyond what I deemed part of my design job. I towel-dried my hair, splashed some moisturizer on my face, blushed, glossed, and called myself ready for my day. On Caterina Orlandini's old Victrola I set Bix Beiderbecke's "Let's Do It, Let's Fall in Love," sat down, and dug into the *sfogliatella* Rosa had brought me.

I set out the four small plastic yeast bags she had dropped off yesterday. They were identical, so I chose one, and turned it over in my hand. It appeared to be about three inches square with an easy ziplock strip with a white ridge across the top. Transparent, it showed pre-measured 2¼ teaspoons of active dry yeast, enough for a loaf. Inside the bag was the pale green label, centered, about half the width of the bag, running fully from top to bottom. Alba Rosa was the manufacturer's name, over an illustration of a rosy sunrise emblazoned with *1927*, and in Italian just below, *secco 100% italiano* -- dry yeast, 100% Italian -- and a brief touting of how easy it is to use and store.

I held it up and considered the bag from the point of view of a murderer. To do the job on Bob Gramm, not too many poisonous shavings would be needed, so this bag would be a handy little killer's tote, easy to slip in a pocket, even a book, almost anything. So, Joe Batta's team had come across one of these bags, empty of everything but a minuscule amount of death cap mushroom, in Annamaria's junk drawer.

The killer had access to these Alba Rosa yeast bags. On the one hand, is that brand sold locally? Is it popular and common? It's the brand Annamaria uses for the villa's yeast breads, but couldn't it be someone else's as well? On the other hand, if the bag in the junk drawer didn't come in from the outside with its murderous purpose, that meant someone in the villa family—other than Annamaria—had swiped one of those little bags, emptied it of yeast, and filled it with *Amanita phalloides*, enough to do the job on Bob Gramm.

I rotated the bag in my hand. By villa family I would have to include Manny Manfredi and our now four Americans, who were undoubtedly in and out of that kitchen plenty since they arrived. My stomach swayed at the thought that it could be one of the Americans. Because even now the field had been whittled down. I didn't believe Glynis had killed her husband; I didn't believe flaky Jenna had killed the man she felt was responsible for her dad's suicide.

Left on the list were Manny, Zoe, and George, and if it was George I'd just have to go and hoover up some death cap mushrooms myself. Still. To be fair, their names had to stick until I could eliminate them. The key question was: What could happy-go-lucky tour guide Manny or Jersey girl Zoe or Brooklyn culinary Robin Hood George have in their personal histories that intersected with Bob Gramm so powerfully that it led to murder? To be investigated, with my death cap cocktail at my elbow.

Whenever I contemplated the murder, I couldn't get past the idea that there was something impulsive about it. Not entirely, to be sure, because unless the guilty person made a habit of collecting poisonous mushrooms for kicks or study, the fungus had to have been "harvested" with Bob Gramm in mind. Maybe the crime hadn't been planned for weeks or years—like poor Jenna who didn't get much further than nursing a need for revenge and stealing one of our knives "just in case"—so if premeditated, it hadn't been for much time at all. Maybe seeing Bob Gramm was a surprise for somebody. And all that occasioned was fear. The planning then was swift and sure. How convenient that day, a field trip to identify good and bad mushrooms! But, according to the testimony, no one lingered long enough to harvest what's probably the deadliest mushroom on the planet.

Back to the yeast bags, where I could at least see a course of action. If Annamaria left them lying around, handy, the killer would have easy pickings. If she didn't leave them lying around, then the killer had insider knowledge of their whereabouts, which should narrow down the field of suspects. I'd ask Rosa or Sofia about where and how Annamaria stocked them. The more I thought about it, the better I liked it. Suddenly the question of how many the box held, how many were missing, how many could be accounted for, seemed pretty much a worthy line of inquiry for the likes of Nell Valenti. But to do that I'd have to get dressed and leave my little Orlandini-free zone. So be it. But first, I followed up the *sfogliatella* with a small, dense, unforgettable wedge of *castagnaccio*, Tuscan chestnut cake, a fall treat, washed down with good coffee.

20

Slipping one of the Alba Rosa yeast bags into my pants pocket, I shrugged into my down vest, closed and locked my door, and headed to where I believed every biped on the villa grounds was competing hard against all comers for the title of *vincitore* in the freestyle marinara competition. I heard the ruckus inside Pete's olive oil production space before I even entered. Windows were open to let in the sun-warmed air, and the daylight was all the illumination the cooks needed.

Pete, who seemed to be presiding, actually looked happier than he had over the last few days, maybe because he had wrangled all the Americans—plus some Baris—into one policeable spot, so his job for these couple of hours was a whole lot easier. The rat-a-tat of dicing, mincing, and chopping filled the air, along with the sizzling harmonies in the sauté pans. The aroma, as always for me, was indescribable. The sort of smell that you want to take away with you on your deathbed. George saw me right away, and saluted.

At one end of a worktable, Rosa and Sofia were furtively manhandling fresh herbs. Apparently they had teamed up, just for the fun of it, breathed Sofia. They made the point, full of shrugs and laughs, that they can take classes anytime, anytime at all, so for them, *nessun grande premio*—not a big prize to shoot for—but Pierfranco had substituted a weekend trip to Paris. (If I didn't know better, I'd swear Pete was deciding to go out of the cooking school business with a pyrotechnic bang.) With pungent herb-scented hands, they patted their chests in happy anticipation.

Chef was making the rounds, blindfolded, hands clasped behind him, inhaling as he went. Glynis showed some life, if a bit like a cafeteria lady dishing up the hash. George looked like he was trying very hard to lose. Zoe was doing mysterious things with what appeared to be rutabaga. Jenna added a couple of drops of some unknown substance into her pan then quickly stashed the small bottle.

Pete hailed me. "Staff meeting, Nell? Five p.m. in the office?"

"I'll be there." And that was it. We were reduced to a work relationship. We were "staff" together. Perhaps for the best, in what little time I had left. I managed to peel off Sofia from the Bari duo, with assurances to Rosa that I would return her sister the ace dicer Sofia as soon as possible. In her very late forties, Sofia, the youngest of the Bari sisters, loped along beside me in her crepe-soled, lace-up black shoes, chattering in blissful Italian what she and Rosa would do in Paris, a quarter of which I understood.

Inside the main building, I followed her to the pantry,

stocked with sacks of farina 0 and 00; cans of San Marzano tomatoes; bags of vialone, carnaroli, and arborio rice, for risotto; jars of passata, basic tomato sauce; bottles of balsamic vinegar from Reggio Emilia; three-liter cans of extra virgin olive oil for needs beyond what Pete can meet; bags of spaghetti for days when homemade pasta is not an option; lines of high-quality dried herbs and spices.

And then there were cardboard boxes with the familiar Alba Rosa illustration. Only one was opened. Sofia waited patiently while I gave it a close look. According to the label, it should contain thirty (30) three-by-three-inch plastic bags of bread yeast, premeasured 2¼ teaspoons. I counted twenty-six still in the box. Not too bad. I'd have to learn from Annamaria how many loaves of bread she'd made since opening that Alba Rosa cardboard box. The correct answer would be three, leaving the fourth pinched by the killer to transport shavings of death cap mushroom and implicate Annamaria.

Sofia lifted a can of the San Marzanos off the shelf to add to their marinara, and we started back. "We take some sauce to Annamaria."

"*Quando?*"

"*Prima di pranzo.*" She beamed, raking her fingers through her hair. *Before lunch.*

"*Bene.*"

Sofia shot me a quick look as we headed across the courtyard. "Fancy dinner tonight," she started.

"So I hear."

"*Una lezione di Theresa?*"

"A wine lesson?"

Sofia picked up the pace as we crossed the cloister

walk and hit the path down to the olive oil production center, past my room, past Pete's cottage. *"Sì."* She raised her eyebrows at me with a smile. "Be very good."

I laughed. "I suppose," I said, then added, "Although this time maybe she won't forget her notes." Sofia looked puzzled, so I cobbled together a crude translation. "Maybe she won't forget"—I tapped my temple—"*i suoi appunti.*" Her notes. I air scribbled on my palm.

Sofia still looked puzzled, but hurried, pumping the tomato can like a free weight. Over her shoulder, she said, *"Theresa aveva i suoi appunti."* Ahead of us stood Rosa jiggling from foot to foot, watching us approach.

"What?" I grabbed at Sofia's arm. "Theresa had her notes?"

"Li ho visti. Rosa!" She waved.

"Sofia!" I made her stop. "Theresa had them? You saw them?"

Eager to please, she gestured at an invisible bag with her San Marzanos. *"Sì. Nella sua borsa."* In her tote. *"Proprio in alto!"*

Right on top.

I could picture it.

At the end of the lesson on wine pairings, it was Sofia who had hurried out to the courtyard with the straw tote Theresa had left behind.

Just then Zoe bounded up to me and asked if I'd judge the marinaras when the time came—maybe in an hour or so? "You," she went on, "were the unanimous choice."

Shielding my eyes from the sun, I said, "I have a reputation inside the entire Cucinavan."

She laughed and squeezed my arm, like there I was, being silly again. "Oh, and it'll be a blind judging."

I nodded, utterly distracted, and turned away. "Just

come get me," I told her, and walked on wobbly legs to the Abbess's room. There I opened the windows but kept the shades drawn, and I sat on the edge of the bed. The mattress hardly noticed. *Theresa had lied to us that night.* It felt remarkable and troubling to me all at the same time. Closing my eyes, I tried hard to remember just what had led up to that moment. Our five American students were seated at the dining table in the chapel, all set to hear Theresa Franchi of Franchi Estate Winery deliver a lesson on Tuscan wines, the Franchi vineyards, and the selection she had brought to suggest pairings with that evening's meal.

I had known Theresa ever since I arrived at the villa a month ago, and all I knew about her were the friendship basics: an American, she arrived in Cortona about three years earlier, met and married the lovely, older Leo Franchi, from a long line of vintners. She learned the business quickly, but she proved better at the public side of things—tours, tastings—and from what I could put together, less good on the financial management, although she was handling it. Leo himself was all about the grapes. Growing, harvesting, pressing, aging, bottling.

Along the way in her life, Theresa hadn't had any kids, or even enough of a single career to carry forward. There was one mention of high-end real estate in the South, but I hadn't asked which South—Italy's or ours? She liked cars, hiking, good food and wine, and everything about Tuscany. Two years ago, times got hard was what she told me once, casually. She thought the vintage wasn't up to snuff. Mother Nature's fault. One year ago, times got harder. She thought Leo was banking too much on what she called eccentric, boutique varietals. So, Leo's fault. She muttered reasons for difficulties like she was flinging chicken feed. Trying them out for size, gauging their believability from our responses. Pete nodded—yet one more Tuscan businessman trying to navigate good and bad times. I just listened, it was all so unfamiliar to me.

So, at dinner that first night in the chapel, Theresa and I had been making small talk while the meal got organized, and then I watched as she lifted her head and looked over her audience, just taking them in at first glance. A quick survey. I do it myself. Who's eager, who's bored, who's skeptical, who's on your side. And then, I remembered, it happened. A look of horror altered her face. I asked her what was wrong. And Theresa Franchi said she had forgotten her notes.

I asked if they were in her car. If so, easy fix. But no, Theresa said she had forgotten them at home. Ah, just a little too far to go for them, so going for them would put undue stress on the timing of the meal and the rest of the plans for the evening. So Pete and I stepped up, reassuring her that we could cover, and she should just pipe up whenever she liked. Instead, she seemed to step back a bit into the shadows, just out of the brightest landings of light.

But Theresa hadn't forgotten her notes at home. At all.

It was just a cover. A quick and credible excuse for her intense reaction at that moment.

To what?

Something remembered? Like what? And why just at that moment?

I recalled how her body tightened up defensively, a cringe. At something, or someone, she saw. No, not a pleasurable meeting. Not an expected meeting. Nothing she could share with a philosophical whisper. Whatever the truth was, Theresa was keeping it to herself, and covering her horror with a quick and easy lie. Forgotten notes, too far to retrieve.

One more image surfaced. Bob Gramm talking to Theresa out in the courtyard as she loaded up her car with her tote, her handouts, her unopened bottles of Franchi Estate Winery wine. Bob Gramm, that way he had of strutting even when he wasn't moving, that was him that evening, with a riveted sneer. Not a pickup scenario, for sure. And even though they weren't being overheard—Sofia had left, no one else was nearby—he was doing almost all of the talking. It came back to me then, what a mean look that man had.

Theresa Franchi knew Bob Gramm. He was old bad news. There was nothing I saw on her tense face that indicated she was dealing with an annoying stranger, someone she'd have to handle nimbly because the winery and the villa did business together. And were friends. Suddenly galvanized, I sprang to the table by the window and booted up my Mac. What was she doing—and where was she—before coming to Cortona and marrying Leo Franchi? First I tried to find anything at all published on Theresa's wedding to Leo, and came up short. I'd have to go into Cortona—assuming they got married there—and check the register from three years ago, somehow narrowing it down. What I wanted was her last name before she became a Franchi.

Could I spare the kind of time it would take to go in person?

Not unless I had no other way into this possible story.

I tried it another way. I Googled Bob Gramm and waited to see if anything interesting turned up. Bob Gramm in a Naples tennis league about five years ago.

Bob Gramm in a photo of a Rotary Club dinner in Naples about six years ago. Bob and Glynis Gramm in front of a new home after Hurricane Irma hit Naples four years ago. Bob Gramm of Gramm's Lams at his Try-a-Palooza sales event just one week after the annual Cars on Fifth show four years ago. The subheader read: **Go on the Lam with your new luxury car!**

Then the copy: **Want to test-drive a Lamborghini? See Bob Gramm at his Try-a-Palooza sales event, where the first six prospective buyers get to "test" their favorite Lam for a full forty-eight hours. Take your honey to a swank restaurant . . . in your Lam! Impress your kid's college roommate when you bring Junior back from break . . . in your Lam! Show up at Rover's vet appointment . . . in your Lam! Drive through the package store . . . in your Lam! Pick up your Viagra Rx . . . in your Lam!**

A second hit in my Google search brought up a photo of the result of Bob Gramm's Try-a-Palooza. **Pictured with Sales Maestro Bob "the Glam" Gramm are the six winners of Lam Owner for a Weekend.** On the hood of a sleek red Lamborghini was the Glam himself, dressed for some reason in tennis whites, surrounded by a clutch of Lucky Lam winners. I scanned the group quickly, not expecting anything, but there she was, third from the left. My heart lurched. I zoomed in and read the names.

(L. to R., Bonnie Duke, Clete Barnes, Terry Dolan . . .)

Terry Dolan. Four years ago she had a pixie haircut with fire engine red highlights, but the smile hadn't changed, or the taste in business casual clothes. Terry Dolan, snapped by the *Naples Daily News* at Bob "the Glam" Gramm's Try-a-Palooza sales event. She was one of six winners, all right, I thought as I studied the picture, but what else had happened? The date of the Try-a-

Palooza was October 20, 2017, a Friday. So the six winners got to tool around in their swank cars for that weekend.

I unfolded the spreadsheet Bob Gramm had used to record dates and figures. The infusion of $60,000 a year for three and a half years began on November 1, 2017. Not quite two weeks after the weekend of the Try-a-Palooza. Was Terry Dolan, Theresa Franchi, paying off the Lam she had tried, loved, and possibly bought? Had Bob Gramm counted on making a sale to at least one or two of the six "winners"? But wouldn't those deals be aboveboard and recorded in the dealership sales records? Certainly not handwritten in a notebook that seemed more for his eyes only.

On a whim, I went to the *Naples Daily News* website and searched the archives for October 20, 21, and 22. No car theft (of a Lamborghini) reported on any of those dates. No Lams sighted in the commission of a robbery on any of those dates—although I would truly have had a laugh if a crook in a Lamborghini knocked over a convenience store. No reported assaults, drug deals, or solicitation, nothing that involved one of these high-end cars. Over the weekend that the winners got to play pretend with these status symbols on wheels, the wheels themselves were well behaved.

At least . . .

I thought it through. At least no Lamborghinis were involved in any known crimes.

But what if at least one of them had been involved in an unreported crime? Or, if a crime was reported, no Lamborghini was spotted. It opened up a whole new line for me. And I was just about to search other news from those three dates when the knock came at my door. Just my luck. Time to judge marinaras and declare one of the participants the winner of a free cooking class at the Villa Orlandini Cooking School, which might end up being as much of a pretend prize as having the use of one of the Glam's fancy cars for a couple of days. I jerked open the door.

Standing there, smiling weakly, was Glynis, wearing her bib apron. "I think we're—"

Nodding a bit like I'd broken a spring in my neck, I pulled her just inside the room. "Glynis, I'm on to something. It's about Bob."

"Bob?"

"The murder. I need to see his business records for the weekend of the Try-a-Palooza back in October of 2017. It's important."

"Right now?"

"Right now."

I thought she'd head for my Mac, but instead she pulled her phone out of her pants pocket, tapped a couple of times, put us on speaker, and got the voice mail of someone declaring herself Patsy O'Toole, please leave a message. Glynis looked at me. "Bob's only employee," she told me. "Considering it's five a.m. in Naples, she's sound asleep." Then Glynis left Patsy the message that she needed Patsy to go into work as soon as she got this message and go into AlertMiner back to—Glynis stopped and raised her eyebrows at me, and I gave her the dates— October 20, 21, and 22 of 2017—"and send those pages immediately to me as a file at this email address—" I rattled off mine, which Glynis repeated into the phone. "Thanks, Patsy. Give me a call back sometime today. I've got some news." At that, Glynis widened her eyes. "*Ciao* for now."

When she repocketed her phone, she said, "Soonest could be in an hour. She gets up early and she's a dutiful sort of gal who deserved a better boss than Bob, but"—she managed a little laugh—"that seems to be a common theme. Maybe I'll hire her in the boutique. Ready?"

I walked alongside Glynis to the olive oil production center. "Did Bob mention anything unusual in the week, say, after the Try-a-Palooza?"

"Not that I recall, Nell, but look at me. I'm not cooking on all burners. I'm hardly cooking on a camp stove."

Inside Pete's beautiful space that was now functioning as the villa's temporary kitchen, everyone was lined up in their chef's aprons facing the door like they were getting ready to film a segment of *Top Chef*. Only Chef himself stood apart, shifting from foot to foot, exercising his ankles in deft little bocce kicks. Glynis joined the line and as I approached the largest worktable, where numbered platters of competing marinara over spaghetti awaited my decision, everyone clapped. Including Pete. With a swift glance at George, I thought he was acknowledging something altogether different from my mere arrival as the judge of their morning sauce production. It was an effort, but I managed to bite the inside of my cheek until I controlled a smile, and stepped up to the platters gravely.

Choosing was easy. Entry #3 was delicious, and since I had noticed in my month at the villa that Rosa Bari had a very free hand with crushed red pepper flakes, I announced this spicy entry as the winner. When the group hushed, I praised the sauce for its exquisite blend of young garlic, red pepper, and Moraiolo olive oil, with a snap of flavor without bitter aftertaste—I was making it all up as I went along—due to the brief company of a peeled potato during the last twenty minutes of cooking. Gasps went up.

Rosa and Sofia hugged and wept. Everyone else seemed pleased the cooking nuns were getting a weekend in Paris, and, except for a general cleanup, the morning was over. As I started to leave, Zoe called, with a bright smile, "Are you joining us on our class picnic?"

"I've got a lot of work to do," I replied, taking in the crestfallen faces, "but I'll try. We'll see."

21

🌿

I hurried back to the Abbess's room, where I peeled an orange and waited for a file from Patsy O'Toole. When it came, Patsy had copied the relevant pages to a Word file, and I read through them slowly. On the twentieth, the names and contact info of the six winners of the Try-a-Palooza were entered, as well as the model and serial number of the specific car they'd be borrowing for the forty-eight-hour span. So Terry Dolan of Venice, Florida, was driving a Lamborghini Huracán LP 580-2. The software, called a "customer experience management platform," kept "transactional, historical, behavioral, and locational" info on the customers of Bob Gramm's dealership. For the twentieth, though, nothing beyond those entries of names, contact info, and borrowed car.

The twenty-first, a Saturday, was chock-full of entries, but nothing on the six. Although Clete Barnes called with a question about the possibility of getting his model but with a silver interior instead of black. That was it. On the twenty-second, however, the cars were returned over a five-hour period. As though he was working for Hertz at a major airport rental return station, Bob Gramm looked over each car as it came back to the dealership. He noted the winners' quick feedback: "Super cool," "Too low to the ground for me," "Where do I sign for it?" "Handles like a Thoroughbred," "I'll make you an offer," and "Thanks."

Two winners had morphed into buyers, Clete Barnes and Hedy Joyce. Not Terry Dolan. Bob Gramm noted the condition of each car in boxes alongside the winner's name. A-OK, A-OK (smells like cigs), A-OK, A-OK (foil condom wrapper, jackass), A-OK (smells like Chick-fil-A), and then there was Terry Dolan's: DINGED! *Right front bumper, blue paint. Assess damage.*

Damage.

Maybe it was the "blue paint" notation. A picture was beginning to emerge.

I Googled "Naples Daily News hit-and-run" and up came this item. What struck me first was the date: October 22, 2017.

BICYCLIST KILLED IN HIT-AND-RUN IN NORTH NAPLES

The body of a boy, 12, was discovered Saturday night by a scooter rider on the shoulder of Goodlette-Frank Rd. The boy, whose name is being withheld because of his age, was heading home after soccer practice when he was struck and killed half a mile north of Freedom Park. Practice ended at seven p.m., and the boy, who was riding his bike, should have arrived home twenty minutes later. Anyone with information regarding the crime should contact the Florida Highway Patrol.

I pushed back from the table, I pushed back from my laptop, I pushed back from this report of a dead boy. But I couldn't push back from the truth. In a borrowed Lamborghini, Theresa Franchi had hit and killed a twelve-year-old boy on a bike. Maybe her foot never even touched the brake. DINGED! noted Bob Gramm. *Blue paint. Assess damage.* How long had it taken him to figure out his Huracán LP 580-2 was involved in an unreported crime?

It took me another ten minutes to find the NBC2 news clip two weeks later of the boy's grieving parents, Jeff and Sandy Shafer, their eyes large with pain, pleading for information leading to an arrest of the hit-and-run driver who killed their boy. "Bobby loved that bike," said the mom into the camera, and the dad added reverently, "It was a blue Evryjourney bike from Sixthreezero." The mom intoned, "It was all he wanted for his birthday, was that bike," and they ran out of anything more to say at that moment about their dead boy.

I stepped outside just to clear my head.

It didn't work. But something inside my skull was happening almost imperceptibly. Like yeast sprinkled over warm water that begins to thicken and erupt without your ever noticing it. Yeast. Zipping back inside the Abbess's room, I did one last search—this time, scrutinizing a clue in the murder itself. I Googled yeast bags, scrolled down through the hits, and clicked on Alba Rosa, the purveyor of premeasured yeast for Annamaria's breads. When I had studied the site before, I was so single-minded I completely overlooked another possibility to the little three-by-three-inch plastic ziplocked bags of bread yeast.

And there it was, at the top, a menu tab.

I clicked, and found, to a satisfaction almost as great as pumpkin-helichrysum bruschetta, what I needed. Bounding over to the nightstand, where I had tossed random items over the last few days, I picked up Detective Joe Batta's business card, and with no hesitation, I grabbed my phone and called him at the general number of the *carabinieri* right in town.

Hoping for a break, I asked for Nina. After a few minutes and some bilingual yelling on the other end, Nina purred, *"Pronto?"*

"Nina, Nell Valenti. Can I possibly see the yeast bag Joe Batta took for evidence?"

After about half a dozen iterations of "no," in case I didn't get the gist, Nina slowed down, and informed me, "No, *signorina*, now it is evidence."

I took a deep breath. Then: "Have you yourself seen it?"

"Sì." No drama. Hardly even a word.

"Can you please describe it?" I ached at the thought she'd launch into another aria of "no."

A languid sigh. *"Momento."* It turned out, by my watch, to be ten minutes until she got back on. "I have it. What do you want?"

"Everything you can tell me about the bag. I assume the removable label is gone?"

"Yes, missing."

"Please, then, Nina, just the bag. Size, color, that sort of thing."

She acted as if she was narrating the latest design to hit the fashion runway, beginning, I believe, with "A simple little bag," and traveling on from there. The bag introduced into evidence in the case against Annamaria bore a strong resemblance to the villa's bread yeast bags, no denying. Both were three by three inches, transparent plastic, the ideal size for two teaspoons' worth of yeast, secured with a plastic ziplock. The ridge along which the "zip" glides, in the Alba Rosa bags from Annamaria's box in the pantry, was white.

"The bag in your hand, Nina," I asked her quietly, "what color is the ridge?"

"Ridge? You mean how the bag locks?"

"Yes."

With perfect nonchalance, she replied, "It is purple."

I breathed, *"Grazie mille,* Nina,*"* and ended the call.

The bag that held traces of *Amanita phalloides* wasn't a bread yeast bag.

It was a wine yeast bag.

I felt forlorn as I waved the Cucinavan down the driveway on its way to a picnic at Lake Trasimeno, half an hour away. All I could tell them when they asked was "I'll come if I can." Manny Manfredi bellowed some directions at me, and George shot me a disappointed look. Even Stella appeared to give me a chance to change my mind before she bounded up the step and into the van when Jenna whistled. To all of them I mouthed *See you later, shooting* a smile I felt quiver just a little bit at the edges.

Inside the van, Chef, dressed in one of his bocce team uniforms I hoped he had washed, was busy announcing the rules of the game of bocce. Rosa, Sofia, Laura, and Lisa were laughing and squealing like they were going to lick the other team of these pantywaist Americans for sure. Off they went, followed separately by Pete, in the Ape, who was passing on a picnic in order to go visit Annamaria. I sent him a quick text. *Please ask her how many loaves of bread she made this week.* All I got back was: *K.*

Standing alone in the sunlit courtyard, I came face-to-face with my plan.

And it meant I was playing a lone hand. Not for any reasons of bravery. If it was just me and Theresa, I believed

I was drastically cutting the odds of anything going too terribly wrong. The fewer the players—especially with this group of Baris, widows, undercover culinary stars, weepy would-be killers, dogs, and let us not for a moment forget the supremely unmanageable Chef—the less the likelihood of blowing it. It was a way too volatile group. Leak anything in the vicinity of Theresa Franchi that gets her wind up, either somebody would get hurt, or she would get away as fast as she had in a red Lamborghini the night of October 21, 2017. How had the woman thought for a moment that she could stiff Bob Gramm over the last few months? In that moment I understood why Theresa had rescheduled the wine cellar tour on the day of the murder—she needed to be on hand during the kitchen chaos of plating the dinner.

I couldn't afford to spook her. So the plan had to be simple and irresistible.

Grabbing the set of keys from the hook in what had been my office, I disconnected two, in particular, then over the next hour, took care of the plan's setup. Then I strolled into the chapel, my favorite room in the entire villa, and let the sunlight shooting through the stained-glass window throw the colors on my face, my shirt, my pants. I was ready. Or maybe I just thought I was ready. But there was no stalling. I huffed out a breath I'd been holding, then I pulled out my phone, clicked to my contacts, and pressed the cell number of Theresa Franchi. "Hello?" came her voice. She still liked answering in English, thinking it added a foreign quality to the winery business.

I have to say I was shocked at how normal my own voice sounded. "Hi, Theresa. It's Nell." And then I switched to seductive. "Wait'll you hear what I've found . . ."

* * *

When she said she couldn't get here before three p.m.—after the Rocciosa disaster a few days ago, she and Leo were taking turns keeping an eye on the workmen—I agreed, but I was increasingly nervous that my plan would get interrupted by the return of the picnickers on the Cucinavan. The red-and-white crime scene tape had been stripped off the kitchen door, so I peeked in. Half cleaned, half restored to normal. I pushed open the door a little wider, picturing the night Bob Gramm's pasta got some shavings of death cap mushroom, and I remembered the chaos of people angling themselves in and out of that small space. Even Oswaldo. Even Theresa, who had moved toward me with a dinner plate ready to go out.

I watched her pull into the courtyard in her small beige SUV—*Franchi Estate Winery*—and went out to meet her, working a dish towel in my hands, just to look casual. In my pocket was my phone. "Hi!" I greeted her, and her face didn't seem quite so haggard. But, then, I had given her some excellent news.

"Where is everybody?" asked Theresa, killer of young boys, killer of middle-aged men.

I lifted my hands and shot her a comical fed-up look. "Out eating hot dogs, I think, and playing bocce, if I know Chef."

Her mouth twisted. "While the rest of us do the work."

To be fair, I thought she was exaggerating—there wasn't a Bari alive who didn't work twice as hard as I did—but I went with it in our spirit of commiseration. "You got it." I almost added "sister," but I didn't want to inject an element of thirties noir, so I clammed up.

"Where is it," she breathed, then bit her lip, "the Rocciosa?" You would think I'd come across a hitherto undiscovered companion piece to the *Mona Lisa*.

"Down in the wine cellar. Come." I nodded toward the building and arm in arm we went, Terry Dolan, now Theresa Franchi, and I.

"Are you sure?"

"That it's the Rocciosa?" I held open the door, gesturing for her to enter before me.

"Yes."

"There's the label. The famous scrawl."

"I know. How did you happen to find it?"

"Them, Theresa." I added to the joy. "There are three, didn't I mention?"

"Right, right. Maybe—"

"I was rearranging the sections. And then I found a whole rack behind a rack."

"Unbelievable."

"Well," I said as though this one word explained anything, "Chef." I wrinkled my nose. "Hoarder." We stopped at the closed door leading down to the wine cellar. Drawing it open, I stepped aside. "Please."

"Will—will you sell them?"

"I would say"—I mused—"there's an excellent chance."

"Leo and I couldn't afford, well—"

"Careful on those bottom two steps, Theresa."

"Got 'em. Leo and I couldn't afford what the Rocciosa would bring on the open market, but—"

"Still," I said, hitting just the right spot between merry and secretive, "the rarity of the Rocciosa."

"Yes, that's it, isn't it? The rarity."

"Rarity," I said sagely, "is what sets us apart from the animals." I had no idea what I meant.

At the bottom, she turned and looked up at me, where I stood smiling down at her on the next to the bottom step. I produced my butane lighter and lit the gas sconce on the wall alongside me. "Right," agreed Theresa. "The animals. Now, where is it?" Her head turned away from me, impatient.

All that senseless killing. "Straight ahead, Theresa."

She picked up the pace, past the graceful old iron gate in the arched entrance to the collection. Earlier, I had come down, unlocked the gate, and swung it all the way open. "So, where?"

"Oh, didn't I say? Past this room. Into the second. Go on. I'm right behind you."

She needed no more directions, and headed out of sight, still trying to talk the Villa Orlandini out of $11,000 worth of wine. I moved to the other side of the entrance and noiselessly swung the gate shut, just as she called to me. "Wait, where—?"

"Second set of racks, Theresa." I nearly whistled. "Then at eye level."

I heard her hand moving along a shelf I had previously emptied, gathering up the only things in sight. As she stepped back into view, I was turning the key in the lock. "There's just these little bags."

I smiled as I tried the gate to be sure it was locked. "Those are some of Annamaria's bread yeast bags, Terry."

It was interesting to see her reaction. She flew at me, shouting, then looking wildly around her in the dimly lighted cellar. The fact of her imprisonment rose around her. "What are you doing?" Her hands rattled the locked gate. "Let me out!"

"The bag you used for the death cap," I said like I was making a YouTube video explaining the differences in yeast, "was one of your own wine yeast bags, not Anna-maria's at all." I raised a finger, and as I stood just out of her reach, I commented, "A big mistake." When I started to explain to her how our problem all along was trying to figure who on the Good Mushrooms/Bad Mushrooms field trip that day had harvested the death cap, she began to shriek. In these five-hundred-year-old stone chambers, the sound was everywhere. "We never even thought the mushroom was harvested by someone *not* on that trip. All it would take would be a local knowledge of where to find it."

"I have to get out of here, Nell. Please, please. I have to get away." I watched her face fall apart. "I had to get away . . . that night."

I snapped. "And Bobby Shafer had to get home."

"It was an accident," she cried. "It was—"

"It was an accident when you hit him. It was a crime when you left him."

She was still shrieking when I hit the top of the stairs and, with trembling fingers, called the cops. Not far into the fifteen minutes it took Joe Batta and two uniformeds to arrive, I heard a wine bottle smash against the wall in the cellar. And then another. "You hear that?" snarled Theresa. "You let me out, Nell, or I'll break every bottle of wine you've got."

The vicious waste of it got to me. And from her, who talked so proudly of which wine to pair with which fish. "Go ahead!" I yelled down to her. "Everything you see, Theresa, every bottle you can get your miserable hands on, is our latest delivery from Leo. Which we haven't paid him for yet. I moved out all the rest. So, by all means, go right ahead. Cheat him some more." A crazy roar erupted from the jailed Theresa, who smashed one more bottle. I waited. After that, she broke down blubbering. Finally, nothing. I closed and locked the door leading down to the wine cellar, and walked out to the courtyard on legs that felt like mismatched sticks.

Pete was climbing out of the Ape. Hesitantly, he started over to me, as I crossed my arms in the midafternoon sunlight and looked away from him. "How's Annamaria?" I managed, my voice strange.

When he said, "Okay," I thought I might seriously lose it. "She said she's made four loaves in the last week."

Of course she had. "She'll be out soon," I told him, just as the SUV of the *carabinieri* pulled into the driveway.

"What do you mean?" Six feet apart, all Pete Orlandini and I could do was look at each other from eyes that held no warmth. Not even truth or welcome news could leap that distance.

"Theresa Franchi is locked in the wine cellar," I said. "She killed Bob Gramm. Here's Joe Batta. I'd better go talk to him," I mumbled. As Pete rubbed his forearm back and forth over his astonished head, I started down the drive, paused, and called back. "I hope I didn't overstep my job description. I'll see you at five."

22

You're under contract, Nell."

It was 5:15 and I was sitting in what had been my office. Less than an hour ago, the cops had wrangled Theresa Franchi, who spat in my direction, her eyes wild, as they struggled to get her into the SUV. I felt oddly unaffected by the spitting. Still, as soon as they pulled away, and the temperature began to drop, I caught a glimpse of the Cucinavan idling at the bottom of the drive. Pete would have to handle it. I headed toward my room, where a shower seemed to be the only sensible answer to ugly truths and possibly a drop or two of spit. And now, in the office, my hair clean, my body clean, my clothes changed, I listened to Pete Orlandini tell me he was holding me to my contract.

I gave him a long look, ignoring the shades that rustled against the window. "What are you talking about? You fired me. That's not holding me to a contract." I didn't add that, by me, no option was good, but at least if I was fired I was free. Maybe unemployable as a cooking school designer by anyone else, but I could get a line chef job somewhere.

He shrugged. "Did I say those exact words?"

My head drooped as I considered. "No, I think you didn't, but that was your meaning."

"I disagree." I waited to see what was up his sleeve. When it came to secret motives, this guy topped George Johnson any day . . . "I believe what I said was that you'd have to stop overstepping your bounds or you'd have to go."

"I'd have to go." This I repeated slowly for full effect. Where did he come up with those words? *You'd have to go.* Just some nameless day laborer working on the railroad a hundred and fifty years ago. "I'm not going to discuss these"—I searched and found the sarcastic choice—"ah, fine points." He shifted in his chair, no doubt wrestling with what a schmuck he suddenly was. "Tell me exactly how you're holding me to my contract." Since the signed contract was in his hand, I eyed it. Forget the lawyer in Florence that drew up that piece of contestable garbage. If I set the lawyer for the Dr. Val empire on the Orlandinis, it would be like releasing a dozen Bob Gramms at their throats. No, better than that. A dozen Terry Dolans. They'd never know what ravaged them.

Pete glanced at the typed verbiage, not even long enough to locate the key phrase, and met my look. "You agreed to develop a cooking school to the satisfaction of the Orlandinis." At that, he set down the document and folded his hands like the revealed jackass he was.

"And you don't believe I have done that." I watched him measure out his truth.

Finally, he sighed. Pete the boss shrank. "Not entirely. No. Not yet." Violently, he pushed himself away from the desk, swiveled, and stared out the window. In that moment,

I felt sorry for him although I couldn't say why. If I had left him sitting there, I'm not sure he would have noticed.

"Pete," I said quietly, "all that's left of the design is the kitchen expansion, and you have the sketches and blueprints for that."

He let out a little snort. "You're really anxious to go, aren't you?"

I flashed, "Give me some credit." And then I said, "I'd rather go knowing I'd met the terms of the contract. I'd rather leave on good terms, and with a great cooking school for you and Chef to enjoy." He gave me the side-eye. "But, Pete, do you really think"—I spread my hands wide, and looked left and right—"you can run a cooking school, ride shotgun on Chef, repair the villa, take care of the olives, and make the oil production space you're dreaming of?" I found a soft spot inside me that remembered my friend Pete, the Pete who could be even more, and maybe I was wrong about all that, but I wanted to help him see. "Do you think you can do that by yourself?"

He sat up straight. "No," he said, all business again. A second time, "No." Something was coming. If he'd had a pencil, right about then he'd be studying it in newfound fascination. "I've got a good friend"—his brows lifted slightly—"a woman—coming from Rome. We used to be—" The smile fled, and he changed direction. "Well, let's just say running the school and working with the olives won't be a problem."

I couldn't resist. "But she's not family."

He bit his lip, but he took it. But I realized from the way he looked past me that he wasn't going to tell me anything more about the new help. The man had resources. Somehow, I had never appreciated that. He had exes with enough good memories about him to pitch in when needed. And

I had foolishly somehow imagined that the lovely Pierfranco had descended on a cloud just for me. "Well, that's good, Pete." But I felt a flash of anger. Just as I was feeling I had been a colossal fool all along, Pete spoke up.

"I'm sorry, Nell," he said with urgency, his words tumbling over each other. "I feel like we took advantage of you." He could barely get the words out. "And you've been a good friend."

Our eyes met. "So have you." How can a truth be both so very much and so very little all at the same time? I didn't understand. Instead, I lifted my chin, which made me feel a bit better, and said, "What more can I do on the cooking school to . . . satisfy the Orlandinis and finish out my contract?" In that moment I understood, I think for the first time, that professionalism had more to do with coming through on what was hard than on what was easy. Sketches and blueprints and spreadsheets and orders and logistics were easy for me, when it came right down to it. And I had thought those glorious moments showed the Orlandinis and other customers just what a pro I was. But as I sat there, devoid of anger, I knew I wasn't leaving the villa for the next few weeks, at least, and I would continue to do my job and keep my disappointment completely to myself. That's when I knew I was a pro.

He looked at me with something like gratitude.

While whatever was on my face I was pretty sure was tinged with regret.

There was something about the last evening of Marinara Misteriosa that felt indescribable for a long time afterward. It was strangely elusive and altogether present. It was colorful; it was stark. The misty rain felt like a blessing. There was no marinara anywhere and nobody missed it. There was Annamaria, freed, in a gray pleated skirt and white satin top, driven home by her sisters. There was really only fond laughter that something awful and wonderful was ending. There were grateful tears that Chef and that Brooklyn waiter George, who showed surprising talent, came up with superb beef braciole for us all.

There was my black polo sweater dress and bare feet. There were two mighty crystal and pewter candelabra Sofia brought to the table from who knew where. There were questions about a dead boy and a blue bike, about blackmail that dried up, about wine yeast and bread yeast, and a desperate sprinkling of death. There was Jenna, wearing a rolled and twisted red scarf around her head, happily announcing she had taken a job as housekeeper to Vincenzo, who could use her help. There was even, in what had to be a dashing act of magic by unknown forces, the dog Stella sleeping at my feet.

Laura was the DJ, mixing it up with pop and Motown and the kind of torch songs we all hold in the recesses of our hearts. Some danced. Some sang. Glynis and George and I tried the Macarena and fell out laughing when we couldn't remember all of it, but really, it was the wine. Chef and Zoe took a Travolta turn when the Bee Gees came on. I slow danced with Pete to Adele's "Make You Feel My Love." At the first few, lone piano chords, there was no mistaking what was coming. Dressed in black wool pants and a brown dress shirt open at the collar, Pete held out his hand and I went. "Bad choice," I sniffed, as I stepped into his arms.

"The song?" he asked me, deadpan. "Or the partner?"

I stifled a laugh. "Dance music for exit interviews."

His voice was low. "No exit, Nell, no interview."

"You're just a sap for Adele."

"I mean it."

I gave a world-weary sigh. "Pete, you've got help coming. I overstepped."

"But with grace and heart."

My voice was tight. "Let's keep it to small talk, okay?"

"Small talk?" He loosened his hold just enough to look me right in the face. "Is that what we're doing?"

I know you haven't made your mind up yet.

"There's a place for small talk, Pete." I thought I might fall apart. "It doesn't hurt."

"Sure it does," he said, pulling me closer, his hand on the small of my back.

We danced past the last notes, and finally stepped reluctantly apart.

O n the morning of my thirtieth birthday, I pulled my fleece jacket over my pajamas and stepped outside. I didn't want to miss any part of the day, even the darkness, even the chill, even the sun that was clinging closer to the horizon until next spring. I took in a breath of the fragrant jasmine pot next to my door. George, Zoe, and Glynis had been gone for two days. Jenna was making herself indispensable at Vincenzo's, where Oswaldo visited often. There was a peace to this darkness that had just the slightest presence of first light. I think on my thirtieth birthday I loved silence more than anything else. And I walked off the path to meet it, to let it surround me, maybe to hear whatever it was telling me. Because there was never any silence at all, really, if you listened. Just quiet.

A treetop breeze starting up, the last of the brief overnight shower plinking from my roof onto the path. A distant nightjar that persisted. A Pete who persisted, sleeping in his cottage. Chef, whose personality made the Villa Orlandini larger than it really was. The Bari sisters, who showed me just how much four good people can accomplish when they simply do their work. George had called from the Florence airport, where he had just learned Zoe was pregnant and would be taking a year's maternity leave when the time came. Without missing a beat, he offered me the job of Stealth Chef's sous-chef. I turned him down, not quite sure why.

There was just enough early light for me to see a dark figure emerge from the dormitory and head on rubber-soled shoes across the courtyard and down the driveway, past the Ape, past the T-Bird. Past the sleepers in their familiar places. From the walk alone I could tell it was Annamaria, out of jail just two days, and I started to follow her. The kitchen was back to normal, but I didn't think she herself was. If Chef commanded fig galettes, she didn't go to bat for plum. Was she off to an early market I didn't know anything about? Was she heading the long way around to check in on Vincenzo and Jenna? Should I catch up, or keep a good distance? Let her know I was here, or just leave her alone? And then I spied a suitcase, and a travel shoulder bag. Her hair was neatly brushed and she wore her dress coat. I caught up. "Annamaria!" I touched her arm. We both stopped as we reached the stone archway that marked the villa off from the rest of the world. And we looked at each other quietly, just more quietness, as though it was perfectly normal for Nell and Annamaria to be out in the Tuscan dark, at the edge of the world, me in my fuzzy slippers, her with her suitcase.

"Ah. Nell." Her voice was low, but her eyes found some light that was still elusive for me.

"Where are you going? *Dove stai andando, Anna-*

maria?" I was a little bit cold, standing there in something less than deep forever darkness, and I felt in asking her I was bringing on an eclipse, a gloom that starts small and imperceptibly.

"*Stai calma,*" she said, *Keep calm,* not touching any part of me. Then she shushed me with only a sliver of a glance back at the buildings we had left behind. "I go to New York."

I wasn't understanding what she was telling me. "New York? Why?" All I caught in the rapid Italian she used was *mia madre.* "Your mother?" Now we were whispering. This was the first I had heard of a Bari mother.

"*Lei ha novantadue anni.*"

"She's ninety-two?" Annamaria nodded with a relaxed smile. I filled in the rest. "And she needs you?" Another smile. Light was appearing in between the clouds of the nighttime.

Annamaria wanted me to understand. "She . . ." she said with some emphasis, and then a pause, "needs me." I saw it all. Zoe was gone, but I saw for Zoe it had never been about love. Not even for Chef. For Zoe it had been about Recipes for All. For Chef it was about feeling like his culinary life mattered again. Mattered more, even, than a cooking school could make him feel. But here was Annamaria Bari, slipping out of the place that had been her home for more than forty years, slipping out, so, no goodbyes. I could ask when she was coming back, if she was coming back. I could ask things she had already answered for herself, but those were private. The two feet between us felt oceanic.

My throat was tight. All I could say was, "It's still your kitchen."

At that, Annamaria's head went back. "*Per quanto,*

Bella Nella?" For how long? *"La cucina"*—the kitchen—
"needs younger." She tried to tell me in very few words.
"I can fight the heart. I can't fight the years."

As she started to move off, I said, "How are you getting to the train?"

"You see me," she said, regarding her sensible walking
shoes.

"I'll drive you." And that's what I did. I eased the Ape
down the driveway, and in piled Annamaria, with her old
suitcase on her lap. A red pom-pom was tied to the handle, so she could tell her green plaid suitcase apart from
all the other green plaid suitcases. The little farm truck
didn't have to go fast or far. We drove through a sleepy
Cortona and on the outskirts picked up the Via Italo Sco-
toni. The sky was lightening, pale pink streams appearing
on the eastern horizon, and we rode in companionable
silence, the Ape's headlamps finding our way when we
couldn't find our own.

At the Camucia-Cortona train station, two others were
waiting for the 6:48 to Firenze. A college student. A businesswoman. I carried the suitcase as Annamaria pressed
ahead to the platform, drawing her coat around her more
tightly. I wondered if the villa was stirring. Rosa pulling
down a bowl to make *sfogliatelle*. Pete carrying logs in
from the stack of firewood. Sofia wondering if she could
get another day out of those socks. Chef thinking perhaps
he should have sent that George Johnson off with a bottle
of Sambuca and let him figure it out himself.

How soon before Annamaria was missed?

I felt my face fall apart. I missed her already. What
would we do? What would we all do?

Next to me, Annamaria was nearly grinning. She leaned
closer. "Is not so bad."

"Yes, it is." I ran my fleecy sleeve over my nose.

"Okay"—she gave in—"is bad, but I come back."

"Promise?" Never since I was ten had I felt so much like a ten-year-old.

She laid her hand on my cheek, and I grabbed it. "To Cortona, yes." She gave me a sly, proud glance. "I run kitchen *al convento*." Cook for the nuns? Still, my heart sank. Annamaria grinned. "Who keep Rosa and Sofia in line, eh?" Then she thumped her chest.

The train as it pulled into the station looked sleek and silver in the near dawn. It exhaled to a stop. All so very easy. Some of the cars looked as cheerful as they could this early in the morning on October 7, in their low light. She stepped up and turned, and I handed her the suitcase. "Keep an eye on it, Annamaria," I said irrelevantly, thinking, I suppose, of thieves. She pursed her lips as though it was excellent advice. I scowled at her because I didn't want to cry. She had been my friend all along. I'm glad at least I knew it. As she set the suitcase down inside, I sprang up and gave her a hug, whirling her to face me. Then I stepped back down onto the platform.

We looked hard at each other.

She was remarkably beautiful.

Suddenly she got serious, glancing quickly behind her at the whistle. "See Claudio get good help." I could tell there was more. At the same moment we both said, "He needs it," and smiled. And then as the train picked up speed, she actually blew me a kiss, and, raising her voice, she said urgently, "Pierfranco." Gripping a railing, she leaned out. "I think—" she started, then stopped. With a catch in her voice, Annamaria said something important in Italian.

"What?" I called after her. "What?"

She gave it her best shot in English. "I pretty sure he loves La Bella Nella."

I stood still.

One arm waved me off like she hadn't given me enough credit. "But you smart," she shouted, "you already know."

I nodded wanly and waved her out of sight.

Day came on.

You smart, you already know.

I stood there alone on the platform, wanting the sunrise to make everything all right.

All it made right was daybreak. And maybe that was enough.

Trembling, I drove back to the villa, pulled in through the stone arch, and parked the Ape.

I headed unhurried for the cottage, not keeping to the path, dew brushing my ankles. There, I knocked like I meant it. When Pete opened the door, he hardly got the name "Nell!" out before I kissed him backward into the room. "What—?" he started, but that didn't seem to be the right question. He was in pajama pants and a T-shirt. "Do you ?" This time he did much better, pulling me close, turning me around, easing me against the wall in the low light. I lost my hands somewhere in his hair, and his own couldn't seem to find their way into my dress. "Is this—?" he tried and gave up. I was seventeen again and plummeting off the high diving board at school, coming up almost not soon enough for air, just air. Like now, like here. Breaking off the kiss with wheezes. "Pete," I said when I could catch my breath, and there was nothing in that moment I could add.

In one swift move, his hands pulled my dress clean over my head, and we both looked amazed. With my arms tight around his neck, I whispered, "I may have to rewrite my rule about fraternization."

"No, it's a good rule," he murmured. Then, with no distance between our lips, he breathed, "But that's just part of your job," he said. "This isn't."

Mirta's Marinara Sauce

*Based in New York City, The League of Kitchens
(leagueofkitchens.com) provides "cooking,
culture, and connection" by offering cooking
classes—many now online!—taught by a
culinary dream team of excellent international
home cooks who share their traditional cuisine.
Mirta, the Argentinian instructor, shares this
version of marinara sauce that she learned at
home with her mother and many of her aunts.
Muchas gracias, Mirta!*

(SERVES 4)
PREPARATION TIME: 15 MINUTES
COOK TIME: 40–45 MINUTES

INGREDIENTS

1 large can (28 ounces) of good canned tomatoes
    (diced, whole, or puree)—I prefer Hunt's Fire
    Roasted
1 medium white onion (peeled and diced)
1 small green pepper (diced)
2 whole garlic cloves (minced)
2 tablespoons dried oregano
2 tablespoons cooking oil
1 tablespoon olive oil
1 tablespoon fresh basil (chopped)

1 dry bay leaf
1 tablespoon sugar
Pinch of salt and black pepper (to taste)

DIRECTIONS

In a large saucepan, add 2 tablespoons of cooking oil until it simmers.

Add minced garlic first and cook for a minute.

Add onion and green pepper (diced in small pieces) and cook until translucent (about 3–4 minutes).

Stir in tomatoes with all their juices and mix all. Rinse the can with a tablespoon of water and add to the sauce.

Add dried oregano and bay leaf.

Add the sugar.

Bring to a boil, then lower the heat to keep the sauce at a slow, steady simmer for 40–45 minutes.

Stir occasionally.

Using a wooden spoon, you can crush the tomatoes as you like.

Lastly, add chopped fresh basil.

Keep the sauce covered and refrigerated for up to 4 days or freeze it for up to 6 months.

ACKNOWLEDGMENTS

Many thanks to my husband, Michael, for the great title and—always—the love and support; my editor, Miranda Hill, and her fine eye for where the best in the story lies; my agent, John Talbot, for standing in my corner, wherever that corner takes me; my Brainstorming musketeers Casey Daniels / Kylie Logan, Emilie Richards, and Serena Miller, for the chemistry and generosity, not to mention the laughs; and my daughters, Jess, Rebecca, and Liza, who always make me proud.

Ready to find
your next great read?

Let us help.

Visit prh.com/nextread

Penguin
Random
House